# DIE ONCE MORE

## LIZBETH LIPPERMAN

# DIE ONCE MORE

## LIZBETH LIPPERMAN

Published by Oliver-Heber Books

0 9 8 7 6 5 4 3 2 1

# PROLOGUE

Sixty miles southwest of Caracas, Venezuela
A laboratory in the forest

Joseph Petrović watched from the two-way window as the young woman struggled against the leather straps restraining her. This one was prettier than the others—younger, too. The way her naked breasts jiggled as she twisted and turned on the table proved they weren't store-bought.

He hated fake tits.

He walked to the door, hesitating momentarily before entering the room. Once inside, he glanced up at the vents. Convinced everything was a go, he approached the woman. The terror in her eyes nearly sent him over the edge as he leaned in and traced the outline of her lips covered by the thick gray tape.

"Be still, my pretty. It won't be long now," he assured her, feeling the familiar ache in his groin. Not long at all.

After dismissing the two soldiers guarding the woman, he trailed his fingers from her chin to her chest, watching her eyes widen at his touch, causing the tightening in his groin to increase. He moved to the left breast, squeezing the nipple gently at first, then harder until she writhed in pain.

He wondered if she was a virgin, although in today's world, finding someone who hadn't had sexual relations by the time they hit adolescence was a rarity. This one looked about twenty and had been plucked from a missionary camp on the outskirts of Caracas in broad daylight. She was probably right out of a seminary school in the States, bubbling with the naïve assumption that she could bring Christianity to this godforsaken country. It wouldn't have taken long to figure out that God had abandoned these people long ago, leaving them at the mercy of the drug cartels and a communist leader.

His heart raced at the thought that because she was a Christian, maybe he would get lucky. Maybe she was saving herself for marriage or for God...or for him.

He moved away and walked to the window, knowing the guards were probably watching, more than likely had groped her before he arrived. They were savages, all of them, but necessary for this project. He usually offered up the girls after finishing the experiments, but today, there would be no consolation prize.

Not if his experiment went the way he hoped.

Pulling the cord, he released the blinds, then locked the door before heading back to the nymph, who was now uncharacteristically still. Did she have any idea what he intended to do to her?

Not in her wildest dreams.

He unzipped his pants, anticipating what she would feel like, especially if she turned out to be a virgin. When he was finished, he noticed her eyes, blank, staring at nothing. He had broken her like all the others. Heading for the door, he flipped up the blinds on the window, stealing one last peek over his shoulder. It was always the same. No matter how many women he conquered, not even a virgin like this one could satisfy his obsession with the only woman he could never completely possess.

The one woman who had betrayed him.

But they would meet again, he was sure.

Positioning himself behind the window, he pushed the button only he had access to. As he watched the gas filter through the vents, he hit the stopwatch. Eighteen seconds ticked off before she stopped breathing.

This was three seconds faster than he had anticipated. The real test would come soon, but he was confident the results would be the same or better.

They didn't call him Dr. Death for nothing.

**1**

# Bucharest, Romania (a.k.a. "Little Paris of the East")

**Time: 1800 hours**

**Mission: Surveillance of a known Middle Eastern arms dealer**

THE RAIN CAME DOWN in a drizzle, enough of a nuisance to interfere with their mission. Griffin Bradley III positioned himself in an old, abandoned brick building that had probably been an architectural treasure before years of earthquakes and war ravaged it. From the twelfth-floor window, he focused his military-grade digital binoculars on a small corner café across the street.

A quick sweep of the area assured him his team was in position. Tyler Jackson, the younger of the two, manned a post in a more modern building catty-corner from him, snapping pictures with a lens the size of a movie camera.

From this vantage point, Griff could only see the back end of the nondescript black car parked around the corner, but he knew Ryan Fitzpatrick, his second-in-command, was there with his binoculars also trained on the café about a hundred yards away.

Talking into his headset, Griff said, "Target out of view."

"I got him," Ty said. "He just sat down at a table in the back, up against the wall."

"I've got eyes on him, too," Ryan chimed in. "He's a big mother."

"The bigger they are... Well, you know the rest," Ty said before reciting a play-by-play into his headset. "Waitress just took his order. He's looking around. Seems a bit nervous. ."

"Wonder if it's going to be our lucky day," Ryan interjected.

Griff slammed his fist on the worn and rotted windowsill. "Damn those umbrellas. I can't see a thing."

"Wait. What do we have here?" Ty's voice rose an octave. "A man just approached the target, and he's taking off his raincoat like he's staying. Hang on, I'm zooming in." He paused. "Holy crap! It's a woman. I've gotta refocus to get a better close-up."

"What the hell's he doing with a woman?" Griff lowered his binoculars. "I'm moving in for a closer look, too." He grabbed his equipment and hauled ass down the unstable corridor, reaching the stairwell and bounding down the steps three and four at a time.

An easy task for his six-foot-two frame.

"Christ! What a woman. Tall, blond, and calling my name. Dirty shame she'll never get to see firsthand what my real expertise is." Ty whistled. "Would you look at those legs?"

Though Griff could no longer see him, he knew his hyper-testosteroned comrade would have that shit-eating grin all over his face. He should have that look copyrighted. Oh, to be young again and still that naïve about the opposite sex.

"Oh, yeah. What a waste to hide them under those baggy pants," Ryan added. "I'm thinking a short, skimpy skirt, maybe black leather."

"When you two are done critiquing the chick, would you mind telling me what the hell is happening?" Griff mumbled, as he made his way to the first floor.

"Yes, sir. She just sat down in the booth across from the target," Ty radioed.

"Don't take it personal, kid. Bradley's messed up when it comes to women," Ryan said, unable to hide the teasing in his voice.

Slightly breathless, Griff said, "Screw you, Fitzpatrick. We're here to watch our Middle Eastern guy, not judge a beauty contest."

Ty pressed on. "She handed him a piece of paper, sir, just as the waitress served them two cups of coffee."

"Two cups? Then he was expecting her." Griff cursed. "And quit freakin' calling me sir, Jackson."

"Yes, sir. Bradley. Griff, sir," Ty answered as if he was saluting his boss over the radio.

Ryan reacted, obviously amused. The whole team knew Ty had a lot to learn and was overly eager to please. "Lighten up, Griff. I can think of a lot worse names he could call you."

Ty continued, "He's leaning in toward her. They're either intimate or whispering."

"Are you looking at the same ugly mug I am? Did you get a load of those scars on his greasy terrorist face? Holy God, that's a face only a mother could love." Ryan focused back on the woman. "My money's on whispering."

Griff positioned himself on the main floor and looked through his binoculars. "Fitzpatrick, will you keep your head in the game? We're here to nail the scumbag, not speculate about his sex life."

"So you agree?" Ryan said.

Griff rolled his eyes, not bothering to respond.

After a few moments of silence, Ty finally reported in. "They're still talking. And for the record, there's no way that babe is dancing with him under any sheet, not unless there's one helluva money exchange. Even then…"

"Think she's a pro?" Griff asked.

"No way. She's way too hot. The only way that ugly dude could pop her is in his dreams."

"The kid's an expert. A genuine lady magnet I've personally seen in action as recent as last night. Within the first fifteen minutes after we walked into the bar, Casanova here got lucky in the bathroom. You gotta be pretty good to talk someone into doing the dirty boogie in that disgusting shithole." Ryan sounded proud, as if he'd taught the kid everything he knew.

Griff stifled a grin and attempted to locate the target as he scanned the café. "For God's sake, would you two—"

Ty interrupted, "They're getting up, sir. He's helping her with her coat."

"Fitzpatrick, move. I want you on their heels." Griff scrambled to his feet and headed toward the front exit of the old building. "Go! We can't lose him now."

STRAIGHTENING UP BEHIND THE WHEEL, Ryan watched the pair closely. The target and the female subject stopped just outside the café door, his hand on her waist in a more-than-casual sort of way. As she opened her umbrella, the man glanced up and down the street before he nudged her in the opposite direction from where Ryan was parked. She linked her arm with his, and they walked briskly as if they were late for an NFL game.

Ryan pulled into traffic, keeping a safe distance behind them as they continued to walk down the street. He saw Ty out of the corner of his eye standing outside the empty building about forty yards back.

Suddenly, the woman stopped, did a one-eighty, and glared at Ryan.

Griff's voice squawked over the radio. "We've been made. Move!"

The car behind collided with the back of Ryan's car a split second after he jumped out and raced after the pair, nearly slipping on the wet pavement.

Horns blared from the bumper-to-bumper traffic, as Griff radioed to Ryan again. "They're splitting up. You take the woman, and I'll take our target."

"Got it, Boss."

Ryan chased the woman through the crowded sidewalks, struggling to keep up as she ditched her umbrella and rapidly covered ground. When she attempted to double back in the same direction the target had taken, he smiled.

Her first mistake.

Within seconds, she was trapped on a street closed off for some kind of festival and overflowing with pedestrians celebrating only God knew what. She tried to skirt the barricades, but Ryan came up on her quickly. Turning to face him, she crouched, apparently awaiting his next move.

In English, he said, "I'm not going to hurt you. I only want to talk." He edged closer.

She lunged and sucker-punched him in the face before he had a chance to react.

Despite his five-eleven frame, he was unable to subdue her, and then it dawned on him why. This was no ordinary chick fighting with flailing arms and legs and high-pitched squeals. This woman was bringing her best heavyweight boxer impersonation and, frankly, outmaneuvering him.

*Enough Mr. Nice Guy,* he thought. Apparently, she'd had some serious training in a jihadist camp, but he was bigger, stronger, and faster. After successfully blocking several of his punches, she took a few blows, but even they didn't seem to stop her. Without hesitation, Ryan back-kicked her in the stomach, knocking her to the pavement, facedown, sending her gun skittering across the concrete.

Walking over, he kicked the Beretta further away, then bent down to lift her up. In one fluid movement, she rolled over, kicked him in the groin, and threw her legs over her head to pole-vault to her feet.

Ryan dropped to the ground with the grace of a falling building, holding his knees against his chest to catch his breath. The woman bent down, picking up her gun with one hand, clutching her stomach with the other. He braced for what he knew would follow. He met her gaze before he lowered his eyes and waited for the bullet.

When nothing happened, he jerked his head up, only to see her running away at a pretty good clip, considering her abdominal injury. He scrambled to his feet and took off after her, thinking he would never live it down when the guys found out the girl had kicked his ass *and* gotten away.

GRIFF SPRINTED toward the fleeing man, taking a sharp turn and heading down a major boulevard. He ran in and out of traffic, avoiding an unusually high number of pedestrians and the sea of umbrellas in his path while attempting to keep a visual on his target.

Using his tall stature and thick torso as a battering ram, the man plowed through the crowd, knocking people to the ground. Griff wondered why there were so many people in the streets as he dodged an increasing number of human barriers the target threw in his path.

Griff was gaining on him. In a final act of desperation, the terrorist grabbed a baby stroller and, in the process of turning it over, lost his balance and stumbled. By the time Griff jumped over the stroller and the now-screaming toddler who had been inside it, the target had grabbed the obviously pregnant mother and was pushing his gun against her temple.

Throwing his Glock on the ground and waving his hands high in the air, Griff stepped in front of the screaming infant, shielding the child from the terrorist. As the mother pleaded with the man, he shoved the gun further into her head, deep enough that Griff saw the indentation. The terrified woman immediately became silent.

"There's no need to hurt anyone. I only want to chat with you," Griff said calmly.

In broken English, the man said, "Stay back or I'll shoot her."

Suddenly, the female subject Ryan had been pursuing appeared with gun in hand. She said something in Arabic to the man in an effort to first calm him, and then reason with him. Griff watched helplessly as the man's finger trembled on the trigger, his attention diverted to the new arrival. There was something vaguely familiar about the woman.

Without hesitating, he dove for his gun on the ground, turning to fire one shot before rolling in front of the infant. Screaming, the mother fell to the wet pavement with gray matter splattered over her face and clothing. The dead man fell on top of her.

Griff quickly turned his weapon on the other woman, who was bent over the man shouting, "No, no."

A warning bell blared in his brain. He'd know that voice anywhere.

Glancing up at him and a pissed-off Ryan who hobbled up to the scene, the woman narrowed her eyes. With both men aiming their guns directly at her, she dropped the Beretta by her side and yanked off the blond wig, shaking her head to unleash long, curly dark locks.

"Nice going, Bradley. You just killed my only lead."

"You *know* her?" Ryan asked, still trying to catch his breath.

"Know her?" Griff laughed, but his eyes remained hard. "I almost married her."

**2**

T op Secret Headquarters, Granger, VA
  Time: 2 Days Later, 1400 hours

MACKENZIE "MAC" Conley knew all eyes were focused
on her as she walked into the room. Glancing around,
she pinpointed the location of each camera recording
her every move. She had a knack for this, a talent that
had saved her ass on more than one occasion.

She followed the young soldier dressed in unfamiliar paramilitary fatigues and armed as if he was
about to enter a cave in Afghanistan looking for a jihadist leader. Why did someone need an AK-47 in an
office building in D.C.?

If she *was* still in D.C.

They'd flown her in an Air Force transport from
Romania to Washington, where they'd whisked her off
to a hotel somewhere in the capital and placed her
under heavy security. The next day they'd blindfolded
her, shoved her into a vehicle, and driven for what
seemed like forever but probably was just a few hours.
At their destination, they'd rushed her into a building
before pulling off the cloth covering her eyes.

They'd practically strip-searched her before escorting her to an underground level. G.I. Joe escorting her hadn't uttered a word despite her many questions. Hadn't even creased his bad-ass Al Capone persona when she screamed obscenities at him back at the hotel, calling his mother a few fairly inventive names to get a rise. Assuming she was being abducted, she'd put up one helluva fight.

At least her captors would remember her, since a few would be needing ice bags if they wanted to wear their tighty-whities anytime soon.

The roomful of people dressed in the same unfamiliar uniform as her escort and huddled around computers across the center of the room was a strong sign of bureaucracy. So why was she was here, and what was up with all the secrecy?

After the debacle in Romania two days before, she'd known it was only a matter of time before receiving her *first* official reprimand. Well, second if you counted Morocco a few years back, but that hadn't been because of a botched mission. She'd been called on the carpet for going so deep undercover that not even her handler knew her location. Mac had taken a lot of heat for that even though it wasn't her fault.

After she returned from Morocco, she'd moved to the West Coast and thrown herself into her job, studying her targets for weeks before moving in their circles, always losing herself in the process. If her role was to be a hooker, her whole life revolved around the transformation, leaving no detail to chance.

It was what made her good at what she did, and also why her personal life was in shambles. It had become increasingly difficult to bounce back from Mac on the job to just plain Mac. She wasn't sure if she knew who that person was anymore, or if she even cared.

Her social life sucked. Period. And now that she'd screwed up the latest job, her work life would soon follow suit.

Griffin Bradley had a knack for making her miserable. Why was he in Romania on her turf, anyway?

She'd spent four grueling months training with a terrorist cell in Jakarta. Another three months pretending Omar Rashid's hands all over her body didn't thoroughly repulse her.

Her stomach rolled just thinking about it.

"First things first," she'd told him, then promised when the job was done to take him wherever the hell obnoxious terrorists went when they had mind-blowing sex—certainly not heaven. Maybe it was the same place suicide bombers met up with their seventy-two virgins.

She shuddered, thinking about his hands on her breasts. But it had been necessary. She'd been so close.

Until Griff killed the lowlife and any chance of discovering where the sleeper cell stockpiled their biological arsenal.

Mac snapped back to the situation at hand, nearly bumping into the soldier she'd been following when he stopped in front of an elevator. After successfully passing both the hand and retinal scan, he stepped aside and motioned for her to enter.

"Not until you tell me where you're taking me, slick," she said defiantly.

Without a word, he shoved her into the elevator and pushed another button. *So much for having a conversation with this yahoo,* she thought as the elevator descended, making her wonder if she was about to enter the depths of hell. When the door reopened, a woman in an identical uniform rushed over and immediately began to frisk her.

"Bet you wish you had her job," Mac said, trying to bait the male soldier for some kind of reaction. He didn't even flinch.

When the woman finished without actually doing a cavity search, Mac smirked. "Find anything new in the two minutes since the last one had her hands all over me?" she asked, sarcasm masking the fear now pushing at her insides.

When neither the woman nor her escort gave any indication of replying, she made a spur-of-the-moment decision to play their game. It would buy some time until she figured out a way to tell them what they wanted to hear and get out of there. She lowered her head and followed the soldier down the long hallway to an unmarked door.

There wasn't time to wonder why she was here before the woman bringing up the rear nudged her into the room. What greeted her was totally unexpected. This was a state-of-the-art surveillance center. Video feeds from security cameras around the world covered an entire wall, and digital clocks displaying military time from every time zone took up another. A large computerized conference room stood off to the right, with an impressive private office, partially glassed in, just beyond.

This kind of technology didn't happen without serious funding.

Several people stopped to stare as she passed, including the guy responsible for the bruise on her stomach. A younger man, who could have been twins with Shemar Moore from the TV show *S.W.A.T.*, stood next to him and brought two fingers up to his forehead in a mock salute. She frowned.

By the looks of it, the buzz had already made the rounds. That figured. All she wanted was to get this debriefing over as quickly as possible, take her hand-slapping or whatever else they dealt, and go back to the familiarity of her undercover world.

There her chances of running into Griff again were minimal.

"How have you been, Mac?"

She was jarred from her scan of the room by a familiar voice and glanced up at the man who had recruited her early in her career for her first government job.

The man who was *still* Griff's boss.

"Good, Dino...but I'd be a helluva lot better if Bradley hadn't killed my only access to the biggest biological stockpile in Eastern Europe."

She stood on tiptoes and planted a quick kiss on CIA Director Lorenzo Dinorelli's cheek, making him grin. Slightly taller than six feet, with a touch of gray sprinkled throughout his jet-black hair, the man could still turn heads. But he'd always been like a father to her, especially since her own father died when she was a teenager.

He cleared his throat. "That's one reason why I wanted to talk to you." He motioned for her to enter the enclosed office and take a seat.

She did as he asked, while her escort—Mr. Personality—saluted and took his leave.

Dinorelli closed the door, then walked around the desk and sat down. Reaching over, he picked up a bowl full of sunflower seeds and offered them to her.

"I see you're still sucking on those things." She watched him pop several seeds into his mouth, an addiction he'd acquired as a young Texas Ranger.

"A habit I can't seem to shake." He spat the shells

into the trash can beside his desk. Never one for small talk, he hesitated briefly before his expression turned serious. "I'm sure you're wondering why I brought you here."

"That and why you felt it necessary to roust me from my hotel room at the butt crack of dawn and treat me like I just traded secrets with the freakin' enemy."

He held her stare. "I knew you wouldn't come any other way. I've been keeping tabs on you since you left my unit two years ago. This won't come as a surprise to you, but you've been scratched from the mission in Romania now that your cover is blown. Rather than see you go somewhere else, I decided I could use a biochem expert on the SWEEPERS team."

She paused a moment, unsure if he was joking about her blown cover. "SWEEPERS? You working with Homeland Security?"

"Nope. We're independent. Only a handful of high-level people even know about us."

She scanned the room. "Where are we?"

"If I told you, I'd have to... Well, you know how that story ends. Let's just say there's not a chance in hell anyone will stumble on us by accident."

Intrigued, she leaned forward, resting her elbows on the desk. "So, what's your mission?"

He pursed his lips as if to hide a smile. He probably knew he had her now. "We're a special unit that goes in and cleans up after others fail."

She looked away. God, it sounded exactly like what she loved to do, stepping in after someone else screwed up. But she couldn't even consider it. "Thanks, Dino. As much as I'd enjoy working with you again, there's no way. You and I both know it."

"It's a shame you feel that way." He popped more

seeds into his mouth, then scooped up some papers and tossed them across the desk.

She picked them up. "Reassignment orders? Don't do this, Dino. You know Bradley and I can't work together."

"I don't believe that. You're the best at what you do, and so is he. I need both of you on something really big. Surely you can put your differences aside for the sake of the job."

"Even if I could, I won't. That part of my life is over. There are other people with my expertise. Get one of them."

"Can't do that. There's a reason I need you. Unfortunately, I'm not at liberty to divulge that information just yet, but what I can say is that it's a job only you can do."

She shook her head.

"If you won't do it for your country, then do it for me."

"I can't."

He stared at her for a moment before sliding a picture across the desk, date-stamped the week before.

When she looked down at it, a wave of nausea threatened to flush out her stomach. "He's been dead for two years." Her eyes pleaded with him to concur.

"So it is him?" He slapped his knee. "I knew it. After you told us he'd attended several of your lectures in Morocco two years ago, I had your handler obtain the surveillance videos from the university lecture hall. Based on your description of him, we singled out a man and ran him through facial recognition."

A shiver pulsed up her spine. "Did you find a match?"

He shook his head. "No. If you remember, he was able to operate totally hidden from satellite imaging, so I wasn't surprised that he wasn't in our databank. Hell, we couldn't even find him even after you told us where he was." He stopped to allow this to sink in. "When this picture came in from one of our operatives shadowing the suspected leader of an Al Qaeda cell, I played a hunch and ran both him and the other man through the program. This time there were enough facial markers to get my attention. I had to find out if I was right."

She continued to stare at him, confused.

"Since you're the only one who can positively ID him, you can see why I need you." He stood and walked around the desk. When he was beside her, he handed her the latest report from Interpol and a satellite photo taken over Caracas, Venezuela.

Mac studied the intel, willing her friend to slap her on the back and say it was all a bad joke. One look at his face told her that wasn't the case.

Joseph Petrović was still alive. She trembled, remembering how dirty he'd made her feel. Instinctively, she reached back to touch her shoulder where she'd had the tattoo lasered off. Where he'd branded her.

After studying the photo for a few more seconds, she laid the papers back on Dinorelli's desk. "Why didn't you tell me he was involved from the beginning?"

"That would have made it too easy."

GRIFF WALKED into headquarters and looked toward the captain's office. *Mac.* He muttered a curse. The operatives in front of Dinorelli's office scattered as Griff halfheartedly knocked on the door before storming in.

"Sorry to interrupt this happy little reunion, but bottom line, I had no choice the other day," he said, never looking in Mac's direction.

"You could have shot him in the arm or leg," she responded, unable to keep the irritation out of her voice.

Griff pursed his lips. "Did you forget he had a gun pressed into that pregnant woman's skull? Not to mention either one of us could have been shot."

"Oh, I see. Now you're saying you were protecting me?" She stood up, ready to leave. "That won't fly, Bradley, since you had no clue it was me. And since when do you take a chance and shoot at a pregnant woman?"

The captain held up his hands like a referee. "All right, kids, let's play nice. Close the door and sit, Griff. You too, Mac."

Griff did as instructed, then purposely chose the chair on the other side of the room.

When he had their attention, the director said, "Bradley, meet our newest team member."

Leaning forward in the chair, Griff glared at him. "You're shittin' me, right?"

"Don't worry. It wasn't my idea, I'm not jumping for joy at having to work with you, either," Mac fired back.

Griff ignored her. "Don't do this, Dino. You know we can't work together. We're like fire and ice."

"That's what Mac said." Dinorelli pointed his finger at them both. "You can, and you will. Now, I suggest if you two have anything to settle, you do it before briefing at 0800." He stood up. "Sergeant Collins is waiting outside to take you back to your hotel, Mac." After grabbing a handful of seeds, he left the room.

When the door closed, Griff was silent, staring

straight ahead, the tension in the room stifling. Finally, he got up and walked to the glass window, observing the activity in the communications center, as if Mac wasn't in the room.

She gave in and spoke first. "I know this isn't the ideal situation for either one of us, Griff, but we're both adults and—"

He turned and faced her. "Save it. The time has long passed when I gave a damn about what we had. I've moved on. I suggest you do the same. You do your job, I'll do mine, and we'll get along just fine."

She glared, unflinching at his words. "Spoken like the jerk I remember." She stood and walked to the door. "Since we're clear on that, I guess I'll see you tomorrow morning." She bent down, slipped under his arm after he opened the door, and marched toward the elevator.

As much as he dreaded having to work with Mac on a daily basis, he had to admit, seeing her green eyes light up in anger had been a turn-on. He used to love igniting that flame.

He scolded himself for going there. What they had was in the past, and he'd damn well better remember that. No way he'd go down that road again.

After the elevator door closed, he walked down the hall to his own office, his thoughts back on the new mission. He was a professional, and he'd do his job the best he could, no matter who was on the team with him.

After slamming things around on his desk for the next few hours, he'd accomplished nothing. Going home made more sense than wreaking havoc in his office. Only a short time into his drive to his apartment in McLean, he decided he needed something to calm his nerves. He made a U-turn and headed back to a seedy bar off the beaten track where his chances of running into anyone he knew were slim.

Drinking in public wasn't something he normally did. Usually he preferred the privacy and solitude of his own home, but tonight he couldn't wait the hour it took to get there. He needed to escape, and consuming a large amount of alcohol seemed like a good idea. For the last two years, he'd tried to forget her. Tried to forget how she'd filled his every thought, his every dream.

*I'm finally over her, dammit! She means nothing to me.*

In a matter of fifteen minutes, he'd already chugged enough liquor to sedate a wild boar, hoping the burning sensation would take his mind off everything else. He reached for the fresh drink the bartender set in front of him, ready to add another empty shot glass to those already lined up on the scarred wooden bar, when Ryan Fitzpatrick approached and flopped down beside him.

"Wanna talk about it?"

"Nope. I just wanna drink."

"Fine. Give me your keys."

MAC UNDRESSED and stepped into the large bathtub overflowing with bubbles and steaming hot water. A glass filled with red wine sat on the marble ledge close by. She picked it up, swirled, and sniffed before taking a modest sip. Savoring the flavor, she let the liquid slide down her throat. She loved red wine even though it didn't love her back. She'd have one helluva headache in the morning. Something about the sulfides set off a migraine every time.

But tonight she needed it. She swirled the wine

again, mesmerized by the deep red color, before taking another long sip and sinking beneath the bubbles. Every muscle in her neck and shoulders ached, not to mention the large bruise on her stomach. It was still in the healing stages and hurt every time she bumped it.

She closed her eyes and leaned back against a shell-shaped bath pillow, trying not to dwell on her incredibly lousy luck. She'd assumed she was at the command center for a major hand-slapping and perhaps even a demotion. Instead, finding she'd have to work with Bradley had taken her by surprise. She'd sworn never to put herself anywhere near him. Never to feel that vulnerable again with any man.

But her knees had gone to jelly the minute her eyes met his when she entered the room. His chestnut hair was longer than she remembered, stopping a little above his ears, and he looked like he'd packed on a few more pounds of muscle, probably due to the daily workout schedule she'd always envied.

She sat up and drained her glass, thinking the one thing about Griff that hadn't changed—probably never would—was the way he could infuriate her in a matter of minutes.

Not this time.

As she stepped out of the soapy water, all thoughts of Griff vanished when a vision of the man in the picture Dino had thrown across the desk flashed in her mind.

*This time I'll get you, you evil psychopath. This time you'll stay dead.*

"So, who's gonna introduce me to the new lady?"
Mac turned to the young man she'd seen the
day before with the guy she'd fought with. At roughly
six foot three, with a bald head that glistened under
the artificial lighting, the Shemar Moore look-alike
was even sexier close up. When he turned his smoky
black eyes on her, she felt her pulse quicken.
"Mackenzie Conley," she said, extending her hand.

"Ty Jackson." He reached for it and slid the tips of
his fingers slowly over the top in a way that sent goose
bumps up her arm.

No doubt this guy scored on that maneuver alone.

"Careful, lover boy," Griff said, entering the situation room. "She'll eat you up and spit you out before
you even know she's there." He plopped down in a
chair at the far end of the conference table. "Ask Fitzpatrick about his blue balls."

Mac shot him a glance. "Yeah, you'd know all
about blue balls, right, Bradley?" She pulled her hand
from Ty's, giving him one last flirty smile before
choosing a chair close to the door in case she needed a
quick exit.

She bit her lip to hide her grin at her ex's scowl

when the younger man lowered himself into the chair next to hers. Watching the testosterone-fest play out might be amusing.

The other man walked over by Griff, avoiding eye contact. Again, Mac worked to hide a smile as he squelched a groan when he gingerly sat down in the hard chair. She didn't regret inflicting bodily harm during their scuffle. Especially since his unexpected kick had not only knocked the wind out of her, but was responsible for the nasty bruise on her abdomen as well.

All eyes turned to the door when Director Dinorelli appeared at precisely 0800 and walked around the table, placing a folder in front of each of them. The word CLASSIFIED was stamped in big red letters across the front.

"I presume you've met Dr. Mackenzie Conley, the best damn biochemist this government has ever been smart enough to employ." It was a statement, not a question, and he barely paused before continuing. "I know Fitzpatrick has." He walked over and stood behind him. "Agent Ryan Fitzpatrick. If you want something blown up, he's your man. Nicknamed Boom for a damn good reason." He took a step to his right to stand behind the man she'd just introduced herself to. "Agent Ty Jackson. There's no computer this man can't hack. Believe me when I tell you that nothing is sacred around him. He can make your doorbell turn on your lamps and rig your toaster to wake you up in the morning." He rubbed Ty's bald head. "Be careful around this one. He knows how to wire the ladies to do exactly what he wants them to do, as well."

Mac nodded a greeting to both men. "So, it's the four of us on the team?"

"Right now, yes. There are two others who work

out of Langley. You'll meet them at some point when their skills become necessary." He moved to the back of the table and opened a laptop, the twinkle in his eyes the only thing exposing the glee at his own joke about the good-looking one named Ty. "Let's get back to the business at hand."

Mac opened the folder, staring at the photograph she'd seen the day before in Dino's office. Dr. Joseph Petrović was either wearing one of his many disguises, or he'd grown a lot of facial hair since their last encounter. She leaned closer, feeling her heart begin to race.

There was no mistaking those eyes.

Trembling, she tried unsuccessfully to look away from the blurred image of the man who had single-handedly ruined her life. The man was reportedly blown apart two years ago in a well-executed raid by a Navy SEAL unit. No one should have escaped the fiery explosion that leveled his laboratory and destroyed everything he'd worked on for over two years.

Mac bit her lip to keep it from quivering before focusing her mind back on the picture, wishing the sadistic monster had gone up in flames with the lab and was now burning in hell for all the horrors he'd inflicted on so many innocents.

But this was no ghost.

"Mac, are you all right?"

She jerked her head up, realizing Dinorelli had been briefing the team. "Yeah, keep going."

He stared at her for a moment as if looking past her façade to the emotions swirling beneath the surface. Finally, he opened a file on his computer, and a picture filled the big screen on the wall. "This is Abdul Hamid, a key Al Qaeda operative thought to be high up the command chain. He's been linked to the bombings of U.S. embassies in both Kenya and Tanzania."

"I've seen him before," Mac interjected, pushing her chair closer to the table.

"Where?" Dino stepped around the table and moved toward her in a rush.

"I..."

The director put his hand on her shoulder. "Did you see him with Petrović?"

For the past two years, she'd spent long hours trying to block out that time in her life. Now, he was asking her to rehash it, and she couldn't. Wouldn't. She shook her head. "I'm sorry. He just looks familiar. I can't remember why."

Dino walked back to the laptop and flashed another picture on the screen. "Khalid al Adel, Hamid's right-hand man and key operations planner. With a Ph.D. from Yale in both psychology and engineering, he's rumored to be the brains behind Al Qaeda."

"Jesus! He went to school here?" Ryan broke in.

"Most high-level terrorists have," Griff responded. "We gave them carte blanche back in the eighties." He shook his head. "We even trained the 9/11 pilots, for Christ's sake."

Dinorelli changed the digital image. "This guy is especially dangerous because it's rumored after only a week or two with him, eighty percent of all the new recruits are ready to strap on a bomb in the name of jihad."

"Now that's the kind of guy I'd like ten minutes alone with in a dark alley," Ty exclaimed.

"Back to the mission," Dino continued. "We know both these men have made trips to Venezuela in the past five months. What we didn't know was why, until this photo was taken by a CIA operative staking out a café frequented by a South American cell they'd been shadowing."

Mac forced herself to look up as Petrović's image filled the screen. She wasn't aware she'd gasped until she felt all eyes watching her.

"Mac, you don't have to do this if it's too difficult," Griff said, his voice a little softer than before.

She met his gaze for a moment before brushing him off with a wave of her hand. It would be so easy to fall back into his arms, to hear him promise she'd never be that afraid again.

But she couldn't.

"Don't even think about treating me like I'm some fragile piece of china." She huffed. "I worked with the guy before. Shit happened. Now I'm here. End of story. So, can we get on with it? We'll be here all day if you stop every time I take a deep breath."

After a pointed stare in her direction, Dinorelli turned back to the screen. "Joseph Petrović, responsible for thousands of deaths in the ethnic cleansing in Bosnia, as well as the slaughter of civilians in Rwanda. He's got his hands in illegal weapons, chemical and biological warfare, and it's even suspected he's behind the nuclear missiles stolen from a Russian stockpile several years back."

Another image flashed up, this one taken at a closer range with better resolution. "What makes him so dangerous is that he holds no allegiance to any country or cause, selling death to the highest bidder. His signature is on too many atrocities in the world to count."

Mac looked away, fighting the overwhelming urge to run from the room after seeing Petrović's picture again and hearing Dino recite his resumé. She had seen up close and personal what the man was capable

of, and she shivered at the possibility of facing him
again. The monster was Satan personified.

"We thought 'Dr. Death,' as he is known, had per-
ished in an explosion. As you can see, he's alive and
well and probably working on his next big money-
maker." Dinorelli paused to let that sink in. "The man
has a penchant for combining numerous fatal bio-
chemicals for faster results and better delivery. We
think he may be working on something like that for Al
Qaeda, and because of Mac's prior connection to him,
we know he's fond of using live subjects as guinea
pigs."

Mac forced herself to focus on the screen, remembering when she'd actually seen the dead body of the
dean of the science department at the University in
Morocco. He'd had the misfortune of being one of
those test subjects.

Dinorelli moved to the next picture. "We have to assume the two terrorists met with Dr. Death and are back
in Iran. For now, we're going to concentrate on Petrović,
since we have no clue what he's up to or even if he's still in
South America." He pointed. "You all recognize the president of Venezuela, Jorge Silva. We know he's in bed with
both the Iranians and the Cubans, the common denomi-
nator being their hatred of the United States. If Petrović
is hiding out somewhere in Venezuela doing God only
knows what, it's a given Silva knows about it and most
likely is getting a kickback for protecting him and—"

"Hold up. Where does SWEEPERS come in?"
Ryan asked. "I thought we only got the call after a
botched mission."

"Unfortunately, we're on this because the now-de-
funct group, Alpha Force, fucked up. Griff, Mac, and I
were members of that group, so you could say we're

cleaning up our own mess. If we'd done our jobs right the first time, Dr. Death would be six feet under, and we'd all be in a bar somewhere tossing back a cold one instead of staring at a recent photo of him in a restaurant."

Dinorelli cleared his throat and approached the message board, pointing to a large map of Venezuela. "We're going in as a news team from ZNN. Mac will be the anchor—Ryan and Ty, camera and sound guys. Griff, you'll stay here and coordinate the entire mission."

He clicked the hand-held control again, and the Taj Mahal in Atlantic City appeared on the screen. He moved to the next picture, and both Ryan and Ty whistled. "This is Marita Rojas, the new Miss Universe as of three weeks ago. We know Silva is strutting around like a proud papa, since this woman is his god-child, the daughter of one of his top generals. He jumped at the chance for us to come in and do a story on his relationship with her and her family. He sees it as a way to show his softer side."

Ryan smirked. "Like the man's got a softer side. He's been linked to the disappearance of so many po-litical rivals that they don't even make the front page anymore."

"And that's probably not the worst of it." Dinorelli cleared his throat. "For now, though, that's what we're going with. You're all booked on Transglobal out of Dulles tomorrow morning at 0600. I'd suggest you make the necessary arrangements, and I'll send a car for each of you around 0400. The driver will have everything you need, so pack light. We're only there for a few days, three max. That should give you enough time to get a feel for Silva and maybe some leads on the mad doctor." He closed the laptop. "Questions?"

"Why can't I coordinate the mission on site?" Griff asked.

Dino frowned. "I figured you'd ask that. First off, it would raise suspicions if too many people are there, and second, it will be easier to work around government red tape from an official U.S. office." He looked around the room. "Any more questions?"

"Did you book us first class? I could use a soft seat on that long-ass flight." Ryan made a gun with his finger and thumb and shot an imaginary bullet Mac's way, flashing a big grin.

For the first time since she'd entered the room, Mac felt her shoulder muscles relax, and she smiled back. "I'd say it's a draw, Fitzpatrick. My stomach, your balls."

He closed the gap between them and shook her hand, holding it longer than normal. "Consider us even."

Mac shut the folder and stood, hearing Griff grunt as he passed Ryan. She glanced up in time to see the steely-eyed look he fired Fitzpatrick's way.

She took a second for a better look at Ryan up close. He was about five-eleven, lanky and redheaded, with a grin that was hard to resist. She pegged him as the comic relief, although she knew from what Dino had said and from doing her homework the night before that that he was an expert with explosives, and all business on a mission.

"Okay, if there are no more questions, it's time to put Mac to work." Dinorelli turned to her. "We do things differently here. The bad guys have the same advanced weapons and technical gizmos that we have but better-trained fanatics who have already outsmarted some of our best operatives. I want the team to go with you to the basement, where we're able to simulate real combat situations." When she gave him a what-the-hell look, he continued, "I wanna see how well you work with them."

"And you can tell this after thirty minutes in the basement?"

"You've been in another unit, Mac, mostly working solo." He motioned to Griff. "Take her down and put her through a trial run with the dummies. Then check her hand-to-hand combat technique. I'll see you all back up here afterwards, and we'll finalize the Venezuela trip." He turned and left the room.

A minute or two passed in silence before Ryan broke the ice. "At least you guys will get a look at her martial arts moves and quit harassing me."

"Yeah, like that's gonna happen," Ty said. He smiled at Mac. "You're too pretty to throw on the carpet."

Griff glared. "You just got yourself the first go-around with the lady, Jackson. We'll see how hot she looks to you when she kicks your ass." He stood up. "Come on. We might as well get this over with."

THEY TOOK the elevator to the basement and entered a large area, divided by plywood separators that created a maze in the gymnasium-size room.

"Ryan, you and Ty sit over there while Mac runs through the exercise." Griff turned to Mac and pointed to a gun resembling an AK-47. "Ever use one of these?"

Her expression never changed. "You know I have."

He yanked a yellow vest off the hook on a wall and

handed it to her. "Put this on over your blouse. The gun shoots paint balls, so we'll know if you made the kill or got yourself killed."

"I get it, Griff. I had the same training you did, remember?"

"They've upped the tempo." He led her to the entrance. "Start here and work your way to the other end. It's designed to check your reaction time in a high-risk situation, but be careful. Innocent civilians are in there, too. Try not to kill too many of them," he said with a little more sarcasm than he'd intended.

He watched her enter the practice area, her face defiant. He didn't know why he felt the need to goad her. She'd always been a damn good operative. So why was he trying to push her buttons?

Because he didn't want to work with her again. It was that simple. After she walked out of his life, she should have stayed out of it. If she flunked this test, he wouldn't have to see her every day for who knows how long.

He focused on the overhead screen to check her score. She was nearly at the other end, and she'd only killed one civilian.

She was as good as he remembered.

When she appeared at the exit and looked up at the board, she smiled.

"Oh yeah, girl, you're looking good," Ty said.

"Shut up, Jackson, and get ready to go up against her on the mat." Griff frowned as Ryan and Ty helped her out of the vest.

"Follow me." He walked across the room to an area covered by a large, circular black mat, similar to what wrestlers used. "Mac, if you step off the mat, it's a point for Jackson, and vice versa. First one to five wins. Remember, no takedowns."

Mac took her position in the center of the circle and winked at Ty. Griff shook his head, knowing what would happen next. His young colleague was so busy trying to impress her that he was caught off guard when she sprang toward him, shoving him outside the circle.

"Who's laughing now?" Ryan teased from the side.

"So you wanna take the gloves off, huh, Mac?" Ty asked.

"I thought we already had," she replied.

After three more tries, the score was tied at two points each.

Griff watched, pissed that Mac hadn't lost any of her skills over the past two years, yet mildly amused at the same time. "Come on, Jackson, quit fighting like a girl," he hollered.

Mac glared at him, then bent over, sweeping her arm in a semicircle, inviting him on the mat. "Put up or shut up, Bradley. You wanna show these guys how macho you are?"

His smile faded.

"Go ahead, Griff, show us how it's done," Ryan bellowed.

"Get out of the circle, Ty, and set your watch. This won't take long." Griff turned back to Mac and nailed her with his eyes. "Ready?"

Her smile annoyed him, and he dropped his guard for a split second. She pounced like a hungry predator, pushing him backward. He tried to regain his balance before stepping off the mat but failed. He didn't dare look, knowing she'd still be smiling as Ryan and Ty cheered her on.

"Don't get used to that," he said, when he finally met her gaze. "It won't happen again." He circled her, moving his feet faster than usual for this exercise. Not

only was she keeping up with him, she'd upped the
speed, forcing him to move faster.

He had to quit thinking of her as a lady and see
her as an enemy. He reached for her and shoved her
out of the circle, giving her his best take-that look as
she walked back onto the mat.

"You got lucky," she taunted him.

He reached again, using his weight to lower her to
the mat, pinning her under his body. Before he realized what he was doing, he swooped low, close enough
to see her pupils enlarge as his head blocked off the
overhead light. She licked her lips as if she knew what
was coming.

It took every ounce of willpower not to kiss those
full lips, now wet and opened slightly.

"I thought you said no takedowns, Bradley," she
said, breaking the spell.

"You don't belong here, Mac. Why not tell Dino
you're not up for this job? Head back to California or
wherever the hell you ran off to and do whatever the
hell it is you were doing before you decided to make
my life miserable again."

The hurt registered in her jade eyes before she
made an effort to smile. "It's always all about you,
right, Griff?" She tried to get up, twisting her body
under his. "Let me up, dammit."

It was his turn to smile. "Say uncle."

"Hey, get a room, you two," Ryan shouted from the
stands.

Suddenly feeling foolish, Griff lifted his body off
hers and held out his hand to pull her up.

She flipped her legs up and stood beside him. "I
don't need your help, now or ever. If we're through
playing games, can we go back to Dino's office? I need
to tell him I remember where I saw that slimy Al

Qaeda guy." She moved past him and headed for the door, leaving him standing there like an idiot.

*Why do I let this woman get under my skin?*

He ran to catch up to her. "You remember where you saw him?"

"Better than that. I remember who he was with."

WHEN THEY REACHED Dinorelli's office, Mac sat down before grabbing the folder with the classified reports, hesitating before flipping it open. The picture had nagged at her all morning, but she didn't know why. Leafing through the pages, deliberately avoiding Petrović's picture, she stopped at the photo of Abdul Hamid.

"You all right, Mac?"

She forced herself to look up at Dino. "I knew I'd seen him before," she said, her voice barely rising above a whisper.

He sat down in the chair next to her and pointed to Hamid. "Think, Mac. Was it something you were working on before Bucharest?"

She rubbed her forehead to stop the dull ache forming above her left brow, cursing the three glasses of wine she'd consumed the night before. "We had eyes on an import/export dealer in Cleveland, Ohio, after internet surveillance was alerted to his sudden interest in the ventilation systems at several locations."

"What kind of locations?"

"A couple of airports, hospitals, even a daycare center in San Bernardino."

"What was your role?" Dinorelli asked.

By now, the other three had walked in and were hovering.

"I was already undercover as a member of New Horizons, an organization the agency set up to look sympathetic to Al Qaeda. My story was I'd lost a brother to friendly fire in Afghanistan and the military covered it up, saying he'd turned traitor."

She rubbed her forehead again as the dull pain escalated. "I was sent to Cleveland to determine if the owner of the shop was part of a sleeper cell suspected of raising funds for terrorist operations. I convinced the guy I was looking for revenge."

All three men leaned in, straining to hear.

"That's where I saw him." She bit her lower lip and closed her eyes for a few seconds. "He came into the store one day about three months ago. Talked to the owner in the back room for about thirty minutes, but I never heard the conversation. I remember him, though." She tapped the photo of Hamid several times with her fingernail. "He looked me square in the eyes and smiled on his way out. It was one of those smiles that makes you long for a hot shower and a scrub brush, you know?"

Dinorelli turned to Griff and the other guys, his frown increasing. "It can't be good that Hamid was in the States. I'm betting these bastards are up to something. With September 11th approaching and this guy showing up in Venezuela about the same time surveillance cameras pick up a dead man having coffee there..." He grabbed the phone on the table. "Get Homeland Security on the horn, Sarge. I want to speak to the director himself. Tell them it's a matter of national security."

"So how does that change our plans?" Ryan asked. "You still want us on a plane to Caracas in the morning?"

"Hell no," Dinorelli said. "That can wait. I'll have

ZNN reschedule with Silva—say the lead reporter came down with a stomach virus or something." He turned back to Mac. "Think you can get your old friend at the import store to talk to you? What'd you say his name was?"

Mac jerked her head around. "Jamil Rashid, the brother of the operative Griff killed in Bucharest. He's actually the one who hooked me up with him." A puzzled look crossed her face. "I thought my cover was blown, Dino. You said that's why I was pulled from the case."

Dinorelli sniffed, looking away. "I might have exaggerated a little."

"Christ, Dino, was her cover blown or not?" Ty demanded.

Dino's eyes hardened. "Not exactly. We made sure the reports out of Bucharest claimed Omar Rashid was killed in an attempted robbery gone bad. There was no mention of a female. As far as the bad guys know, he was in the wrong place at the wrong time."

"You lied to me?" Mac couldn't believe what she was hearing.

"Had to," Dino said. "I knew you wouldn't come any other way, and I need you on this, Mac." He raised his hands in the air. "The team needs you. You're the only one who's ever seen Dr. Death up close without one of his many disguises."

Mac swallowed several times in succession, suddenly feeling as if her throat was closing up. Of all the men she knew, Lorenzo Dinorelli was the one she thought would never lie to her, the one who always played by the book. She would've bet her life on it.

And she would have lost that bet.

"That's low, Dino," Griff said. "You should've been up front with her—with all of us."

Mac stole a peek across the table at Griff, noticing the muscle in his right cheek twitching the way it did when he was trying to control his temper. Despite their differences, she had to admit Griffin Bradley would also be included on that short list of men she trusted.

"Like it or not, my job's to keep the bad guys from bringing down more buildings. I did what I had to," Dinorelli responded. "Mac's vital to this mission. If you want to be pissed at me because I put the safety of our country above my personal feelings, so be it. Now get over it. I need your heads in the game a hundred percent, because we might be playing catch-up here."

Mac lifted her head and locked eyes with her new boss. She'd deal with his lie another day. Right now, she agreed with him. If Al Qaeda had something planned, it might already be too late, but they had to try.

"When do you want me to make contact?"

**4**

Mac opened the heavy door and walked into the Global Market House, assessing it quickly for any traps or hidden cameras. Although Dino had assured her Jamil Rashid had no idea she was with his brother when he died, it never hurt to have a backup plan. She touched the upper part of her shirt to make sure the wire was in place, then made eye contact with Rashid.

Sipping a latte at an outdoor café across the street, Griff was set up to monitor the verbal exchange. Ty and Ryan were posing as city workers repairing the traffic light on the corner, ready to rush in if they heard Mac's distress call through their earpieces. The assistance team from the Ohio ATF was in place in various positions on the busy sidewalk, also ready to converge if Griff gave the word.

"Have you heard from Omar?" Mac asked, crossing the store to where he stood behind the counter.

"You don't know?"

She heard the sadness in his voice. "Know what? He was supposed to meet me for dinner before I left Budapest. He never showed."

"Omar was killed in a robbery." Rashid's eyes turned angry. "A couple of street kids or something."

Mac forced herself to remember how she'd felt watching her mother wither away with cancer when she was just a kid, and a few tears rolled down her cheeks. "I'm so sorry, Jamil. I know how much you loved him."

"And you, Katrina. Omar said you and he became very close while he was training you. He said I should find a girl like you for myself. Even asked me to take your name off the possible suicide candidates."

"No!" Mac shouted, hating the way her undercover name rolled off his tongue. "Now more than ever, I want to be a part of it. I owe it to your brother—to my brother."

Rashid walked out from behind the counter and nudged her to the back room. After checking the store again to make sure there were no customers, he whispered, "Yesterday, we received a shipment of weapons from our sources in Venezuela."

Mac pretended elation at the news despite having to hold her breath. "All that money we raised has finally paid off?"

"It's better than we hoped."

She heard Griff's sharp intake of breath through the hidden earpiece.

"That's fantastic! When do I get to see them?"

Rashid studied her face. "Why?"

"Come on, Jamil. I worked as hard as you did to get that money. Let me enjoy the fruits of my labor, if only for a few minutes."

He took a step closer, giving her another whiff of what must have been several days without bathing. "Do you know the area around the Rocket Mortgage Field House—where the Cavaliers play?"

She nodded, having no idea where the arena was, but it should be no problem finding it. She mentally crossed her fingers that the Cavs wouldn't be playing tonight, since she was pretty sure Dino would give the order to destroy the cache of weapons before they left the area. A lot of innocent civilians milling around would only complicate things. "What time should I meet you there?"

He glanced at his watch. "I close in a couple of hours, but it's not busy, so I'll lock up earlier. There is a row of storage units down the street from the Coliseum. The Cavs are on the road tonight, so traffic shouldn't be too bad. I'll pick you up on the corner. Can you find your way there by seven thirty?"

"Seven thirty it is. Praise Allah." She said goodbye on the way out and got into the cab waiting outside.

Thirty minutes later, the team hooked up in Griff's hotel room downtown to analyze the new information. The general consensus was that Rashid either didn't know anything about Petrović, or he was a damn good liar, although the weapons from Venezuela seemed too much of a coincidence. Normally, they would pack up and get out of town, turning over the info to the ATF guys to take care of.

But this was different. Since they'd stumbled onto a new piece of information that could lead to disastrous consequences and time was of the essence, the plan was to take out the storage building with the weapons before getting on a plane back to D.C.

Within two hours, Griff, Ty, and Ryan headed out to the north part of town to scout out the units. Their mission was to make sure the blast didn't put any occupied buildings in harm's way. The fact that the arena wouldn't be packed with basketball fans was an added plus.

After hailing a cab, Mac arrived at the rendezvous point at precisely seven fifteen. She didn't see the rest of the team but knew they had her in their sights. Testing the tiny microphone taped to her chest, she called Griff's name.

His voice came through loud and clear in the nearly invisible microphone in her ear. "You're in view. We're waiting for the exact location of the weapons. You okay?"

"Yes," she replied, reassured they had her back.

As soon as she relayed that information to the crew, Ty and Ryan would enter through a window in the back and set up enough C-4 explosives to turn the weapons into scrap steel *after* she was safely back in her hotel room, away from Rashid.

Standing under a streetlight on the corner, she waited, glancing frequently at her watch. Seven forty-five.

Had he figured out somehow that this was a setup?

Just when Mac decided Jamil Rashid was a no-show, a black Hummer slowly approached from a side street and stopped in front of her. The back door swung open and Rashid leaned out. "Get in, Katrina. Quickly."

She slid across the seat to the opposite side, hating the way he lifted his body to make contact with hers as she passed. Along with the driver, there was another Middle Eastern man in the front seat. "I'm so excited," she said, rubbing her hands together.

Rashid smiled. "Maybe after I show you the weapons, you'll join me in a late dinner. We can talk about Omar."

*Not in this lifetime, dirtbag.*

"Sounds like a plan," she said, smiling seductively.

The Hummer inched down the paved road between the buildings before suddenly making a U-turn and heading in the opposite direction. Her heart raced when she realized they were traveling away from the arena—away from her backup.

Griff whispered, "Got eyes on you," which had a calming effect on her. She knew somewhere out there he sat in a rented van and wouldn't let anything happen to her.

Ten minutes later, they came to a stop in front of a huge red brick structure tucked in the middle of several others. The driver pushed a button, waited for the doors to slide open, then pulled into the belly of the oversized building that looked like an old, abandoned railroad station.

Through the darkened windows, Mac saw shipping crates stacked almost to the ceiling across both sides of the room.

"Wow! There must be over a thousand containers," she exclaimed, making sure Griff and the others heard.

Two heavily armed, thick-necked men appeared out of the shadows and opened the back door, waiting for her and Rashid to step out.

Obviously pleased with her reaction, Rashid hurried toward her, excited. "I can't wait to show you."

He motioned to the hired guns to lift one of the crates off the stack and place it in front of him. After prying off the top, he flipped up the lid.

*Jesus!* She was expecting AK-47s and maybe a few grenades, but this was some serious killing machinery. There were rocket launchers, M16s, and surface-to-air missiles powerful enough to take down a jetliner. Where had this type of weaponry come from, and why in the world did they need it?

She whistled. "Why so much firepower, Jamil? Are

you planning to take out the entire state of Texas or something?" She meant to sound impressed, hoping Griff got the message, but the minute she saw Rashid's furrowed brow, she knew she had gone a little too far with her enthusiasm.

"Why so many questions?"

"I'm just excited, that's all," she said, hoping she hadn't blown it. She leaned closer to touch one of the rocket launchers. "There are some powerful weapons here that can make a big impression with our enemies. When are we planning to use...?" She gasped as her eyes caught site of a stainless-steel canister tucked between two more launchers.

"What is it?" Rashid asked.

It was as if she suddenly had lockjaw. She attempted to speak but couldn't. Finally, she made herself look away from the rattlesnake curled up, ready to strike, staring up at her from the steel container. She hated seeing the emblem she'd seen so many times in Petrović's laboratory in Morocco, hated the memories it forced into her mind. Hated that just looking at it now still sent shivers up her spine and made her feel like she was under his control once again.

"What's the matter?" Rashid stepped closer, eyeing her suspiciously.

Mac recovered somewhat and blew out a breath before she murmured, "I'm overwhelmed. It's definitely better than we'd expected." She hoped her voice didn't betray her.

Rashid continued to stare a few more minutes before he grabbed the front of her blouse. With one violent jerk, he ripped it down the middle, exposing the wire taped directly above her left breast.

"You whore!" he shouted, pulling out his gun. "I'll kill you for this."

Before he could get off a shot, Ty ran out from behind a stack of crates with Ryan right behind him and fired off four rounds. Both of the thugs and the other Middle Eastern passenger crumpled to the concrete as Rashid grabbed his lower leg and hobbled to the car. The driver, who'd remained with the vehicle, quickly backed out with the squeal of the tires reverberating off the walls of the building. Both Ty and Ryan fired at the car but quickly discovered it was bulletproof.

Ty grabbed Mac's arm and ran toward the back where he and Ryan had entered the building. Once they were safely outside and far enough away, Ryan positioned his finger on the detonator.

Ty's eye lit up. "Blow, you mother."

"Wait!"

Ryan halted as Griff's voice rang out in all their earpieces.

"Don't blow it up," he said.

In a matter of seconds, a van appeared at the end of the street and raced toward them. After the vehicle screeched to a halt, Griff climbed out and shouted, "Now that there's no longer a threat of the weapons being used, it's a perfect opportunity for the alphabets to come in and scour through all this. Maybe some of the markings on the guns will give them a clue as to where they originated. Finding the supplier is just as important as getting these out of the hands of the terrorists. ATF is on the way with a backup team right behind them."

When Ryan nodded and gingerly held the detonator away from his body, Griff turned to Mac, anger flashing in his eyes. "What the hell happened in there, Mac?"

"I...I was only trying to let you know—"

"Let me know what? That you blew your cover

when you hesitated? You might as well have flashed your government ID."

She lowered her head, pulling the torn edges of her blouse closer together.

"Leave her alone, Griff," Ty said. "It all worked out. We got most of the bad guys and their toys." He pointed to the building where an ATF unit had arrived and was rushing toward the entrance in full combat gear.

Griff ignored them for a minute and turned his rage on his youngest team member. "Damn it, Ty. She nearly got you killed. That's not acceptable on my watch." He walked back to the car, hesitating briefly before he slid into the driver's seat. "And in case none of you noticed, Rashid and one of his thugs got away."

"I'm sure Dino called in reinforcements to pick them up," Ryan said, moving to stand next to Mac as if to shield her from Griff's anger.

"He doesn't know we're here," Griff said. "He thinks we're somewhere behind the arena. I didn't have time to tell him the location had changed. Get in, Mac," he commanded. "Ryan, you and Ty stay here and disarm the C-4. I'll see you back at the hotel." He slammed the door after Mac climbed in, as if to emphasize how upset he really was.

The drive back to the hotel was shorter than it seemed. Mac stole an occasional glance at Griff, noticing the twitch on the right side of his face had finally settled down. But the scowl on his face left no doubt he was still really angry.

And he had every reason to be. She knew better than to react so out of character with Rashid. That was the first thing she was taught when she trained for undercover work.

What had she been thinking?

She had to tell Griff about the emblem. That Petrović was involved somehow in the weapons showing up in Cleveland. The snake was an instant giveaway and had conjured up every horrible moment she spent with him in the mountains. She opened her mouth, but nothing came out.

At least now she wouldn't have to go to Dino and ask to be reassigned the way Griff suggested. After her performance tonight, it was a given that her future on this team, or any other for that matter, was no longer in her hands.

She blinked several times in rapid succession to keep the lone tear that had formed from rolling down her cheek when reality finally hit. *Dammit!* The last thing she needed was for Griff to see her crying, to accuse her of yet another weakness. But she couldn't help it, and the tear trickled down her cheek.

She'd almost gone to her grave tonight because of her own mistake. But what was worse, she'd almost taken her teammates with her.

SHE PRESSED her back into the cold tiles of the shower, sliding down until she sat crouched on the floor. The hot water flowed down her face, blending with the tears. The only thing left in her life giving her any pleasure was her job, and now, even that would be gone. No one would want to work with her, knowing they'd have to worry about her getting them killed. Griff was probably on the phone right now with Dino demanding a replacement.

At the thought of Griff, she wondered what bothered her more. That he went off on her in front of the guys, or that he had every right to? The only emotion she seemed to have left him with was mistrust. For a while, she'd let herself believe maybe they could at least work together.

Who was she kidding? Working together wasn't what she'd hoped for today. She imagined being in his arms again, especially after the *almost* kiss on the mat back at the training facility at headquarters. But he'd sent the message loud and clear. That would never happen. How could she expect him to love her again when she didn't even love herself?

She grabbed the soap from the floor and scrubbed until her skin was the color of strawberries, but even then, she didn't feel clean. She was damaged goods.

The shrill ringing of the phone snapped her back to reality, and she sprang to her feet. After several rings, it stopped. She figured it was Ryan or Ty checking on her after Griff's verbal spanking. She'd seen the way both of them looked at her when Griff was reaming her out. She didn't want their pity right now—or ever.

*Get a grip, Mac. You've never been a wimp or a quitter.*

She let the spray of warm water wash over her for a few more minutes before stepping from the shower. Tomorrow, she'd tell Dino about seeing the snake emblem on the canister and have a chat with him about setting her up at a desk job, or something else less likely to prove detrimental to her own health as well as that of her teammates.

Or maybe she should just head back to California and buy a little house on a private beach. At least there, she wouldn't be responsible for getting someone she cared about killed.

And she wouldn't have to be in the same room

with Griff every day or see the disgust in his eyes when he looked at her.

But that would all happen tomorrow. Tonight, she decided she needed more than a hot shower to get past the events of the day before she could even think about tackling anything else. She walked to the mini-bar, pulled out two small bottles of vodka, and emptied them into a tumbler. Lifting the glass to her lips, she chugged, hoping the burning sensation would get her mind off the mess she'd made.

It didn't.

She went back to the minibar, intent on drinking enough liquor to do the trick. Before she could decide if it was worth a trip to the ice machine, there was a knock at the door.

"Mac?"

*Griff!* She tiptoed to the door and peeked out. He looked so good, dressed in a navy-blue shirt and jeans, his hair still wet from his own shower. But she wasn't about to let him come in and lecture her again. He'd already made it perfectly clear to her and the rest of the team that he found her undercover skills woefully lacking. Tomorrow was soon enough to hear any remaining thoughts he might have about her incompetence on the job or the consequences of it.

"I know you're in there, Mac. Don't make me pull rank and order you to open this door." When she didn't respond, he added, "Because I will, you know."

Just when she thought the day couldn't get any worse.

She grabbed the heavy white robe from the bathroom, pulled it on, and belted it as she crossed to the door.

When she finally opened it, Griff stared at her

face. "You been crying?" He walked past her and plopped down on the bed.

Closing the door, she pressed against it, chewing on her lip to keep the tears from re-forming. Sometimes she hated being a girl. "Say what you came to say, Griff, then let me get back to my pity party."

He tilted his head as if he were analyzing the situation before a hint of a smile crossed his face. Rising from the bed, he walked over to the dresser and picked up the two empty mini vodka bottles. "This your idea of a pity party?"

"Cut the small talk. You've already told me what a screw-up I am. I don't need more proof."

She expected him to react with anger and rush out. Instead, he opened the minibar and grabbed two bottles of tequila. He poured one into her empty glass and the other in a clean one from the dresser.

Carrying them to where she stood glued to the door, he handed one to her. "Drink this. It will help you sleep." He tilted his head back and drained his. After she did the same, he took the empty glasses and put them back on the dresser. "I've thought about this ever since we got back. I was pretty hard on you in front of the others, but hell, Mac, I know you're better than—"

"Petrović had something to do with the shipment," she blurted.

His eyes softened at the mention of the guy he knew had terrorized her. "How do you know?"

She swallowed the lump in her throat, praying for the courage to tell him without her mind dragging her back to the place she had fought so hard to forget. "One of the canisters had his emblem on it. When I saw it, I froze." She met his gaze. "I'm sorry, Griff. I know I put the team in danger, but I reacted before I had time to process it. I guess thinking I could do this mission was a big mistake. I'm sure after you tell Dino what I did, it will all be a moot point, anyway."

He sat back down on the bed. "I talked to the guys before I came down here, and we're all in agreement. I'm not going to tell Dino the entire truth about you blowing your cover—only that Rashid was suspicious and discovered the wire. Although we have to tell him about the emblem, he doesn't need to know that it completely threw you off your game."

Relief washed over her. He had just offered her life back. No matter how hard she tried to convince herself it didn't matter if she lost the only job she'd ever loved, she couldn't. "I don't know what happened today, Griff. I was so surprised by what I saw..." She couldn't finish—couldn't tell him why seeing the snake had unnerved her so badly.

He stood and sauntered toward her, stopping a few feet from the door. "This isn't a free pass, Mac. I'll be watching everything you do. Fuck up one more time, and you're off my team for good."

He reached for the doorknob at the same time she did. When his hand closed over hers, she gasped, the electricity sending jolts all the way down to her toes.

He grabbed both her hands and entwined them with his, pinning her against the door with his body. Slowly, he inched her arms up the length of the door, over her head, until his body was so close to hers that she could feel his heart racing against her chest.

She held his steel-blue gaze until he lowered his head, pressing his forehead to hers. She felt his warm breath brush across her eyelashes, his five o'clock shadow tickling her cheeks, and every nerve in her body awakened with the sensations. She loved this man, always had.

Suddenly, he dropped her arms. "I can't do this again."

He pulled the door open and was gone, leaving her feeling the same way she'd felt all those months they'd been apart.

Alone and unlovable.

**5**

G riff kept his promise and didn't tell Dinorelli
about Mac's mistake, even when he got his own
ass chewed out for not calling for backup after the location was switched. Although he avoided making eye
contact with her for the next few days, it was business
as usual. The Venezuela trip was rescheduled for the
following day, and Mac was looking forward to it.
With the rush of feelings that overwhelmed her when
Griff was in the same room, she needed distance to
stay focused.

The knowledge that Joseph Petrović was involved
in the arms shipment had the director even more excited about what the team would find in Venezuela. It
was the first real connection to the mad scientist since
the intel picture had captured his face on an unrelated
mission.

At six the next morning, Mac, Ty, and Ryan
boarded the plane in Washington, their aliases intact,
and after a quick layover in Miami, they transferred to
a 757 for Simon Bolivar Airport in Caracas. Since D.C.
and Venezuela were in the same time zone, they
would arrive in Caracas before one, and they'd need to
get on the road as soon as they landed. A van would

be waiting to take them to the reigning Miss Universe's home in Calabozo, about one hundred and ten miles from the airport. Though a thirty-minute helicopter ride between cities would have been faster, the team had decided on a road trip. It would provide the perfect opportunity to get an up-close look at the landscape and to watch for anything out of the ordinary. If Dr. Death was in Caracas, it was a sure bet they wouldn't find him in the heart of the city.

Mac reclined her seat and closed her eyes, hoping to snooze away at least an hour of the nearly four-hour flight. As promised, Dino had come through with first class. Just as she was drifting off, she heard a familiar voice then felt a rush of warm air across her cheek. Opening her eyes, she saw Ryan next to her, obviously having talked the former occupant into exchanging seats.

"Thought I'd keep you safe on the flight." He moved closer. "My way of making up with you."

Mac cocked her head his way. "Didn't I make it perfectly clear back at command that I don't need protection? Or have you already forgotten what happened two weeks ago in the rain?"

"Ouch!" He raised one reddish-brown eyebrow. "Okay, no protecting. Let's just say I want to get to know you a little better. Does that work for you?"

"As long as you're aware I 'chew men up and spit them out,' according to Bradley. He's full of it, by the way." She extended her hand. "I'll take you up on the offer of friendship, but trust me, I'm not in the market for anything else."

"Fair enough. You're not my type, anyway. I prefer women who can't kick my ass." He leaned in. "Is it true you hold the unbeaten record for marksmanship at Langley?"

She frowned. "That story is exaggerated. Now, please, new friend, be quiet so I can get some sleep." She moved his hand, which had drifted dangerously close to the side of her breast, and growled at him.

Closing her eyes again, she tried to fall asleep but couldn't. Flashes of the other night in her hotel room with Griff monopolized her thoughts. She'd wanted him to hold her, reassure her things would be all right again, but how could he? She'd thrown away any chance of that happening when she ran from him two years before without telling him how badly Petrović had scarred her, how the man's touch still haunted her dreams. Now, she wasn't even sure they could be friends.

Erasing those thoughts from her mind, she turned up the volume on her headset and watched the newest *Mission: Impossible* movie, thinking Tom Cruise's mischievous smile reminded her of Ryan's. Sometime after that, she must have dozed off, because the next thing she heard was the pilot making the landing announcement. She shook Ryan, who was snoring softly with his head on her shoulder.

He shot up in his seat and reached for his piece before realizing he'd left it at home, per the director's instructions. Arrangements had been made for weapons to be distributed upon landing.

Deplaning in Caracas took longer than expected, but after ninety minutes, they were settled in the van with their equipment and heading southwest to Calabozo. Thankfully, Venezuelan weather in September was much like D.C.'s. It was actually pleasant, and Mac guessed the temperature was in the seventies, although she knew from the internet that they were still in their wet season.

As promised, Raul Perez, a longtime informant

acting as their driver, had brought each one a 9A-91, the smallest assault rifle made, but insisted they keep them under the seats unless needed. "Calabozo sits between the mountains and the plains, so there isn't much scenery of interest other than the farmlands," he explained. "However, we may encounter a few bandits on the way."

Mac sat in the front seat, scanning the countryside for something, anything that might suggest a clue to Petrović's whereabouts. About an hour into the trek, they passed through a village with absolutely no visible activity. No kids playing, no cars on the road, no sign of life anywhere.

She was about to mention it to Perez when twenty or more armed men suddenly appeared in the road, their automatic weapons trained on the van. She reached under the seat and wrapped her fingers around the gun.

"No, miss," the driver said. "Stay calm and let me do the talking."

She straightened in the seat, her instincts on high alert, her hand positioned to grab the automatic weapon.

An older soldier approached the driver's side and motioned for them to step out of the van. Against her better judgment, Mac opened the door and got out, then watched Ty and Ryan slide the side door open and do the same. One look told her both were as apprehensive as she was about leaving the guns in the van. Immediately, they were surrounded by the soldiers, none appearing old enough to need razors.

As if in slow motion, she watched Perez slowly open the door. With the hair on her neck standing at attention and the air crackling with electricity, she held her breath as the drama played out. When Perez stumbled, several of the armed men rushed up, shouting as they discharged their weapons. The driver crumpled to the ground as the baby-faced soldiers fired several more rounds into his already lifeless body.

Her body numb with horror, the metallic smell of Perez's blood spreading over the dirt road, her years of training kicked in and she made a move toward the armed men. But Ryan beat her there and grabbed the killer's gun before another soldier stepped in and stopped him with the butt of an AK-47. Blood spurted from the nasty wound on his forehead as he fell backward, landing almost on top of the dead Venezuelan.

"Stop!" Mac screamed when the soldiers circled Ryan, their guns aimed at his head.

GRIFF PACED the length of the communications center, his eyes trained on the screen and the satellite images. He still had a bad feeling about sending Mac and the others to Venezuela without him but had to admit Dinorelli's reasoning made sense. Being close to Washington was a definite plus if something went wrong.

So far, everything was operating on schedule. The group was on their way to Calabozo, where they would meet with Miss Universe for the interview and photoshoot. They were scheduled to have dinner at the presidential palace and do a follow-up interview with Silva. The next day they would shoot a short documentary about Venezuela. Two days in, then they'd be on a plane back to D.C., hopefully with some insight as to what Dr. Death was up to.

The man was supposed to be dead. How he had escaped the laboratory explosion was a mystery to everyone and the reason Griff hadn't slept all night. He'd tossed and turned, reliving that day like it was yesterday. When the SEALS plucked Mac from the lab hidden in the Middle Atlas Mountain of Morocco, he'd made a promise to himself that he'd never let anything like that happen to her again.

But he couldn't keep his promise. Mac was in South America right now, and he was stuck in a large building hidden in small-town Virginia.

He glanced again at the satellite images, relieved everything still looked good. Like other SWEEPER missions under his command, his job was to make sure things went down as planned. He hated surprises. Every mission generated a surge of adrenaline that came with not knowing the outcome, but this one was causing more raw nerves than usual.

This one was different.

And he hated knowing the reason why.

He walked to his office in the back corner of the room, grumbling under his breath. Seeing Mac again after not hearing from her for so long had taken him by surprise. Despite being thinner, she looked the same, her long, dark curls still unruly. It had triggered memories of the days when they were so in tune with each other that they didn't even have to speak to know what the other one was thinking or feeling.

But he had to quit thinking that way and look at her only as a member of his elite squad. Things could get complicated if she was able to invade his brain from clear across the globe. After what almost happened in her room the other night, he would be wise to keep a safe distance.

He meant nothing to her now, was only a teammate, and he vowed to keep it that way. He could take only so much rejection in one lifetime.

To this day he had no idea what had gone wrong between them. They'd both been working for the CIA on a mission to find a suspected biochemical dealer in Morocco. After two weeks without finding anything, the rest of the team had returned home, leaving Mac with a handler to stay another month to finish out her cover as a visiting university professor.

Just when they were convinced the Moroccan trip had been a bust, Joseph Petrović, an exiled war criminal, nicknamed Dr. Death because of his penchant for using human subjects to test his nerve gas delivery system, had made contact with her. Nobody knew how obsessed the man who claimed to be the lead chemist for a large chemical company had been with her until it was too late and she was in his clutches. Held prisoner in a mountain hideout overlooking Morocco, completely hidden from satellite surveillance, Mac had been on her own while they scrambled for any clue as to where she was.

Griff remembered those eight days well, unsure if she was dead or alive. He'd nearly gone crazy, feeling so helpless, and begged Dino to let him go back to Morocco to search for her himself. Somehow, Mac had found a way to get a message to them, but she was unable to pinpoint her location.

With a lot of luck, they were able to trace her last signal to the mountain laboratory, and a SEAL team had worked quickly to extract her. After they had her safely out of the building, they blew it apart, along with the ruthless kidnapper trapped inside.

Or so they'd thought.

But Mac was never the same after that. The sparkle in her eyes disappeared, her ability to be around people gone. No matter how hard he'd tried to help, she wouldn't let him in, leaving the details of her ordeal with Petrović to his own vivid imagination. In the end, she'd confessed she no longer had feelings for him, left the agency, and moved to the West Coast. All in the space of two weeks. He'd tried to talk her out of it but eventually realized she wasn't ready to share her feelings or anything about her captivity with him.

After a year, he gave up on her ever returning to D.C. and tried to move on. And he thought he had until she yanked off that stupid blond wig in Romania and looked him in the eyes. For an instant, he'd wondered if they could work it out, but that thought quickly vanished when he faced her again in Dinorelli's office. She'd made it perfectly clear her feelings hadn't changed.

It really didn't matter anymore. He had a job to do, and that meant keeping his personal feelings separate from the mission. She'd nearly been killed the other night after a stupid mistake. He should have told Dino about her screw-up before they'd even left Cleveland —should have insisted she be yanked from his team. And he'd fully intended to, but when the moment came, the words didn't come.

A telephone ringing in the main room snapped him back to attention. He picked up the folder labeled RESURRECTION, denoting Petrović's rise from the ashes, and tried to concentrate on the reports.

After a few minutes, he slammed it shut. He might as well face it. He would be useless until the team stepped back on U.S. soil in a couple of days. All he could do was watch and wait.

He sucked at both.

"Agent Bradley!" a young Navy ensign called. "You'd better get out here ASAP. We have a situation."

Knocking his desk chair back as he sprang out of it, Griff raced from the office. "What kind of situation?" He focused on the satellite shot and pointed to the Venezuelan soldiers. "Why have they stopped the van?"

The soldier hesitated before responding. "They showed up out of nowhere and shot the driver. We're trying to get a better look."

"Where's Director Dinorelli?"

"Downstairs in a meeting with some bigwig from the Pentagon. That's why we called you."

"I don't give a rat's ass who's with him. Send someone down there and tell him we need him here *now*." Griff moved closer to the satellite image, hoping it wasn't as bad as he'd originally thought.

It was.

He drummed his fingers on the table, eyes glued to the screen. This was supposed to be a relatively danger-free mission. Get in—get out. What had gone wrong?

After what seemed much longer than the five minutes it actually was, Dinorelli rushed through the door and moved quickly to where Griff and the others were watching the screen.

"What the..." he muttered. "Who are they?"

"Our best guess—paramilitary, sir," the ensign began. "We're waiting on a call from Venezuela to find out more, but at this point, we can only speculate."

"Damn it, Dino! I knew I should have gone with them." Griff slumped into the nearest chair, lowering his head into his hands, a helpless feeling overwhelming him.

"I need you here," Dinorelli responded.

"No!" Griff shouted when he looked up in time to see one of his teammates fall to the ground. "Pull whatever goddamn strings you have to before it's too late." He jumped up, pointing to the screen. "Where the hell are the weapons the guy was supposed to give them?"

"Calm down, Griff. You know as much as I do." Dino's tone was harsh before he softened it a little. "Let's let this play out. They're all professionals, and they've been in worse situations than this. Hell, you trained Fitzpatrick and Jackson yourself. Give them a chance to work it out on their own." He reached for the phone the soldier held out.

Griff listened as his boss spoke to someone in the capital building in Caracas under the guise of a ZNN executive who'd received an SOS from one of his employees on the job over there. Hearing that conversation did nothing to allay his fears. The last time Dino gave the team more time to work it out on their own, Mac had paid the price. Now, here Griff was again, unable to do a thing while she and the team were in Venezuela facing a bunch of renegade soldiers who probably killed for kicks.

They were *his* team. He was supposed to keep them safe.

The painful truth was that whatever was going to happen would play out in the next few minutes. Even the Venezuelan president couldn't get help there quickly enough. Griff could only stand by and watch the drama unfold.

He closed his eyes. He couldn't lose her again.

MAC FUMBLED WITH HER JACKET, reaching for her press credentials. "We're American journalists."

One of the soldiers slapped her hand away before reaching in himself. His eyes held a hint of a smile as he lingered a few moments, roughly cupping her left breast under the jacket before pulling out the papers and handing them to an older man who appeared behind them. Then he walked back to Ryan and hovered, almost daring him to move.

The new arrival, obviously the leader from the way the others reacted, scanned the credentials before giving her a skeptical look. "You expect me to believe you're reporters? Why is ZNN in Caracas?"

Ty held up his hand, indicating to Mac he would take the lead. He pointed to the documents sticking out of his shirt pocket. "My passport. We're on our way to Calabozo to do an interview with the reigning Miss Universe."

At the mention of the beauty queen, the soldiers began to chatter. One flick of the commander's hand silenced them. "Why would you want to interview her? The world doesn't seem all that impressed. Nobody came around last year when we had another winner."

Ty, who looked almost as young as the Venezuelans, took a step forward. "One Miss Universe is not big news, but two in a row? America wants the story about your country, your culture, and the many beautiful women here."

The solders began whispering to one another again.

"Silence!" The commander moved to Mac, scanning her as if he could see under the dark blue suit. "Why did your driver pull a gun on my men?"

"That's a load of crap!" she exclaimed. "Your men—"

She stopped mid-sentence when his eyes turned cold, and she glanced toward Ty, who shook his head. Turning slightly, she made eye contact with Ryan, who was finally allowed to stand and was now pressing a handkerchief to his forehead. He tried to smile to reassure her that he was okay.

"We have no idea unless he thought you were trying to rob us," Ryan interjected. "We didn't hire him ourselves. The van and the driver were sent by your president."

Mac watched the scene play out, grateful Ryan had stepped in. If she had her way, these thugs would pay for killing the driver in cold blood. But she wasn't stupid. Three against twenty only ended well on the big screen in Hollywood. Her anxiety increased as a soldier jumped from the van, carrying the guns from under the seats.

The commander smirked as he examined them. "I can't wait to hear why reporters need to carry state-of-the-art automatic weapons."

"The driver gave them to us in case we ran into trouble. None of us even knows how to use one," Mac said in her best girlie-girl voice.

The commander narrowed his eyes. "And I'm supposed to believe this?"

"Call President Silva yourself," Ryan said. "I'm sure the driver was simply following orders."

For a few moments, the commander stared at Ryan before pulling out a cell phone. Before he could call, the phone rang, and he turned away from them to talk. After a string of "yes, sirs," he hung up and did a 180, barking orders to clear the road to allow the van to continue to Calabozo. Mac guessed the caller had been Silva, and from the scowl on the leader's face, the president hadn't been pleased.

This project was important to the head of the country, and it was a given he wouldn't look kindly on anyone messing with his plans for his goddaughter. She'd told the whole world when she was crowned

Miss Universe that she wanted to live in New York City and work as a dancer. What better way to get attention than to have her face splashed across televisions all over the world?

After confiscating their weapons and phones, the commander instructed one of his soldiers to drive and positioned another in the back seat, wedged between Ty and Ryan in case they encountered another band of thieves along the way. After a brief nod to each other, Mac and her teammates settled in, exchanging relieved looks when the van headed south again.

GRIFF STARED AT THE SCREEN, wondering why one of the soldiers was now behind the wheel of the van and another was crowded into the back seat with Ty and Ryan. This couldn't be good. When Dino walked up, Griff twisted around to face him. "Have you made contact with any of them?"

Dino shook his head. "My guess is they either don't have access to their phones or, more likely, there's no service. As I mentioned earlier, they're professionals, Griff. They'll handle it."

Griff couldn't help thinking about that night in Cleveland when Mac lost her cool. "I worry about Mac. She's not a hundred percent since she joined the unit."

Dino moved closer so he could whisper. "Cut her some slack. You have no idea what she's been through."

Griff stared at him suspiciously. "Since when did you start going soft?"

The director held Griff's eyes for a moment, almost as if deciding whether to say something. Finally, he

pulled Griff to the other side of the room, away from
the others. "Since I found out Petrović did a number
on her. The bastard tortured her for the entire eight
days he had her, battering her both physically and
emotionally. What she's been through most women
wouldn't recover from."

Griff was stunned by what his boss had just said.
He knew Mac was a changed woman when she returned from Morocco, but she never gave any indication that her time with Petrović had been that bad.
"How do you know this?" he asked, sad that the
woman he had been prepared to spend the rest of his
life with felt safe enough to share that kind of info
with Dino and not him.

"Let's just say there's very little about any of you
that I don't know and leave it at that." Dino pointed to
the screen. "Looks like the crisis has been averted.
Guess my call to President Silva reminding him that
unless he intervened with my ZNN crew, his goddaughter would never see her dreams come true, had
an impact."

"Glad that worked. I don't even want to think
about what might have happened if it hadn't."

"Keep your eye on them until they return to the
hotel. I'll be in my office if we need to make another
call to Silva." He turned and walked out of the room,
leaving Griff staring at the satellite image, unable to
think about anything except how he was going to
make Petrović pay for what he could only imagine
he'd done to Mac.

**6**

## Sixty miles southwest of Caracas, Venezuela
## A laboratory in the forest

JOSEPH PETROVIĆ ADJUSTED THE BINOCULARS, training them on the lone female of the group, positive his eyes were playing tricks on him. He moved to a better spot on the balcony. Hidden by the forest draping the mountain, the laboratory was out of sight of aerial surveillance. Because of that, this was the only spot in the eight-thousand-square-foot building where he could see the road when something interested him.

And something definitely interested him.

When the woman turned her head, moving directly into his sight, he got a better look at her and gasped.

It couldn't be, could it? He'd heard she'd left the CIA after he was supposedly killed. He narrowed his eyes, remembering that time like it was yesterday.

Was it really her?

Dr. Mackenzie Conley.

What was the CIA doing in South America?

Memories of their time together two years before

flashed in his mind. After three weeks of sitting in her classroom at the university listening to her lecture on biochemical weapons, watching her move gracefully around the podium, occasionally smiling at some young student in the front, he'd known he had to have her for his very own. Very few things excited him beyond his experiments, and when he found something that did, he could be very persistent. Before he knew it, she'd become an obsession, occupying all his thoughts.

Disregarding the fact that he was risking his entire project that already had a buyer willing to pay enough money to finance the rest of his life in luxury, he'd found a way to lure her to his laboratory in the mountains with the help of her boss and the promise of a tour of his facilities, as well as a large monetary contribution to the university. Once he'd isolated her on the mountain, he started the mating ritual, leaving a fresh orchid and a chocolate kiss on her bed every day.

He'd possessed a lot of women, most of them through force, but this one was different. He wanted—needed—her to come willingly to his bed. But she'd been a hard one to crack, and in the end, he'd had to drug her and bring out his favorite toys. He felt the familiar ache in his groin at thinking how terrified she'd been when he strapped her to the bed and did things to her that he knew would break her. Chuckling to himself, he reasoned that not even the best CIA training in the world could have prepared her for him.

Even when she'd found a way to overpower the soldier stationed outside her bedroom door and make her way out of the building to use the satellite phone and call for help, he hadn't worried, convinced his lab was hidden too well to be discovered.

But he'd been wrong, and paid with the total destruction of everything he'd worked so hard to accomplish.

His attention was diverted back to the roadside scene when he saw the Americans get in the van and drive away. Quickly, he rushed into the bedroom and grabbed the phone.

"Yes, Dr. Petrović?"

"Who were those people you just released?"

Though Silva had assigned the men exclusively to protect the lab and his experiments, Joseph had allowed them to participate in extracurricular activities for the revenue necessary to support their drug habits. Today was a special treat for them, a payback of sorts for not getting sloppy seconds on the dead girl a few days ago.

"A news crew from the States."

He recognized the voice as Rolando, the commander of the group.

A news crew? Not likely. It sounded like Mackenzie was back in the spy business again. "Why'd you let them go?" Usually, the soldiers killed their victims and hid the bodies. That way, nobody ever came snooping around.

"Direct orders of President Silva himself," the officer reported. "They're here to do a story on the reigning Miss Universe."

Petrović bit his lip to keep from laughing at the absurd idea. Another example of how easy it was to do a snow job on the man who ran the country. "And they're on their way to Calabozo?"

"Yes, doctor."

Petrović smiled and hung up. So Mackenzie was up to her old tricks again. Walking to the bookshelves lining the far bedroom wall, he pushed the button behind a biography of the Great Houdini. As the secret door opened, his excitement about seeing the woman he would never forget reached a new level. She wouldn't come willingly this time, either, but he was up for the challenge. He'd had two long years preparing for it.

From the massive collection, he chose a disguise even his beloved Mackenzie wouldn't recognize.

BY THE TIME they arrived in Calabozo, the trio was tired, sticky, and in a hurry to get the job done and head back to Caracas. From every account, traveling on the back roads after dark was an open invitation to be robbed. Or worse.

When they reached Calabozo, it was as if they'd entered another country. The small farmhouses dotting the landscape sharply contrasted with the modernized Caracas. It was like stepping away from New York City and landing in a small town in the Midwest.

Marita Rojas's residence looked much the same as the rest of the houses on the block: small, run-down, and sporting an elevated tank in the front yard that held their water supply. Miss Universe turned out to be a delight, and the interview went as planned. It was entertaining to watch the two guys compete for her attention, although Ryan hadn't stood a chance. One glimpse of Ty, and the attractive young woman never looked away.

The two-hour return trip was uneventful, with Mac sitting on the edge of her seat most of the way. At the hotel entry, the soldiers handed over their phones but kept the weapons. The debacle on the trip had unnerved them all more than they'd thought, and it was more than a little stressful to know that if there were more surprises in store for them, they would be without protection.

The plan was to tour the capital building and add the interview with President Silva to what they already had gotten from the beauty queen, but they were exhausted.

Ryan made a quick call to the presidential palace and convinced Silva he wouldn't get their best work if he insisted on filming the interview that day. He flashed a grin toward Mac after disconnecting. "See, princess, even the president thinks you need your beauty sleep."

"Cut the crap, Fitzpatrick. I look way better than you." She stepped in for a closer look at his head wound. "Get room service to send up a roll of tape and some bandages and bring them to my room. I'll patch you up until you can get it looked at back home."

Ryan wrinkled his nose. "How about I bring a bottle of wine with me?" He paused and raised his eyebrows. "Since we don't have any Novocain, of course."

Ty and Mac burst out laughing.

"I'm getting disillusioned, my friend. I thought you had better moves than that," Ty deadpanned.

It felt good to share a light moment after what they'd been through, even though they were all still edgy.

As they walked into the lobby, Mac whistled. President Silva had insisted they stay here and made the arrangements himself, definitely his way of trying to get more favorable coverage. A crowd milled around, a few tourists but mostly Venezuelan men in business suits and local women dressed in brightly colored dresses and heels that had probably cost more than Mac's entire wardrobe. Even the lighting screamed

luxury, with the massive crystal chandelier overhead
casting dancing reflections around the room. She
couldn't wait to see her room, deciding she didn't even
want to know how much it cost, since the Venezuelan
government was footing the bill.

Alone at last after the bellman delivered her luggage, Mac stripped off her suit and headed for the
shower. After their close call, it was comforting to
know Ryan and Ty were in rooms next to hers. She
shivered, painfully aware the young guerillas would
have unloaded their weapons and left their bodies
with the driver's along the side of the road, for sheer
pleasure alone, if their leader hadn't spoken to the
president.

She sighed, not sure she could handle this undercover work much longer. Maybe it was time to have a
heart-to-heart with Dino about working a desk out of
the Virginia office from now on. But that would mean
she'd probably run into Griff every day.

Although the thought was not revolting, it was
reason enough not to pursue it. As soon as she was in
her room, she called Dino to check in, then phoned
Griff. He answered on the first ring, not even bothering to say hello.

"Is everything okay?"

"Yes," Mac responded. "It got a little hairy for a few
minutes, but we're back at the hotel. They confiscated
our weapons and our phones, so this is the first
chance I got to report in." She tried to keep her voice
light so he wouldn't pick up on how shaken she had
really been watching their driver get shot in cold
blood.

"And nobody got hurt?"

"The driver's dead, and Ryan has a nasty cut on his
forehead from when he tried to stop them from killing

us. I'm going to patch him up as best I can, but he'll need medical attention when we get back to the—"

"Which will be first thing in the morning," Griff interrupted. "I'll have tickets for the early nonstop out of Caracas sent to the hotel tonight."

"No," she said emphatically. "We pushed back on the interview with the president until tomorrow afternoon. Although the chances are not great that we'll find anything, we have to go through with this on the slim chance that there might be some connection between him and Petrović."

"No," Griff said, just as emphatically. "It's too dangerous. Even Dino will insist you kiss off the meeting with Silva and come home. He's—"

"I've already spoken to Dino. He agreed we've come too far to give it up now."

"Why would he allow you to further risk your lives after what just happened? And why would you call Dino before me?"

She heard the frustration in his voice and wondered what that was all about. "Dino was still the boss the last time I checked, Griff. He said he called President Silva, pretending to be a CEO at ZNN. Told him he'd received a distress signal from his team. Said Silva nearly flipped when he heard and ensured him something like that wouldn't happen again."

"Yeah, like the man never lies. We were lucky this time, Mac, but I still think you should abort the mission and get out of Venezuela."

As good as that sounded, they had to stay. President Silva had a vested interest in keeping them safe, and so far, they'd learned nothing about Joseph Petrović. Although they'd all kept a watchful eye on the countryside, no one had seen anything remotely suggesting he might be in the area.

"We're okay, Griff. We'll interview Silva tomorrow afternoon and be on the first flight back early Thursday morning. That's a promise."

After a moment, she heard him take in a deep breath. "Guess that will have to do, but say the word and I can have you home in a matter of hours."

What was up with him? He almost sounded like he cared about her.

*Just my imagination,* she thought as she hung up. A knock startled her, and she nearly screamed. A peek showed Ryan outside her door with a silly grin, holding up a first aid kit.

After she let him in, he flopped down on the bed and opened the kit. "We know how good you are as a biochemist, Mac. Let's see you do your best Nancy Nurse impression." He sat quietly while she first cleaned the wound, then put several Steri Strips on it.

"You're good to go," she said after applying a large Band-Aid over the area. "Try not to get this wet."

Still grinning, he got up from the bed. "Without a doubt, sharing a bottle of wine with you would have taken the pain away."

She laughed. "Get out of here and get some sleep. We have a busy day tomorrow."

After she closed the door behind him, she pulled off her blouse on the way to the shower. As the hot, steamy water trickled down her tired body, its soothing fingers massaged away the tension. Her thoughts went back to Griff and his reaction when she phoned.

She'd run from him after her extraction from Morocco when he hinted at a relationship with more commitment. Being engaged was one thing, but actually walking down the aisle scared the bejesus out of her. She loved the man too much to drag him down with her. And down was definitely where she'd been headed in the months after her move to California.

She reached for the shampoo and lathered her hair, remembering how Griff had done that very thing for her on more than one occasion.

*Oh God, Mac! Don't go there.*

Quickly, she rinsed out the suds then stepped from the shower. After toweling dry, she slipped on a nightshirt and slid under the luxurious, silky sheets, an audible sigh of approval escaping her lips. Despite her being totally exhausted, sleep evaded Mac as the image of Petrović's eyes flashed across her mind every time she closed her own.

MAC AWOKE with a start and glanced at the clock on the nightstand. Eight twenty. Why did she still feel so drained? Probably because she'd lain awake until well after two, and as much as she hated to admit it, the trip to Calabozo had taken a big toll on her.

Over breakfast, she and her cohorts discussed exactly how they'd work Silva at the shoot, scheduled for one that afternoon. It was a given that if Petrović was holed up somewhere in Venezuela, the president knew about it. The hard part would be getting him to slip up.

"So, let's talk about how we're going to do this," Ty said, shoving the last bite of scrambled eggs into his mouth.

"You and I aren't doing anything," Ryan reminded him. "Today, it's all on Mac. She's got to convince Silva we're legit, and at the same time, try to get him to brag a little. Hope he'll slip up and mention anything that could be related to Petrović or a joint project between them. You and I are only there for camera and sound."

"Second only to who has the biggest package, most of you guys like to boast about yourselves, which is a real turn-off to most women, by the way." Mac swallowed the last of her orange juice and gave them a thumbs-up. "So, it shouldn't be too hard getting him to talk about himself."

"Not true about the package," Ty protested.

Mac nodded. "I said most men. We know that Silva considers himself an international playboy and a lady-killer. I'll make sure to wear something less conservative—no dark blue business suit like I had on yesterday."

"Can't wait to see you in something sexy," Ryan said, waggling his eyebrows with a ridiculous up-and-down motion that wrinkled his nose.

"Oh, give it up, Fitzpatrick," Mac teased before getting serious again. "Here's my game plan. For starters, get him talking about his beloved country and how he played a big part in the success."

"Yeah, like how Venezuela, under his control, is rolling in drug and oil money while a large percentage of his people are starving to death," Ty interrupted, shaking his head. "I read somewhere they're so hungry, they're now eating the zoo animals."

"Gross! Common sense tells me not to lead with that, though. It will be hard enough to smile at him, knowing he's such a monster." Mac scrunched her nose before glancing down at her watch. "Come on. We've got a few hours before showtime. Let's go out and snoop around, see if we can get lucky and find a clue or two. The perfect way to do that without looking suspicious is to do some shopping." She slapped her forehead. "I can't tell you how much I'm gonna hate that—not!"

"Want Ty and me to go with you?"

"You're joking, right? Every man I know hates going shopping with a woman. I couldn't put you through that pain, number one, and number two, the three of us shopping together might arouse suspicions." She patted his cheek. "Thanks for the offer, though." She held back a grin at the look of relief that flashed across their faces. She stood and walked toward the door, waving back at them over her shoulder.

Heading down the street, her thoughts reverted to Petrović. Although it was unlikely he was hiding out in a place this visible, it was worth a shot. Then again, what better place to hide than a bustling, overpopulated city? Caracas was the most urbanized city in Latin America and the largest in Venezuela, housing a block-long capital building. Its population exceeded five million people. The huge multistory buildings lining the square were a testament to the wealth.

For her sightseeing adventure, Mac chose Plaza Caracas, located in the Simon Bolivar Center at the foot of the *El Silencio* district. Although it was built in the early days before the modernization of the city, no one would ever call it *silent* now.

She walked across the cobblestone courtyard and entered the thirty-story mecca for shopping enthusiasts. The directory was digitalized in a seven-page display, accessible by the numerous escalators already filled with shoppers even at this early hour.

To an observer, Mac was simply a tourist on a shopping expedition, fingering brightly colored silks, even haggling before buying a couple of yards at a few places. After two hours, her arms full of her purchases, she knew about as much as she did when she'd left the hotel. Perhaps there was nothing to find.

Deciding to head back after stopping at the last two stores on the floor, she made her way back to the street. Maybe if she had a week, she could see all the shops, since she'd only made it to the eighth floor. Resigned to the fact she wouldn't find out anything useful, and excited about snatching up a few of the gorgeous purses at a third of the price she'd pay in the States, she entered a leather store.

As she casually browsed through the merchandise, she noticed two young girls standing by a shoe rack, their hands moving in animated conversation. She made her way toward the back until she was close enough to hear bits and pieces of the conversation. She stepped closer.

"I know," the taller one said. "But my mum's insisting I come home. The story of the girl from the mission is all over the news."

"My mum's upset, too," the other one said. "Everyone's scared to go out alone, but we can't leave now. We're just starting to see progress."

Mac recognized the accent as British and moved even closer. Tapping the taller one on the shoulder, she said, "Excuse me. I couldn't help overhearing. Should I be concerned about going out by myself?"

After they exchanged glances, the girls huddled closer. "Yes. In the past month, three girls have disappeared. Last week, a missionary student who was alone in her room one afternoon just vanished into thin air. No one saw or heard anything."

Mac covered her mouth with her hand in an exaggerated show of horror. "Oh my gosh! Do the police have any idea who might have done it?"

"That's the scary part. There are never any signs of

a struggle or any clues left behind." The girl pointed to her friend. "We're both serving the Lord here, and everyone at our mission school is afraid."

"Thanks for the warning. I'll be extra careful while I'm here."

Mac paid for a small clutch then walked out of the shop, unable to think about anything else except the story the girls had told her. Starting for the last shop, she glanced at her watch. She had about ten minutes to spare before she needed to get back and prepare for the interview.

The story of the missing girls resurrected a plethora of unpleasant memories, and she couldn't help wondering if Joseph Petrović was involved. Not only did he have a thing for young, pretty girls, but Dino had mentioned that he sometimes used humans in his experiments. Could the disappearance of three girls in a month somehow be connected to him, or was it simply a coincidence?

Probably a coincidence, she decided. South American women disappeared all the time, the *modus operandi* for the many gangs who kidnapped the girls for huge ransoms. Just recently, she'd read about young Latino girls being kidnapped and sent to other countries as sex slaves.

Still, it would be wise not to blow off the information, since she knew firsthand what Petrović was capable of. For the kidnapped girls' sake, she hoped it was nothing more than coincidence, but if her gut was right, God help them.

As the light bulb went off in her head, she realized they might have just uncovered proof that Petrović was very close.

As she dodged through the crowd, the little voice inside her head that had kept her alive all these years warned Mac she was being followed. She slipped into another leather store and pretended to check out the purses next to the window, a perfect spot to see who stopped, who lingered, and to study the passing faces. When she walked out of the store, she was relieved to see that other than the throng of midmorning shoppers scurrying by, carrying their day's purchases and chatting with one another, and the few vendors hawking their goods outside the shops, nothing seemed out of the ordinary. She took another look at her watch, deciding to forgo the last store and return to the hotel instead.

Walking briskly, Mac still couldn't shake the feeling of being watched. When turning a complete circle produced nothing, she concluded her overactive imagination was running amok because of the missing girls' story.

Once inside the hotel, she pushed her suspicions out of her mind, concentrating, instead, on what she would wear when she met the womanizing general face to face. President Silva was sending a limo for them in a little over an hour, giving her just enough time for a quick shower.

When she stepped off the elevator, the feeling of someone watching her returned. Her CIA instincts kicked in as she slowly walked to her room. Wishing she had her trusty Beretta with her, she checked the door for any signs of tampering.

There were none.

Once inside, she stripped off her clothes and headed for the dresser to grab underwear to take into the bathroom with her. Housekeeping had already been there, and the scent of fresh lilies from a vase on the dresser filled the room. She pulled out a drawer, grabbed her panties and bra, and then glanced up at the mirror.

That was when she saw it, not recognizing the scream that filled the room as her own. She barely made it to the restroom before she threw up her breakfast. After flushing the commode, she made her way to the doorway and stared at the reason for her violent reaction.

In the center of the newly made bed, there was an orchid and a chocolate kiss.

# 7

Mac reached for the hotel phone and began punching in Ryan's room number before thinking better of the idea and dropping the receiver onto the bed as if it was about to explode. If Petrović was able to gain access to her room, more than likely he'd bugged the phone. She lunged for her purse on the edge of the dresser, but her hands were shaking as if she desperately needed a fix. She was only able to grab one end before the entire contents spilled onto the carpeted floor. Swearing, she scooped up her cell phone, fully intending to call Griff, but knew he'd insist they abort the mission. She couldn't do that. Even if there was only a slim chance of finding a connection between President Silva and Petrović, it was too compelling to turn back now.

The thought of Petrović in her hotel room was terrifying, though, and she had to tell the guys. Together, they'd decide what to do. She called Ryan's number again.

When he answered on the third ring, his voice was low and gravelly. "Jesus, Mac, this better be good. I was right in the middle of going over all my notes about the trip to Calabozo, and Ty is taking advantage of the last thirty minutes of sleep before we leave for the interview."

Swallowing back fear, she opened her mouth, but nothing came out. "I'm sorry," she finally managed. "I..."

Griff's words in Cleveland came back to her, and she couldn't finish. He'd made it very clear if she screwed up again, she'd be off the team for good. Now that she'd seen Petrović in the photo in Venezuela, she couldn't let that happen. She had to be involved in putting him six feet under, and this time for good. Confronting him once more, actually looking into his eyes when he took his last breath, was the only way she could move on with her life.

"You what?" Ryan interrupted her thoughts, a little annoyed now.

She debated whether to tell him, then made a split-second decision to keep the candy and flower a secret for now. Ryan and Ty would insist on investigating, and their cover would be blown.

"Should we mention what happened on the way to Calabozo yesterday?" She blew her hair off her forehead. How much lamer could she get?

"You don't think Silva already knows about his men shoving guns in our faces?" Ryan sounded confused, and she worried she would blurt out the real reason she'd awakened him. "He called the leader himself to verify our story. Remember?"

She played innocent. "Oh, God. I'd forgotten. Sorry."

His voice softened. "I probably should start getting ready now, anyway. Our flight leaves early in the morning, and I plan on catching up on all the sleep I've missed as soon as we get back."

"How early?"

"How early what?" he asked.

"Our flight. What time does it leave?"

"Eight in the morning. We can go over our notes on the plane and maybe get even more shut-eye."

While he was talking, Mac did another scan of the room, looking for anything that could be a hidden camera. Although she couldn't find one, she was sure it was there. "I don't suppose I could talk you into going home tonight, right?"

There was a silence, and Mac worried he'd guessed why she was acting so weird, even though that was ridiculous. No one knew about Petrović's nightly ritual of leaving a chocolate kiss and an orchid on her bed. In all likelihood, the good doctor was long gone, too smart to hang around and risk being discovered. This was merely another of the cruel mind games he loved to play. So why blow the mission now?

But a niggling thought wouldn't leave her. What if he was arrogant enough to hang around, knowing she was onto him? They hadn't been too concerned when they realized they would not be getting the weapons back, since this was a simple fact-finding mission. That all changed with the discovery of the candy in her room—but only she knew that.

She decided it was worth the risk. If Petrović was in cahoots with Silva, as suspected, it was vital they keep up the pretense of why they were in Venezuela in the first place. Besides, there was no way Petrović could know they hadn't acquired more guns on the black market, which was to their advantage. Somehow, she'd get through the interview then tell Ty and Ryan as soon as they left the presidential palace.

"Mac, is everything all right?"

"Of course," she responded way too quickly. "Why wouldn't it be?"

"I don't know. I'm getting vibes that say otherwise."

She forced herself to keep her voice calm. "There you go again, Fitzpatrick. Getting all macho and wanting to take care of me. Need I remind you of your blue balls again?"

"Oh, hell no!" he responded with a huff. "Okay, then, I'll see you in the lobby in a half-hour." He paused. "Actually, we only have fifteen minutes now."

"See you there," she said, already planning her next move.

As soon as she clicked off her cell phone, she retrieved the plastic laundry bag from the closet and carefully slipped Petrović's gifts in, wrinkling her nose as if they were disease-infested. Highly unlikely, but still possible, he might have gotten sloppy and left a fingerprint or two. Next, she grabbed the ice bucket from the dresser, filled it a third of the way with tap water, and carried it back to the bed. After pulling back the covers, she tossed the entire contents across the bed.

Then she picked up the house phone and dialed the front desk. "Hi. I'm in room 817, and I'm such a klutz. I spilled a glass of ice water all over my bed, and there's no way I can sleep here tonight. Any chance you have another room available on this floor?"

"Let me see."

She waited while he checked.

"Yes," he said a moment later. "There's one a few doors down that is—"

"Perfect," she interrupted. "Could you send someone up with the key? I have a busy afternoon ahead of me and would like to make the move right now."

"Of course, ma'am. I'll take care of it immediately. And I'm sorry for the inconvenience."

*Sorry for the inconvenience?* She'd just deliberately spilled a bucket of water on her bed, and he was apologizing. That was a benefit that came with a fancy hotel.

She retrieved her suitcase from the closet and threw her clothes into it. Grabbing the bathroom trash can, she tossed in her cosmetics. She was already fully packed when the concierge himself knocked on the door.

"I'm so sorry this happened to you," he said, picking up her luggage. "If you'll follow me, I'll show you to your new room."

She grabbed her purse and the trash can before taking one last look around the room. "Bite me, you bastard," she murmured.

She fell into step behind the concierge. "Lead the way."

When she was alone in the new room, she did a thorough search, even though she knew the likelihood of Petrović having enough time to put a camera in every room on this floor was remote. Satisfied she'd outsmarted him for now, she unloaded the cosmetics from the trash can onto the bathroom counter, stripped off her clothes, and jumped into the shower. Because she couldn't shake the feeling there might be a camera in this bathroom, she was in and out of the warm water in less than five minutes.

As soon as she was dressed, she made her way downstairs, preferring to wait in the crowded lobby for her teammates. Standing off to the side, she surveyed the room, searching for any sign of Petrović. The probability that he was no longer there was high, knowing she was onto him. The man took pride in the fact that his disguises were so good that not even the

best intelligence agencies around the world had com-
piled any information about his appearance.

She was the exception, the only one who could
identify him.

She scanned the room once again, and when she
was satisfied he wasn't there, she made her way to a
leather chair near the door, sat down, and picked up a
magazine. Pretending to read it, she glanced up every
few seconds to re-check the room, searching for
anyone remotely resembling the man who had nearly
destroyed her at the mountain hideout.

She had no doubt she'd be able to pick him out of
a crowd. She'd been his prisoner for eight days, which
was more than enough time to study every wrinkle on
his face, every mannerism he displayed, including the
way he carried his arms when he walked. Even the
most masterful disguise wouldn't conceal his identity
from her. Shivers traveled up her spine at the thought
of coming face to face with the man who still terrorized her dreams. She had no idea how she'd react if
she actually looked him in the eye. Just the sight of his
emblem on the weapons canister had freaked her out.

Getting impatient now, she tapped her fingernails
on the arm of the chair, anxious to get the Silva interview over with and be on a plane home. Even if she
couldn't talk Ryan and Ty into an earlier flight, she
was definitely spending the night with one or both of
them.

When she saw Ryan and Ty step off the elevator,
she waved, blowing out a sigh of relief.

"Ryan's worried something's up with you, Mac," Ty
said. "Is there anything you're not telling us?"

A glance at Ryan's face verified that Ty wasn't exag-
gerating. She stood and playfully punched his shoulder. "You're just being a big brother, and although I

appreciate it, nothing's wrong. I want to get this interview over and go home. That's all. I guess yesterday's confrontation with those rogue soldiers affected me more than I'd thought, and I'm just reacting."

Ryan studied her for a full thirty seconds before nodding. "Booked us on the eight thirty back to Washington tonight. We'll have you in your own bed by midnight, princess."

Mac struggled to keep from tearing up, knowing how much he'd been looking forward to hitting the sack the minute they returned from the presidential palace. "Thanks," she said softly.

"Don't thank me yet. You have no idea what this will cost you." He grabbed her arm and nudged her toward the door, where a white stretch limo had just pulled up. "There's our ride."

Mac stood on tiptoes and gave him another kiss on his cheek before walking toward the chauffeur, who was now holding the door open. Sliding into the back seat, she glanced one last time over her shoulder before they sped off. Just as she expected, there was nothing there.

So why did she feel like the eyes of the devil were still on her?

❦

HE WATCHED her taking in every inch of the hotel lobby more than once, enjoying the fear he saw in her eyes. Knowing she would probably recognize even his best disguise, he'd stayed one step ahead of her and had his contact at the hotel install a camera in the lobby so he could sit back and watch when she left. He hadn't anticipated the added bonus of seeing her there alone while she waited for the two men accompanying her. Dressed in a sleeveless navy dress with a high collar that showed off chiseled arms and gorgeous legs, she seemed frazzled.

Smiling to himself that his little surprise for her had her off her game, he concentrated on the screen as she relaxed and leaned back in the chair, obviously satisfied he wasn't in the lobby. Seeing her yesterday on the road to Calabozo had been an unexpected delight. He'd come very close to letting down his guard and ordering the soldiers to kill the men with her and bring her to him right then. But he knew it hadn't been the time or place to make his move. That would come later.

He wondered how the CIA had found out he was in Venezuela, certain that was the reason for their presence in Caracas posing as reporters. He'd been extra careful once his experiments began to produce results exceeding his own wildest expectations. He was very close to finding the most potent delivery system for his fatal gases, and after one final test, he intended to auction off his discovery to the highest bidder. With the money he was sure to make from the sale, he would settle down on the remote island he'd recently purchased and live out the rest of his life in luxury.

And he intended to have Dr. Mackenzie Conley at his side.

He was jerked back to attention when she rose from the couch and headed toward the two men as they emerged from the elevator. It killed him to see her run to the lanky one and hug him. He wanted the intimacy of her breasts touching his chest, and no one else's.

He vowed right then to make sure if he couldn't have her, no one else would. But for now, he'd have to be patient. He gathered his equipment and hurried from the room onto the balcony overlooking the driveway just as she got into the limousine that had pulled up in front of the hotel. He couldn't see her through the tinted windows but knew she'd probably taken one last look back to search for him in the crowd before the limo pulled away. He didn't need to follow her to know where she was going.

He clapped his hands in glee, anticipating the look on her face when she discovered his final surprise for her before she left Venezuela. He was sorry he wouldn't be there to see it for himself.

THE MINUTE they stepped out of the limousine, four young Venezuelan soldiers appeared to escort them up the steps of the massive white palace with a striking terracotta roof. All were around the same age as the hooligans they'd encountered on their way to Calabozo.

One of the officers, who appeared to be a few years older than the others, gave them a salute and introduced himself. "Welcome to the *Palacio de Miraflores.* I'm First Lieutenant Martin Bautista, special events officer for President Silva." He held out his arm to her, and when she took it, he led her up the steps, with Ty and Ryan following close behind.

"The interview will be held in the Boyacá Room," the young lieutenant said. He released Mac's arm and motioned for them to follow him.

Mac heard Ryan whistle softly as they walked down the ornate hall decorated with some of the most impressive paintings she'd ever seen.

"They're lovely, aren't they?" Bautista said when he

noticed her interest. "The famous Julián Oñate painted them in the 1800s for Joaquin Crespo, our president then. The furniture was imported from Barcelona, Spain."

"Unbelievable," she replied, thinking there was no other words to describe them.

When they rounded the corner, the sight that greeted them nearly took her breath away. In the middle of the hall was a huge fountain surrounded by four gigantic rock crystal mirrors.

"This is the Peruvian Sun Hall," Bautista explained. "The decorations are made from gold donated by the government of Peru," he added when they passed the fountain and continued down the hallway.

He stopped in front of a massive wooden door that could only be described as exquisite. "This is the Boyacá Room. You and your crew can set up in here, and President Silva will join you in a moment."

"A shitload of bucks went into this building," Ryan commented when they were finally alone. "Did you see all that gold back there?"

"Drugs are a lucrative business, my friend," Ty said, setting up his camera equipment. "Are you ready for the interview, Mac?"

Ryan answered for her. "She's ready, all right. No man in his right mind could possibly resist her in that sexy dress." He ruffled her hair playfully. "Silva will have a hard time concentrating on your questions."

"Oh, give it up, Ryan," Ty teased. "How many different ways does she have to tell you she's not interested?" He moved closer. "On the other hand, I've noticed she hasn't totally shut me down yet."

"You're like a little brother to me, Ty." She blew him a kiss, walked around the table, and poured a glass of water. After taking a long drink, she licked her lips. "I'm anxious to get this interview over with."

Ryan's amused expression quickly changed to one of concern. "Are you ready to tell us what's bothering you?"

"Not yet. I need to get through this before I can talk about it." She shook her head and attempted to smile. "I love that you're worried about me, though."

Just then, the door opened, and they got their first look at the Venezuelan president. General Jorge Silva was slightly shorter than her, but his sculpted body left no doubt there was a personal trainer on his payroll. With his dark black hair slicked back and his smoking black eyes that homed in on Mac's chest, it was obvious he considered himself a player.

She resisted the urge to say, "Hey, I'm up here."

When his eyes finally found her face, he extended his hand. "It's a pleasure to meet you, Miss Conley. I'm anxious to tell the world about my beautiful godchild."

"Call me Mac." She pulled her hand away when she thought he'd held it too long.

He sat down at the head of the table and motioned for her to join him at that end. When she was seated next to him, he instructed Ty and Ryan to begin filming.

"It's my pleasure to welcome ZNN to my beautiful country to talk about our rich culture, our people, and, of course, our gorgeous women. But first, I'd like to give you a little history about this room." He spread his arms out as the camera panned over the room. "The Boyacá Room is one of the largest in the palace and was named in honor of the battle won by Simon Bolivar in 1819—a battle that freed Colombia from the British invasion. The room was built in the early 1960s and is decorated with rich parquet flooring and wooden ceilings."

"It's striking," Mac said. "Can you tell us about the paintings?"

Silva smiled as he pointed to a large piece of art hanging in the center of one wall. "This was done by muralist Gabriel Bracho, and it represents the faces of Bolívar, Francisco de Paula Santander, and José Antonio Anzoátegui, all heroes of Boyacá. It was inaugurated by President Rafael Caldera during his first term of office in 1973."

"You must be very proud," Mac said, reaching for her water for a quick drink before proceeding. "As I know you are proud of your goddaughter, the reigning Miss Universe, Marita Rojas."

His smile widened enough to show several gold fillings in his back molars. "She is a delight and a hero to all Venezuelans. Besides being beautiful, her talent as a dancer is unequaled in this country, the result of many years of instruction and hard work. Hard work that will hopefully pay off with a career in your great city of New York."

There it was. The only reason he'd allowed foreign journalists in for a private interview. Mac used the opportunity to let him drone on and on about his goddaughter, figuring it was a small price to pay for the opportunity to check out the palace. As hard as she tried to pay attention to him, her mind kept wandering back to her hotel room and finding Petrović's personal calling card on her bed.

Although she knew she was safe in the presidential palace, she couldn't shake the feeling that Petrović was still watching her somehow. As preposterous as that seemed, she surveyed the room as Silva was busy flashing pictures of his goddaughter for the camera.

Just when she decided she was being totally ridiculous, she spotted a framed photograph in the bookcase directly behind the general. Quickly, she covered her mouth to hide the gasp.

It was a picture of her at the café in Morocco where she'd first met Petrović. She remembered the day he'd taken it like it was yesterday. There was only one person with access to that picture. One person who could have sent it to the presidential palace or brought it here himself.

And she shivered to think that Joseph Petrović could quite possibly be in the building right now.

She couldn't stop herself from interrupting Silva. "Where did you get that picture?"

He gave her an amused look before turning around to see it. "Oh, that. It came by special messenger this morning, and since I knew you were coming, I thought it would be a nice surprise. Do you like it?"

*Special messenger, my ass!* "I do." She faked a smile. "I'm wondering if we can wrap this up. As you know, the reason we postponed this trip last week was because I had a stomach virus. I'm afraid it has left me a little lightheaded still."

"We've only just gotten started," he protested.

Ryan stepped forward. "We have more than enough footage to use to get your goddaughter the exposure she needs. I'll make sure a copy of this interview, along with all the pictures, goes to the directors of the five best dance studios in New York City."

That seemed to pacify the general, and he nodded. "As soon as you pack up your equipment, my driver will take you back to the hotel," he said to Ty and Ryan before turning to Mac. "I was hoping you'd join me for an early supper, Miss Conley."

*When hell freezes over,* she wanted to say.

Instead, she smiled. "It would have been my utmost pleasure, but my stomach is telling me I shouldn't have eaten a big breakfast this morning. I'm afraid I wouldn't be very good company right now. I will take a rain check, though, and come back at a later date. Maybe we can finish the interview and have that supper *alone.*"

He did a slow inspection of her body. Lust sparkled in his eyes as though he was already anticipating what might happen after the dinner. "I will await your call and make the arrangements."

"Thank you," she said as she practically ran from the room with Ty and Ryan right behind her.

"Let's get the hell out of here," she whispered to them. When both men gave her a questioning look, she said, "That picture of me in there could have only come from Dr. Death himself."

**8**

Halfway down the hallway, Ryan stopped abruptly and turned to Mac. "You think Petrović knows we're here?"

She nodded. "Let's wait until we get out of here to talk about this." Her voice wavered at the thought that the man who had stolen any chance of her returning to a normal life might actually be close enough to touch her right now. She couldn't stop the fear that passed through her.

Silva suddenly appeared with two of his soldiers. "My men will help you load your equipment and see to it that you get back to the hotel safely."

Something about the way he said the word *safely* felt like more than casual conversation. Was he warning them somehow? Was he aware of how much the picture had affected her?

When he smiled and grasped her hand, Mac decided her paranoia might be working overtime. Petrović was a solo act, and it was more plausible that the general didn't even know his buddy was up to his old tricks again.

After Ty and Ryan shook his hand, they helped the soldiers load the cameras into the limousine. The look on Ryan's normally mischievous face was so serious that Mac would have teased him about it if the situation weren't so dire.

But it was critical they get back to the hotel and on a plane to the U.S. as fast as possible. Both of Petrović's covert messages had done exactly what he'd intended they do—put her on edge and knock her off her game. But she had no intention of letting him get to her on his turf—or any, for that matter.

The ride back to the hotel was somber, with only small talk in front of the driver. As soon as they exited the limo, Ryan grabbed Mac's arm and led her down the sidewalk away from the hotel—away from any listening devices or cameras. Ty fell into step behind them, and they walked several blocks before anyone said a word.

When they were far enough away from the hotel, Mac stopped and sat down on a bench. "He's here," she said.

Ty's eyes widened. "Are you saying Joseph Petrović is here right now?" He did a quick 360 around the area. "Did you see him, Mac?"

Again she shook her head. "He's playing games with me."

"What kind of games?" Ryan asked. "Has he hurt you?"

"No, nothing like that, but he was in my hotel room this morning. I'm sure of it."

"Fuck!" Ryan said. "Is that why you were so upset earlier?" When she nodded, he got right in her face. "You should've told me right away, Mac. We would've canceled the interview and gotten on the next plane back to D.C." He threw his hands in the air. "Hell, we don't even have weapons."

"I didn't think he'd be stupid enough to expose

himself and risk being captured just yet. He likes to think of himself as a cat and me as a mouse. He wants the satisfaction of seeing me squirm."

"How do you know he was in your room?" Ty asked.

Mac sighed, knowing she'd have to dig back into memories she'd suppressed for so long. She wasn't sure she could do that.

But she forced herself to say the words. "When I was his prisoner in Morocco, he would put a chocolate kiss and a white orchid on my bed every night. It was part of a mating ritual in his sick mind." She looked away just in case she couldn't stop the tears she felt forming behind her eyes from spilling over. The last thing she needed was for her teammates to think of her as a girl. "This morning when I got back from shopping, both the candy and the flower were in the middle of my bed."

Ty sat down beside her on the bench. "Could someone else have known about his ritual and tried to scare you?"

"I thought about that, then decided it was probably Petrović," she answered in a monotone. "He's a loner. Even though I'm sure he's in the country with General Silva's knowledge, I'm guessing the relationship is strictly business." She looked up and met their concerned gazes. "The display was meant to scare me. Even when I was his prisoner and at his mercy, he loved playing mind games with me. Seeing the fear in my eyes turned him on."

"The sick prick," Ryan said. "I'd like to turn him *off* with my bare hands right about now."

"You and me both," Ty said, reaching for Mac's hand. "Come on. Let's get back to the hotel, pack up, and head out to the airport. You stay in Ryan's room while I throw your things into a suitcase. We're not letting you out of our sight."

Ordinarily, Mac would have balked at the obvious show of male protectiveness, but she felt comforted now, knowing she didn't have to put on an act in front of them. The truth was that she was more terrified than she wanted to admit, and the sooner she got away from this place, the better.

"Thanks, guys," she managed as they headed back to the hotel.

Ryan called the airport and found out there was an even earlier flight than the one he'd booked them on. If they hurried, they could be in the air in less than two hours.

It wasn't until they were in the taxi on the way to the airport that Mac's breathing returned to normal.

But even then, she still felt Joseph Petrović's presence close by.

"YOU THOUGHT Dr. Death was in your room and you didn't get on the horn to me immediately?" Dinorelli huffed and shook his head. "Need I remind you this is exactly what happened two years ago, Mac? You went off the grid when you made contact with Petrović without alerting any of us. We all know how that worked out."

Mac glanced around the room at the other team members, who were all anxiously waiting to hear her reasons. Ryan and Ty, who had lately become her closest allies on the mission, were the only ones who looked like they agreed with her. She opened her mouth to tell her boss she'd been afraid she'd be pulled from the mission if she called him, then

quickly closed it. Dino, of all people, should understand why catching Petrović and watching him die
once more was so vital to her.

But if she admitted she'd been worried about
losing her job, she'd also have to fess up to her
screw-up in Cleveland. Griff had kept his word and
not mentioned it. If Dino knew how she'd totally
come unglued at merely seeing a symbol she remembered from Petrovic's lab, he'd have yanked her off
the mission before she even finished the sentence.
Couple that with this new Petrović thing, and her
butt would be clinging to a desk chair before the day
ended.

"And what would you have done, Dino?" she asked
him defiantly. "Swooped in and rescued me?" She
slammed her hand on the table. "I told you before. I'm
not some fragile doll who needs a wall of testosterone
around me. I figured by the time I got back to the hotel
room yesterday that Petrović was long gone. Scrapping
the mission would have only given him the satisfaction of knowing how deeply his little surprise had affected me."

Ryan stepped forward to stand beside her. "Cut her
some slack, Dino. You hired us because we're able to
think on our feet, which is exactly what she did. She
made sure she got out of the room immediately. Even
bagged the evidence. Can you imagine how not seeing
her panic must've pissed the bastard off?"

"Yeah," Ty said, moving up to stand beside them in
an apparent show of solidarity. "You're always
preaching about how an angry man makes stupid
mistakes."

Dinorelli stared at all three of them, his eyebrows
in a deep V, before he pointed to Griff, who was seated
on the other side of the table. "You haven't said a word

through all this. I'd like to know what's going on in that head of yours."

All eyes turned to Griff, who up to this point had been quietly nursing a cup of coffee. He chugged the last of the drink and set the cup on the table, while holding Mac prisoner with his eyes.

She shifted from one foot to the other, determined not to let him see how his stare affected her. Was he about to tell Dino about Cleveland? He'd threatened her job if she made one more mistake. Would he toss her from the team and relegate her to in-house-only duty?

"I agree with Mac on this one."

Dino's frown deepened. He'd apparently been expecting his number one guy to side with him, not with the other three. He walked over to the satellite photo on the screen behind his desk. "You got lucky, Mac, and I'll go along with you this time, but let it be known"—he nailed her with a glare—"if you suspect even for one minute that the sadistic asshole is anywhere near you, I want to know about it before you take your next breath. I'll be the one to decide how to proceed if that happens. That goes for all of you. Understood?"

All four heads bobbed in agreement. Mac decided now was not the time to remind her boss that she could handle herself. In her heart, she knew Dino was right. Not relaying information to the team was the reason she'd ended up strapped to a bed in Petrović's fortress in Morocco two years before. You'd think she had learned her lesson.

She vowed to be extra vigilant now that Petrović knew she was looking for him.

"So, we're concentrating on the area between Caracas and Calabozo, since that's the only place he could've seen you, Mac. That's if he saw you at all. More than likely some official at the airport is on his payroll and alerted him the minute you stepped off the plane." He grabbed a handful of sunflower seeds and shoved them into his mouth before pointing back to the picture. "That's a lot of ground to cover, and frankly, I think the man is too smart to make it easy on us, even if he is pissed off. His lab in Morocco was totally invisible on satellite photos. Ten bucks says this one is, too." He spat the shells into the trash can and clicked the remote.

A picture of Mac, Ty, and Ryan standing outside the van with guns pointed at their heads filled the screen. "If Petrović did see you, my guess is that he is —or was—somewhere near here." Dino pointed again at the photo on the screen. "Usually, soldiers aren't stationed on a deserted stretch of road, and thugs don't wear government-issue uniforms. I'm thinking the men were sent to protect him and decided to score when the opportunity presented itself."

"Did the satellite pick up any trace of Petrović ever being there?" Griff asked.

"No, but remember, our man is a master at hiding. It doesn't mean he wasn't there. At any rate, all we can do is to keep looking."

"So what now?" Ty asked.

Dino shook his head. "If all my calculations are correct, the doctor is getting closer to accomplishing his goal. It's our job to make sure that doesn't happen, but unfortunately, there's nothing we can do except wait for his next move and hope he makes a mistake."

Mac felt Griff's eyes on her and turned to him. "Thanks for the support" was all she managed to get out under the scrutiny.

He stood up and walked around to the other side

of the table before leaning in and whispering, "Don't thank me yet, shortcake. I happen to agree with you on this one. That's all. I'm still watching you, though." He straightened up and walked to the door. "I'll be in my office for the rest of the afternoon if anyone needs me."

*Well, there it is.* She'd hoped his agreeing with her meant he was softening a bit toward her, but his whispered words destroyed that theory. She was convinced the man would never forgive her, and frankly, she didn't blame him.

She resigned herself that she and Griff could never be more than team members, but at times like this, she'd settle for that.

JOSEPH PETROVIĆ WALKED through the slum area on the outskirts of Belo Horizonte. It was just after dusk, and a swarm of children, most of them under fifteen, were congregating around a fire in a barrel, even though the weather was only mildly chilly.

He stopped to watch, noticing one group of kids inhaling from a can of spray paint. A glance at another group showed them passing around a cigarette, probably coca paste. He knew that coca paste was the drug of choice for these street kids because of its easy availability, and although it was made from coca leaves and was a precursor to cocaine, it was actually more harmful to the kids. It contained dangerous levels of toxic processing chemicals such as kerosene, sulfur, and methanol, which were normally removed from regular cocaine.

Even if he did feel a touch of remorse for what he

was about to do to these kids—which he didn't—they would be dead in a few years anyway.

And if the drugs didn't kill them, the death squads would. It was a known fact that the problems created by the increasing number of street children were so numerous that vigilante squads earned as much as fifty dollars for every child they killed. No one would miss the ones he'd use for his experiment. Hell, no one would even notice they were missing.

He'd been planning exactly how he would do this ever since he saw Mac and the phony news crew in Venezuela. Almost immediately, he'd begun making inquiries about all of them and discovered she had just recently rejoined the group that operated in a remote town in Virginia, according to his highly paid sources. He opened his phone and stared at the photos his inside man had obtained of Mac and her compadres, some from even before he'd met her in Morocco. One man, in particular, had piqued his interest. His sources identified him as Griffin Bradley, the leader of the present unit. When a photo popped onto the screen of Bradley with his arm around a smiling Mac, the green-eyed monster resurfaced, just like the first time Petrović had viewed it. It was obvious there was more than a coworker relationship between the two, which infuriated him. Mac was his, and the sooner she accepted that, the better.

But he'd figure out how to deal with that later. Right now, he needed to focus on the job at hand. With the CIA on to him, it was only a matter of time before he slipped up, even though he was more cautious now than ever. He was so close to walking away with hundreds of millions of dollars, and he had no intentions of watching all his hard work go up in flames like the last time.

He glanced at his watch. Seven thirty. If all went well, he'd be on a plane back to Caracas by ten—before anybody discovered what he'd done. He'd arrived in Brazil at Tancredo Neves/Confins International Airport yesterday afternoon and had driven directly to the small, abandoned building about a half-mile away from where he was standing right now. After setting up his equipment, he'd slept on a cot in the back room, unwilling to leave his work in the hands of the flunkies he'd hired to make the arrangements.

His attention was diverted when he heard someone holler and saw one of his hired helpers rounding up the group of boys who had just inhaled the paint fumes. The other four adult assistants were gathering up clusters of kids. Knowing these children usually formed peer support groups, known as terminus, he figured this one numbered about seventy.

Perfect.

He turned and walked toward the building to make the final preparations as the street kids followed the men who'd lured them with the promise of a free meal and drugs.

Entering the building, Petrović made sure every window had been tightly sealed, as he'd instructed, before he went to the back office and watched the boys marching into the building like lambs to the slaughter. The pathetic wretches were probably wondering where the free food was. When they were all in, one of the helpers closed and locked the door.

After reaching for his gas mask and pulling it over his face, Petrović grabbed a small canister from the corner and opened it up at one end. Immediately, a stream of gas gushed out. Quickly, he opened the door and walked into the room, clicking his stopwatch at the same time. He counted off the seconds out loud as the lethal gas flowed into the small room. One by one, the children dropped to the floor, screaming when they saw their friends dying. The five adult men, who had no idea what would happen after they brought the street children to the building, began running to the door, but it was too late.

In less than twenty seconds, everyone in the room except Petrović was dead.

He stepped around the bodies on his way to the door, satisfied that his product was ready to be auctioned off to the highest bidder. Right before he exited, he pulled a single white orchid from his coat pocket and dropped it on the body of one of the dead children.

She would know it was his private message to her.

## 9

M ac awoke with a start and reached for her alarm clock. *Damn!* She'd overslept and would now be more than fashionably late for work. She'd stayed up until after three, researching Venezuela and its landmarks, searching for something—anything—that might shed some light on where Petrović was hiding out.

Logic told her he'd need a building big enough to conduct his experiments, and one that would be hard to hide from the eye in the sky. But this wasn't Petrović's first rodeo. His other lab in the hills of Morocco had been hidden so well that even the most high-tech surveillance equipment in the world had missed it. Had it not been for Mac remembering his men throwing the dead body of the university dean over the cliff, God only knew what would've happened to her back then.

After a quick shower, she grabbed a cup of instant coffee and headed out the door, hoping nothing important had happened at headquarters while she slept. Things had been unusually quiet since they'd returned from Venezuela a few days before. Petrović seemed to have simply dropped off the radar. As much as she wanted to believe that, she knew it was wishful thinking. More than likely, he'd gone deep under-cover, waiting for the perfect opportunity to expose her vulnerability again. Even on U.S. soil, she found herself looking over her shoulder everywhere she went.

Thankfully missing rush-hour traffic, she made the drive from D.C. to Virginia in under an hour. With a little luck, no one would even notice she was late. However, the minute she stepped off the elevator at headquarters, she knew that wasn't going to be the case. The usually busy front office was nearly vacant.

She greeted the officer manning the desk with a nod. "Where is everyone?"

He didn't even glance up. "In Director Dinorelli's office—waiting for you."

*Crap!* The one day she was late, there was some kind of important meeting going on. Walking there, she braced herself for the tongue lashing she knew she'd get. As soon as she opened the door, every eye in the room focused on her. Besides the team, there was an Asian man, whom she didn't recognize, sitting at the table with the others. She made eye contact with Ty, and he patted the seat next to him. Heading that way, she couldn't help noticing the scowl on Griff's face. Smiling to herself, she sat down next to the good-looking computer expert and reached for a bottle of water from the center of the table.

"Well, I see you decided to grace us with your pres-ence this morning, Mackenzie," Dino said.

*Oh boy!* It was worse than she thought if he was calling her by her full name. Like a parent, he only used it when she was in trouble.

"Stayed up late researching last night and overslept." She took a sip of water before meeting his eyes innocently. "Did I miss anything?"

"What were you researching?"

"Venezuela. I thought if I studied the landscape long enough, I might see something that jumped out at me about where Petrović's lab might be hidden."

"And did it?" Dino's voice had softened.

She shook her head. "I know he has to be there, although it will be hard to flush him out of Venezuela under all that presidential protection."

"He's not in Venezuela," Dino said. "At least, he wasn't there yesterday."

She knew it was crazy thinking he could get to her here, but she was suddenly glad to be surrounded by four of the strongest men she knew. "Where is he?"

"That's what we're here to talk about." He opened up his laptop, and a picture of a mass of bodies lying on the floor of a dilapidated building flashed on the screen behind him. He stood up and moved to the side so they could get a better look.

"Oh my God! Are those children?" Ryan asked, leaning forward on the table.

"Street kids in Belo Horizonte, Brazil. Sixty-three of them, to be exact, along with five adult men."

Dino clicked the remote, and a close-up of the same scene replaced the first picture. This time there was no mistaking the bodies of small children.

"Son of a..." Griff exclaimed. "Do we know how they died?"

"Nerve gas." Dino clicked again, and a close-up of an empty canister appeared on the screen.

Mac gasped, recognizing the unmistakable image of the curled-up snake imprinted on the outside. "He gassed innocent children?"

Dino nodded. "Homeland Security is pretty sure

he's in the final testing stages for his new chemical weapon. They think he chose the street kids because who would give a rat's ass if they were killed? Hell, the Brazilian police will probably thank him for it." Dino tsked in disgust. "So we've got to come up with a more aggressive approach than sitting around with our thumbs up our behinds waiting for him to strike again."

"I've advised every airport and harbor in the country that Petrović might try to slip in, but it will be extremely difficult to pick him out of a crowd with no real pictures," the Asian man said before screwing the cap of his water bottle off and on three times and finally taking a sip.

"I agree. As much as I'd like to say that alerting every possible port will keep him out, I can't—even if we had a picture. We all know how skillful he is with disguises and identities." Dino turned to Mac. "Now's as good a time as any to introduce you to another member of our team." He pointed to the man who had just spoken. "Dr. Mackenzie Conley, meet Dr. Jiang Lo, affectionately known as J-Lo. He heads up our security division."

"Wish he actually looked like his namesake," Ryan said, biting back a grin.

"Wish you looked like Angelina Jolie, but that ain't happening anytime soon either," Jiang fired back.

"Touché," Ryan said.

"J-Lo's here because we think it's time we stepped up our game. He's got satellite eyes and international ears everywhere just waiting for Petrović to come out and play," Dino explained.

"Maybe we ought to think about baiting him?" Mac said softly, knowing that would involve her.

As repulsive as that idea was, she couldn't get the image of those dead children out of her head. Petrović was pure evil, and if stopping him from committing more senseless killings meant putting her life on the line, she knew she had to do it.

"No way!" Griff said, slamming his fist on the table. "If he gets his hands on you again..." He stopped mid-sentence and lowered his head. "There has to be another way."

"For once, I agree with Griff," Dino said. "The man is far too obsessed with you, Mac, and although I don't doubt you could draw him out, I worry that we wouldn't be able to keep him from absconding with you. He's a genius when it comes to staying under the radar." He shook his head. "We'll have to come up with another solution that doesn't involve you."

"There is no other solution," Mac said, then swallowed hard. "I trust all of you with my life. Besides, he's concentrating on making millions from his new weapon of mass destruction. He probably isn't even thinking about me anymore."

Dino clicked the remote button once again and zoomed in on one of the young bodies. A single white orchid lay on his chest. "Does this look like a man who has lost interest?" he asked, his voice barely a whisper now.

Instead of being fearful, Mac was outraged. "All the more reason to use me as bait. Maybe chasing me will distract him, and we'll get lucky."

She glanced around the table at the horrified looks on all their faces. She'd just volunteered to be the cheese in a mousetrap in order to stop a madman from committing atrocities so evil, she couldn't even imagine. She glanced toward Griff, who was unusually

quiet and was now looking down at the table, avoiding
her gaze. When he finally looked up, she begged him
with her eyes to come up with some way to stop her
from becoming a sacrificial lamb.

With a grunt, he stood and exited the room.

GRIFF PULLED into the parking lot at what was fast becoming his favorite bar. Although he'd never spoken
to any of the customers when he was there, he was
now on a friendly first-name basis with the bartender.
He'd lied and told the guy his name was Brad Smith, a
computer software designer in the city. Had even fixed
the bar's computerized cash register once.

Lately, he'd been dropping in for a quick one after
an unusually hard day at headquarters. It was just
enough to take the edge off. At least once a week he'd
have a few beers, make small talk with the bartender,
and then head back home to D.C.—if you could call
his apartment home.

Hell, he'd never even finished decorating it, and
he'd been there over two years. He couldn't help remembering how excited Mac was when they picked
out the living room and bedroom furniture together. It
was supposed to be *their* apartment when they moved
in together. Now, he couldn't look at it without seeing
her finagling the salesman into taking off the delivery
charges. When she dumped him and left town, he'd
lost all interest in any further furniture shopping.
Who needed more than a couch and a bed, anyway?

Mac's suggestion right before he stormed out of
Dino's office that morning still haunted him. He hated
that she was willing to be used as bait to coerce that

slimy asshole out from under whatever rock he was hiding beneath. Yet he knew that Petrović was getting really close to perfecting his new chemical weaponry. God help them all if it fell into the hands of Al Qaeda or some other equally horrific terrorist group.

The reports out of Brazil suggested that whatever Petrović used on the children had killed them quickly, and this new creation took longer than other nerve gases to dissipate, making it even more lethal. When the first responders entered the building to investigate after an anonymous phone call, they hadn't worn protective equipment. Five police officers died before they realized what they were dealing with and quarantined the building. Only then was a team of HAZMAT-trained officers able to enter the building safely. And even *they* hadn't stayed long.

Because of the toxicity of the chemical and the uncertainty of not knowing exactly which gas had been used, the abandoned building was simply boarded up, leaving the bodies where they'd fallen. The Brazilians weren't about to risk contaminating the rest of the small city until they knew exactly what had been used.

Griff knew she'd wanted him to beg her to reconsider, but the truth was that the team took risks all the time. They'd used an operative as bait many times before, and probably would again. But Petrović was crazy, and this was Mac. Griff had had to get out from under her gaze to think clearly. Later, when he and Dino talked privately, both had agreed the idea was too risky, and they'd have to come up with something else.

Right now, he needed alcohol to chase away the look on her face when she'd volunteered to act as bait. After what Dino shared with him about how Petrović had tortured her, how could she even think about the possibility of ever being in the same room with him again?

Griff climbed out of his pickup and headed for the door, noticing with relief that there was only one other car in the parking lot. Occasionally, one of the customers would try to engage him in small talk, and that was the last thing he wanted tonight. He knew if the team didn't come up with another way to flush Petrović out—and fast—Mac would eventually talk Dino into putting her out there to tempt the psycho.

And Petrović wouldn't let her live this time. Griff was certain of it, and was pretty sure Mac suspected that outcome too.

He pushed those thoughts from his mind. He'd think about all this in the morning when his brain was fresh. Tonight, there was an icy-cold beer with his name on it waiting for him inside the building.

He glanced around as soon as he entered, glad to see that the lone customer was by himself in the opposite corner and didn't look like he was interested in a conversation with a stranger.

"Hey, Brad. The usual?"

Nodding to the bartender, Griff plopped down on the barstool closest to the TV in the corner, where a replay of the Washington-New York game was on.

"Hate that they blew it yesterday," Mike said, setting the cold bottle in front of him. "I had fifty bucks riding on that game."

"I hear you," Griff said. "That fumble in the last two minutes makes me wonder if one of the players had money with a bookie."

Mike snickered and slid over a bowl of pretzels, just as someone sat down on the barstool next to Griff.

"I had my money on New York, so I made a killing. Drinks are on me," a woman said.

Turning slightly to acknowledge the newcomer and praying she wasn't a talker, Griff was pleasantly surprised. Wearing a tight sweater that stopped a couple of inches above her waist and a pair of black jeans that could have been sprayed onto her slim figure, the blond woman smiled when she noticed his reaction.

"Heard you make a mean martini," she said to the bartender. "That true?"

Mike smiled, obviously having the same reaction to her as Griff did. This far away from the city, the usual customers were farmers and good old boys. Not many women who looked like her ever wandered in.

"Not much call for martinis around here," Mike said, still smiling. "But I'll whip one up, and you can decide for yourself."

"Deal." She reached over and grabbed a pretzel from the bowl in front of Griff. "Mind sharing? I had a light lunch, and I'm starving."

"What brings you to our neck of the woods?" Mike asked when he set the martini in front of her.

"Boredom."

Griff shoved the pretzels her way. "That's as good a reason to drink as any, I guess."

She nodded. "Sitting behind a desk all day long solving other people's problems takes it out of me. Sometimes, I just need to get away and think about my own." She reached for the drink and took a sip. "I decided a ride in the country sounded peaceful, and when I saw this bar, I knew it was a sign from up above that I needed to chill." She took another sip. "I don't know if this is the best martini I've ever had, but it's pretty damn good."

Mike beamed. "Glad to hear it. And you've come to the right place to relax." He pointed to the only other customer in the place. "Harry's wife just called, so he'll be leaving real soon. We may have to sneak him out the side door if she gets antsy and comes looking for him. Then it will just be Brad and me here."

She gave Mike a bewitching smile that seemed to work before she turned back to Griff. "So that's why I'm here. What's your story?"

Griff took a swig of the beer, trying to decide how to cut off the conversation without being rude. When he failed to come up with a good way, he shrugged. "Basically, the same as yours. This is on my way home after a long day at the office." He hoped that would appease her, but just in case it didn't, he glanced down at his watch. "I'll just finish up here and let you and Mike shoot the breeze."

As he lifted the beer bottle to his lips, she touched his hand, sending an electric current up his arm. Maybe it was because her skin was soft, and she smelled so good. More likely, though, it was because he hadn't gotten laid in months, and she was definitely easy on the eyes.

"Why not stay and have one more drink. I'm buying, remember?"

As good-looking as she was, he resisted the urge to take her up on the obvious invite she was sending his way. He had too many other things on his mind, and he was anxious to get to them. He reached into his back pocket for his wallet just as his cell phone rang. Glancing down, he noticed there was only one bar.

He stood up. "I'll be back in a second to even up, Mike. This call may be important." He walked outside to see if the reception was better, but even with two bars, there was no reception. He checked his missed calls, not recognizing the number.

He'd hoped it was Dino with good news about Petrović—news like they'd found the monster and sent him to hell where he belonged. But he knew it wouldn't be that easy. After putting the phone back in his pocket, he reentered the bar. There was a fresh beer waiting for him when he sat down.

When he didn't touch it, the blond gave him a pouty look. "Oh, come on. What's five more minutes gonna hurt?" She glanced at her wrist. "I need to leave soon, too. We'll both go after this drink."

He thought about it momentarily, and decided it wasn't a good idea. In his frame of mind, one more would lead to another, and before you knew it, he'd be calling a cab to take him home. "As much as I appreciate the offer, I'll just finish up the one I have and head home."

"Party pooper," she said, reaching for another pretzel and making sure her breasts made contact with his arm.

After taking a long drink to try to neutralize the sensations his brain was sending south of his belt buckle, he looked up and didn't see anyone behind the bar. "Where's Mike?"

"In the back. He said he had some work to do and trusted that we wouldn't rob him blind."

Griff finished off the beer. "I wouldn't be so trusting if I were him." Suddenly a wave of lightheadedness hit him. He blinked several times to clear his head, but the feeling wouldn't go way.

"So, Griff, are you feeling a little woozy about now?"

The alarms went off in his head. No one in here knew him as Griff. He tried to focus on the blond to ask how she knew, but the room began to swirl around him. He laid his head on the granite bar to keep from falling off the stool.

The blond massaged the back of his neck seductively. "Too bad, Griff. I would've loved to check you out under the sheets." She tsked. "You must've pissed off a lot of powerful people."

He tried to think clearly, but he couldn't. Reaching for his cell phone was impossible, since he couldn't even feel his hands.

He felt her warm breath in his ear as she whispered, "Rashid says when you play with explosives that don't belong to you, you end up getting hurt." The amusement was apparent in her voice. "And Joseph sends his regards as well. Says to tell you the girl was meant to be his all along."

When she leaned over to kiss his cheek, he tried to reach for her, but couldn't.

"Be back in a minute, handsome. I'm just gonna bring your truck a little closer. Then you and I are going for a drive."

He felt her hand in his jeans pocket and heard the jingling of his keys when she found them. Then she was gone, and he heard the side door to his right opening and closing. He cursed himself for allowing himself to fall victim to something as amateurish as having his drink spiked. He knew better. My God, he was a trained CIA operative.

But this was no dope-and-rob scam. The fact that she'd mentioned both the terrorist arms dealer from Cleveland and Joseph Petrović told him he was in deep trouble. He'd faced dangerous situations before, but this time he was certain he wouldn't make it out alive.

At the same time he heard a massive explosion, he

was lifted off the barstool and thrown across the room. Landing in the corner, he was able to open his eyes just enough to see flames shooting into the bar, dangerously close to him, but there was nothing he could do about it. A mental image of Mac caught in a net with Petrović laughing in the background was the last thing he remembered before his world went black.

## 10

"**C**an you hear me?"

Slowly, Griff opened his eyes and tried to sit up before screaming in pain and falling back onto the pillow. A forceful hand on his chest kept him from trying it again.

"Stay down, partner. You're banged up pretty good, and two of your ribs are broken. Experience tells me that can be a bitch."

Even if he could sit up, Griff wasn't stupid enough to chance a repeat of the searing pain that would have felled a large animal. Instead, he nodded and focused on the man standing beside the bed, holding him down. "You can let go now, Dino. I guarantee I won't be trying that again anytime soon—at least not without morphine or a bottle of that good scotch you keep hidden in your office."

"I see the explosion didn't affect your sense of humor."

*Explosion?* Griff took a painful breath and wondered how he'd ended up in a hospital bed with tubes coming out of everywhere. Little by little the details came back to him, and he remembered being blown off his stool and tossed like a rag doll into the far corner of the bar. "What about the girl?"

"What about her? We think she was sent by someone who wanted that beer to be your last," Dino said.

Griff reached over and tugged at the bedrail until the remote came loose. With the hand not hooked up to an IV or oxygen monitor, he stabbed at it until the head of the bed rose. Although it didn't come without pain, he was now almost in a sitting position and able to glance around the hospital room. Ty and Ryan were both in the corner. He did a quick scan of the room, searching for the one person he really wanted to see right now.

She wasn't there. Had Petrović gotten to her, too? Immediately, his heart rate upped a notch. "Where's Mac?"

"She's fine," Dino reassured him. "As soon as we got the call about the explosion, we whisked her off to a safe house in case Petrović was behind it and you weren't the only one he was targeting yesterday." He scratched his head. "I don't understand it. Nobody could have possibly known about SWEEPERS or our location, but even if they had, there's no way they'd get anywhere near the building. J-Lo has security so tight that I personally was denied entry into the compound once when I forgot my credentials, though the guard knows me by sight."

"So how'd they figure out you'd be at *that* bar at *that* particular time?" Ty asked from his seat in the corner. "If they had no idea where our base was, how'd they track you after you left work?"

"It's not his first time at the bar," Ryan responded. "I followed him after he killed that arms dealer and he came face to face with his ex. I knew he'd be upset, and I didn't want him doing anything stupid."

Dino looked first at Ryan and then back at Griff. "Is that true?"

Griff nodded, suddenly feeling like a newbie instead of a seasoned operative. "I stop there once or twice a week for a drink on my way home. Like you, I believed our location was a guarded secret."

"It was. But this explains a few things," the director said. "Someone knew your routine and was standing by to decorate your pickup with a little C-4 while you indulged in a biweekly ritual." He pounded his hand on the bedrail. "Dammit! How many times have I told you guys not to do anything routinely?"

Griff knew Dino was right, but at the moment he was more interested in what his boss had said right *before* he chewed him out. "Wait. That was *my* truck that exploded?"

Dino nodded. "Apparently, you were supposed to be in it. The girl was obviously collateral damage. If she'd been a genuine suicide bomber, she wouldn't have started the car and detonated the explosives without you beside her." He tapped his forehead with his fingers, as if that would make him think clearer. "My guess is she thought she was taking you somewhere and had no idea your vehicle had been rigged to blow." He paused and leaned in closer. "So why weren't you in the car with her?"

Griff lowered his head, embarrassed to have fallen prey to the terrorists. It was hard talking about this with Dino, knowing his screw-up had nearly cost him his life. How could Griff explain how he'd been off his game ever since Mac arrived at headquarters? But that was no excuse. Even a CIA trainee knew better than to drink something that had been out of his sight for more than a nanosecond. Hell, his mistake was worse than the one Mac had made with Rashid back in the warehouse in Cleveland.

"There was a side door, and she must have decided it would be easier to drag me out that way instead of through the front into the parking lot. I think she went to bring the truck around." Griff drew in a sharp breath as a sudden pain sliced through his chest.

Both Ty and Ryan were on their feet and next to the bed even before Griff closed his eyes with the agony. Reopening them, he waved his hand to let them know he was okay. "What about Mike?"

Dino's eyes narrowed. "Mike?"

"The bartender. Was he in on it?"

"If he was, he was also collateral damage. It looks like she killed him before the car blew up," Dino answered. "If it hadn't been for an irate woman looking to drag her husband out of the bar, you might be dead as well. Seems the good old boy left the bar after his wife called, then decided to stop at another pub closer to home for one more drink. When he didn't make it to the house, she came looking for him, madder than hell. She got there in time to pull you out of the burning rubble." His eyes hinted at mischief. "You're lucky, but I almost feel sorry for the poor devil when that woman finally got her hands on him."

Griff looked upward and said a quick thank you for the man who was probably still getting verbally abused by his wife. With the bar situated in the middle of nowhere, who knew how long it would've taken for someone to discover the fire and call for help if she hadn't arrived?

"So back to this girl," Dino said, interrupting Griff's thoughts. "Had you ever seen her before?"

"No, but she definitely knew who I was."

"What do you mean?"

"Right before she left to pull my car to the side of the building, she whispered a message in my ear from Rashid."

"That's strange. For the life of me, I can't figure out why a terrorist from Cleveland would target you specifically." Dino leaned over so far that Griff thought he was about to have a bedmate. "Any ideas?"

"Yes. The woman said he wanted me to know that when I play with someone else's explosives, I can get hurt." Griff looked up just as the nurse walked into the room.

"Sorry, boys. This will have to wait. It's time for Mr. Bradley's pain medicine. I've been watching him through the window, and his face tells me everything I need to know." She pushed her way between Ryan and Ty and set her tray on the bed. After swabbing the rubber stopper with an alcohol pad, she injected the medicine directly into the IV tubing.

Within minutes, Griff felt the pain in his chest easing. He had no idea who had invented morphine, but right this minute, he would kiss them if he could. He felt himself drifting off when he suddenly remembered that he'd forgotten to tell them the girl also mentioned Petrović. It was important that Dino know this, as it was the first time they could actually connect a terrorist cell with the psychopathic doctor. But the morphine had already begun to work its magic, and he closed his eyes.

"They fucked up," the voice over the phone said. "I told you I should have been the one to kill Bradley."

"I'm sorry I didn't listen to you. You're the only one

I can really trust," Petrović said before slamming the phone down and uttering a string of choice expletives. He didn't need anyone to remind him that hooking up with a moron like Rashid was a major mistake. How hard could it be to isolate one operative and kill him?

But Rashid had assured him the woman was his best assassin. Said if anyone could take care of business in a hurry, it was her. She took care of business, all right. The incompetent bitch had gone and blown herself up, leaving the target alive inside the bar. Petrović wasn't surprised when Rashid reported that the local newspaper hadn't even mentioned the incident, other than a brief story buried toward the back about a car fire that caused an explosion. Apparently, the CIA didn't want the world to know how inept they really were.

The next time the opportunity presented itself, he'd use his own people—or do it himself. He saw Griffin Bradley III as a major obstacle in getting to Mackenzie, and one way or another, the man would not be long for this world. Petrović would make sure of that.

He walked over to the window and watched as the juvenile soldiers restrained the young woman on the table in the lab. This one was a fighter, but her valiant efforts to get away only served to turn them on even more as they groped and taunted her.

They'd found her all alone on the streets of Calabozo after eleven the night before and had no problem abducting her. He wondered what she'd been doing walking the dark road by herself, imagining several different scenarios. Had she fought with her boyfriend and rushed out, totally disregarding the danger that lurked outside? Or was she a working girl?

Either way, he had no interest in her and decided

to let the guards have their fun before he did his final test with the nerve gas. Ever since he'd seen Mac on the road below his lab pretending to be a TV reporter, his interest in other women had all but disappeared. He hated that one woman could have that much power over him, and he vowed to possess her no matter what.

In the meantime, he needed this one last trial to see if the latest improvements he'd made to the delivery system had decreased the time it would take for the gas to kill its victims. He took a final glance into the window before tapping on it. When the soldiers looked up, he motioned for them to get out of the room.

After the last one had departed and the door was sealed shut, he pushed the red button on the control panel at the same time he started his stopwatch.

As SHE STEPPED off the elevator on the seventh floor, she immediately spied Griff walking to the conference room. For a moment, their eyes met, and she was sure she saw a hint of a smile before he looked away. She wondered if he blamed her for what had happened at the bar. Before she'd been kidnapped and taken to the cabin, Dino called to explain why she had to go. Said someone wanted Griff dead, and until they ruled out Petrović, they had to isolate her. His logic was that if they'd been able to get to Griff so easily, they might already have her in their crosshairs.

Nodding to the woman at the front desk, she followed the two agents to the back and was forced to stand outside the conference room while they waited for the okay to leave her there. They would probably be glad to be rid of her, since she'd bugged them the entire trip, trying to get information. She could be a real pain in the butt when she didn't get her way.

"Bring her in," she heard Dino say before the men turned and moved aside for her to enter.

As soon as she walked in, Ryan jumped up and gave her a bear hug. "Thank God you're safe."

"I appreciate the concern." She allowed her eyes to roam around the table, nodding acknowledgments to both Ty and Dino. When she came to Griff, she smiled, and as hard as he tried not to, he smiled back. She said a quick thank you to the gods that he hadn't been hurt too badly.

Then she noticed the woman sitting next to him, and before she could stop herself, she frowned. With skin a beautiful shade of brown, the newcomer could only be described as gorgeous. Immediately, a pang of jealousy took over. Why was a woman who looked like that sitting next to Griff?

"Looks like a week in the mountains didn't do much for your disposition," Dino said, noticing her frown. He motioned for her to sit.

She chose the seat between Ty and Ryan, directly across from the woman who was brazenly staring at her now. Reaching across the table, she extended her hand. "Mackenzie Conley. And you are?"

"Ah! You're the one the crazy doctor is so obsessed with."

"That would be me," Mac retorted, uncertain how she felt about being labeled that way. "Who did you say you were?"

"I didn't," the woman said, seemingly enjoying being so vague.

"Mac, this is Selena Martinez, the best tech expert

out there. If you think James Bond has the coolest equipment, you haven't seen GG's."

"GG?"

"Gadget girl," Griff said without looking up.

Martinez shook Mac's hand. "Although I usually don't work well with women, I have a feeling you and I can figure it all out."

Before Mac could respond, Dino waved his hand in the air. "Okay, enough with the chatter. They'll be time for that later. Right now we need to talk about how Griff damn near bit the dust, and more importantly, what our next move should be."

"And we believe Rashid acted alone with the assassination attempt?" Ryan asked. "Griff mentioned that the lady referred to him before she blew herself up. Is it possible this was just retaliation for us destroying their weapons?"

"Rashid was behind this?" Mac looked first at Griff then back to Dino. "I get why he'd want to see me dead, but why Griff? He couldn't have known he was the leader of the team that had confiscated his precious weapons. Besides, weren't our identities kept secret?"

"We think the weapons had a lot to do with why they targeted him," Dino responded. "We also believe there might be a mole in the building and are investigating the possibility." He clicked on the screen, and a picture of the Cleveland arms dealer stared down at them. "But we also now know that Petrović was involved."

"What makes you think that?" Ty asked.

"The woman mentioned him, too," Griff said softly.

"Shit!" Ryan exclaimed. "So the two assholes have

teamed up?" He turned to Griff. "What exactly did the woman say?"

Griff looked down as if he didn't want to answer. Finally, he raised his head and looked directly at Mac. "She passed on a message to me from Petrović. He said the girl was meant to be his all along."

Hearing those words made Mac's skin crawl, and she closed her eyes to get control of her emotions. Suddenly, she understood completely why she'd been awakened in the middle of the night and driven into the mountains. It also explained why they'd guarded her like she was Fort Knox. Petrović *was* certifiably crazy, and he would stop at nothing until he had her in his clutches—again.

"Damn!" Ryan exclaimed. "He is one sick fuck."

"That he is," Dino agreed. "It's obvious he'll do whatever it takes to get his hands on Mac again. But that's not what we're here to discuss." He clicked the remote, and the screen went blank. "What you're about to hear is a conversation that J-Lo received this morning from one of his friends at Interpol." He turned up the audio, and they all listened to a brief conversation in Arabic.

Although there were no pictures, Mac immediately recognized one of the voices. "That's Rashid."

"Yes, and we think the other voice is the head of a sleeper cell in Pakistan," Dino said. "J-Lo is working now to identify him. But right now, we're more concerned about what they said."

"And that was?" Ty asked, leaning forward on his elbows, waiting for Dino to interpret.

"Rashid said it was a go for Miami," Griff replied.

"Forgot you spoke Arabic," Ty said. "So, do we know when whatever is being planned in Miami will go down?"

"He mentioned final preparations will take six more days." Dino glanced at the calendar on the table. "That gives us until Saturday to figure it out."

"And how are we going to do that?" Ty asked. "Do we even have a clue what they're targeting down there?" He shook his head. "Miami isn't some little suburb with only a high school football field and a Dairy Queen, you know."

Dino nodded and pointed a finger at Ty. "And therein lies our dilemma. We have no idea what we should be watching. Hopefully, J-Lo will be able to provide us with more info in the next day or two. He has his buddies all over the world listening to every conversation that comes over the wire. We'll know something as soon as it's out there."

"It's not enough," Mac said suddenly.

She'd been following the conversation, hoping to hear anything that might give them hope, but there was nothing. In less than a week, something catastrophic was going to happen in Florida, and they were helpless to stop it.

"We know it's not much, but for now, it's all we have," Dino said.

"We can't just sit back and watch them win. We have to go on the offensive." She lowered her eyes, knowing what she was actually going to propose.

"And how do we go about doing that?" Ty asked. "We don't even know what they're going to do. Are they going to blow up a terminal? Poison the water supply?" He shook his head and let out a noisy, frustrated sigh.

She kept her eyes fixated on the floor, unable to look at any of them. Finally, she looked up. "You all know what we have to do, but none of you will actually say it." She waited for someone to respond, but no one did. "Petrović wants me. We have to give him access."

Griff hammered his fist on the table, then groaned in pain. "Dammit, Mac. We've been down this road before. There's no way we'll allow you to be his prey. It's too risky."

She met his gaze and tried to hide the fear she knew must be in her own eyes. "It's the only way." She looked away before he convinced her not to do it, focusing on Dino instead. "The cabin in the mountains has a fake floor in the bedroom leading to a dirt tunnel that ends up in the old storage shed out back."

"An underground tunnel? How would you know about that?" Dino asked, unable to hide the confusion from his face.

She gave him her best impression of innocence. "I may have slipped away from your maximum-security detail a couple of times to enjoy the view when I was bored."

"Well, I'll be damned. Wonder why the old man who lived there would need a secret tunnel."

"The Allegheny Mountains were popular for hiding Confederate soldiers during the Civil War," Ty said. "What? I watch the History Channel," he explained when they all stared at him.

A silence prevailed around the table before Dino finally nailed Mac with his eyes. "It could work," he said. "Because of the location, though, we wouldn't be able to have men standing guard."

"I know," she said softly. "No one can come up the road without being noticed. But I can use that and the tunnel to my advantage." She paused to swallow the big lump that had formed in her throat. "By the time the bad guys discover that I'm hiding in there, you guys will be charging up the hill to rescue me."

"I can arm her with hidden weapons and alarms," GG said, now staring at Mac with interest. "If you're gonna go, I can make it way more fun for you."

Mac nodded. "I'm looking forward to seeing your talents in action."

"I'm going with you," Ryan interjected. "We're talking about me, here. I can blow the crap out of them."

"No," Mac said, reaching for his hand on the table. "Petrović is too smart for that. He'd know you were there and find a way to pick you off."

Before Ryan could argue, Griff spoke up. "I'm going. End of discussion." With that, he pushed his chair back and walked to the door. "We'll need to leave in the morning. Make it happen, Dino."

**11**

___

"I
s that the second time that chopper has flown by
us?" Mac asked from the back seat of the Lincoln
Town Car.

"Yeah," Ty answered from up front. "It's got the call
sign of a local TV station on the side, so I radioed
headquarters to check it out. According to the station
manager, they have no helicopters in the air right
now."

"So they've taken the bait." Mac looked down at
Griff, who was lying on the floor at her feet.

Griff wasn't sure how he felt about that. On one
hand, he was glad their plan had been set in motion,
but on the other, it meant that Mac was now vulnerable to whatever Petrović had planned for her. He
hoped he'd be able to protect her from that demented
doctor.

He'd awakened at the butt crack of dawn even
though they weren't scheduled to leave until noon.
They'd chosen that time because there'd be more
traffic and it wouldn't look so staged. When he
stepped into the car, he'd had a good laugh seeing Ty
dressed in a blue suit instead of his usual jeans and t-
shirt, and had ribbed him the entire way to Mac's

apartment. Crouched low in the back seat, he'd stayed out of sight, even though the windows were tinted so dark that no one could see inside the vehicle anyway. As uncomfortable as that was with his Kevlar vest on, he'd resisted the urge to complain. Dino insisted the entire team wear vests at all times, even when they slept.

When they pulled up to Mac's apartment, Ty had made a big deal out of putting her luggage in the trunk and helping her into the back seat. They had no idea if whoever had tried to kill Griff was watching, but just in case they were, they'd put on a show.

About fifteen minutes after they'd picked Mac up, Ty noticed a dark Escalade a few cars behind them and radioed Ryan, who was driving an industrial van about a half-mile back. Just as he drove into the last tunnel before the exit that would take them up the mountain, Ryan pulled in front of the Cadillac and slammed on the brakes. It was all the other driver could do to keep from plowing into the back of the van, and he skidded off the road, finally coming to a stop on the shoulder. That gave Ty just enough time to pull over in the tunnel and scramble out of the limo into a waiting, nondescript agency car.

As soon as Ty was out of the vehicle, Griff climbed into the front seat and immediately put the car in gear. Catching a glimpse of himself in the mirror wearing a suit he'd had to borrow from Dino, he decided he deserved the teasing he was sure to get from his cohort back at the compound. When the Lincoln exited the tunnel at the other end, no one could have possibly known it had a new driver.

"I hope Ryan can handle the driver in the SUV who must be calling him every name in the book by now," Mac said. "It wouldn't take much to get his Irish temper fired up."

"He took off before they had a chance to ream him out," Griff said just as the chopper reappeared overhead. "Our friends are back."

"I guess this means Dino was right about them hacking into our secure line." Mac shook her head. "That's kinda scary, if you think about it."

"Dino used a line the IT guys specifically created so that a good hacker could intercept messages without realizing it was a setup. It comes in handy when we want the bad guys to think they know what our next move will be. Using a code we knew they'd crack, we put it out there that we were taking you to a safe haven in the Alleghenies." Griff exited the interstate and turned down the road that led up the mountain.

"And we're sure they intercepted the post?"

"We're definitely being followed, so they had to know our plans. I guess there's always the possibility they weren't able to hack the line, since we had to make it tough enough to ward off any suspicions. But if that's true, it means they've been watching you, me, or both."

The minute the words were out of his mouth, he glanced up at the rearview mirror and wished he could take them back. Although she attempted to hide the fear that flashed in her eyes, he knew her well enough to know what she was thinking. Knew she'd rather die than be in Petrović's hands again. Although she'd never really told him much about the time she spent as his prisoner, from what Dino said, it must have been devastating. Mac was one of the strongest agents, man or woman, that he knew, and if Petrović had been able to compromise her, he must have used ways that were unimaginable. Just thinking about it made Griff renew his vow to kill the bastard very slowly when they finally caught up to him—and he had no doubts they would, eventually.

For now, though, they had to play his little game. Reel him in slowly and then hang him with his own rope.

"Griff?"

Her voice jerked him back to the present. "Yeah?"

"I'm glad you came with me," Mac said softly.

He was about to say that he'd been the only logical choice when the chopper made a third pass overhead before executing a sharp left turn and heading back in the opposite direction.

"Guess they don't need eyes in the sky anymore, since this road only leads up the mountain. Right now they must be thinking they have us cornered," Griff said, feeling the anxiety creep in. "Are you sure you're up for this, Mac?" He looked in the rearview mirror again and saw her nod.

"I just want to put it all behind me."

Not any more than he did. The thought of her being in so much danger scared the hell out of him. He decided to change the subject and get her thinking about something else. "They checked out that underground tunnel and reinforced it, so there's no chance of it caving in on us. We could actually hide out there if they stake out the storage shed for some reason. And Dino made sure the shed was stocked with enough ammo to fight a war. Even gave us a four-wheeler if we need it. And from what I hear, GG also left us a few surprises as well."

She nodded again before glancing out the window.

Seeing her so vulnerable had him shifting into

protective mode. He wanted to stop the car, take her into his arms, and reassure her that he would protect her with his own life. But for many reasons, the least of which was that he'd screw up the entire operation, he knew it was out of the question and scolded himself for even considering it.

What had he been thinking insisting that he be the one to go with her to the secluded cabin? Somewhere in his head, he had to have realized that meant spending time alone with her. It was hard enough being in the same room with the rest of the crew there. No matter how many times he tried to convince himself that she was just another teammate, he knew she wasn't—and never would be. What they shared before her time in Morocco had been special, and regardless of what happened over the next day or so, they would never go back to that relationship. He wasn't sure they could even be friends again.

"How much farther?" she asked, her voice catching.

"Another hour or so."

They drove the rest of the way in an awkward silence, and Griff used the time to figure out the best way to ward off the attack he knew would be coming. As Dino had warned, there was only one road leading to the cabin, and any effort to place backup in strategic places along the way would more than likely squelch any chance of Petrović taking the bait. The success of the operation depended on him thinking he had the upper hand.

As they rounded a sharp curve, a small log cabin came into view. Hoping they were up to the challenge, Griff drove down the gravel road almost to the front door and parked the limo.

"If my estimations are correct, they'll probably

wait until dark to make a move. They don't know we're onto them, so it's to their advantage to surprise us while we sleep."

"I'll be glad to get this over with," Mac said, repeating her earlier statement as she climbed out of the car and attempted to smile at Griff when he held the door open for her. A sudden hint of mischief brightened her eyes. "You look adorable in Dino's suit, by the way."

"Don't start on me. I'm going to take enough grief from Ty as it is." He took one final glance toward the mountain road before checking his watch. "Go into the house and try to relax. We've got a couple of hours before the sun goes down. I hope Dino remembered to stock the place with groceries. I'm starving."

That was enough to break the ice, and she smiled. "Just like a man. We're about to face God only knows how many evil terrorists, and you're thinking about a sandwich."

He couldn't help it and smiled with her. "How am I going to protect you if I don't keep up my strength?" Without waiting for a response, he grabbed her suitcase from the trunk and followed her up the steps.

After retrieving the key from under the mat, Mac opened the door and walked through. Griff was close behind her and got his first look at what very well might be the last place he would ever see. As confident as he was in the skills of his fellow SWEEPER teammates, the position of the house made him and Mac especially vulnerable to a lethal attack.

And they weren't even sure who was coming or why.

What if they were wrong and Petrović's ultimate goal wasn't getting his hands on Mac? What if his intent was simply to kill her? If that was the case, it would dramatically change their method of attack. If keeping her alive wasn't an issue, they could use sophisticated weaponry to destroy the cabin and everyone in it without any advance warning. There would be no defending against a guided missile attack. Even if they did manage to get in the tunnel beforehand.

As much as he hated thinking about it, he prayed whoever was out there had orders to take Mac alive.

He placed her suitcase in the corner and opened it. Inside there were two AK-47s, several magazine clips and hand grenades, and two gas masks. That should do nicely until they reached the storage shed and the cache of weapons out there.

"Where's the tunnel entrance?"

She pointed to the corner of the living room. "Do you want to check it out before we settle in?"

"Yes. I have no idea how far behind us they are or how long they'll wait to make their first move. I want to be sure there are no surprises when we go underground."

"Good idea. Come on. Let's give it a test run."

She grabbed a flashlight from the counter and waved for him to follow her. When he was beside her, she lifted the carpet in the corner.

"Nice," he said when he saw the trapdoor leading to the tunnel. "Let me."

He reached around her and lifted the heavy door, noticing the *what the hell look* she gave him. When she slid past him to be the first into the tunnel, he fought to keep from grinning. After climbing down the makeshift steps, the first thing he noticed was the overwhelming smell of fresh turned earth and wood from the reinforcements Dino had authorized. He knocked on the side to make sure it was stable.

"It's fine," she said, grabbing his arm. "Come on. I want to see what kind of goodies Dino left for us."

It took less than a minute to reach the other end, where there was another handmade ladder exactly like the one in the living room. He was about to step in front of her and push the door open but stopped cold when she sent him another of her looks. He raised his hands in mock surrender and bit his lip to keep from smiling as he bowed to allow her to go ahead of him.

He tried not to watch her climb up the steps, but the view of her backside in the tight jeans was too much to resist.

The door opened after she gave it a few nudges with her shoulder. When he heard her squeal, he nearly broke his neck trying to get up the steps in a hurry. "Damn it, Mac. I thought you were in trouble," he said when he saw her with her back to him in the corner of the shed.

"Check this out." She pointed to the large metal container now standing open in front of her. "There are two more AK-47s, more grenades than we can possibly use, a couple of Browning pistols, and holy crap! There's even an RPG-7."

He joined her in the corner and stared into the container. "How much do you want to bet these came from the stash we confiscated from Rashid in Cleveland?"

"Poetic justice," she said, picking up a grenade and rolling it around in her hand. "Dino did good. If we're going to go down fighting, he made sure we'll be able to hang with the big boys."

"What did GG come up with for you? Are you impressed with her yet?"

A huge smile covered Mac's face. "She's growing on me." She held up her left hand with a huge turquoise ring on her middle finger. "Don't get too close to me. This little baby sends a squirt of pepper spray out right before it launches a needle." She chuckled. "If some dirtbag gets too close to me, he'll be looking for a new eye."

"Pretty impressive. Now we need to get back to the business at hand, and that's checking out the refrigerator to see if the man remembered that we haven't eaten all day."

"I have to admit I'm pretty hungry myself." She led the way back through the tunnel.

When they were safely in the cabin, Griff replaced the carpet over the trapdoor.

"Looks like you're in luck," he heard her say from the kitchen. "Remind me to kiss Dino when I see him. Not only has he stocked the refrigerator with my favorites—ham and hot pepper cheese slices—but he's also included a six-pack of beer."

"I think I'll kiss him myself," Griff said, coming up behind her and looking over her shoulder into the fridge. "A cold one is just what we need to take our minds off why we're here."

He reached over to grab a bottle just as she turned to say something to him. For a minute, their chests touched, and an electric current pulsed through his body. He jumped back as if she were a torch.

"Sorry," she said before turning and getting the beer for him. "Sit down while I fix us both a sandwich." She pulled the meat and cheese from the refrigerator, along with a beer for herself.

As she busied herself with the sandwich preparations, he used the time to study the cabin. If he was right and the attack did come after dark, they'd need to know every nook and cranny in the place so they wouldn't be in the line of fire. Whoever was out there must know he was the only one protecting her. They'd need to take him out first. He had to make sure that didn't happen.

He estimated the cabin to be about fourteen hundred square feet, if that, with the tiny living room sparsely furnished in the ugliest decor he'd ever seen. The green and gold plaid accent pillows on the worn brownish-gold couch made it even worse. The small kitchen was adequate, with a table for two and a few small appliances, and off to the left was the bedroom with a bathroom no bigger than the closet beside it. He looked toward the bedroom, immediately sorry when his brain painted a vivid picture of what he'd like to do to Mac in that room.

"If you're still hungry after you eat this, there's plenty more," she said, placing the paper plate with a sandwich and a handful of chips in front of him.

Knocked back to reality, he chugged the last of his beer and set the empty bottle on the table. "What I'd really like is another one of these," he said, before reaching for the sandwich. That was a lie. What he'd really like had more to do with the bedroom than the kitchen. "But I don't want to get so relaxed that they're able to sneak up on us." He took a bite and nodded. "You always did fix these exactly the way I like them, with extra mayo and double cheese."

She sat down opposite him and met his gaze. "I am good at something, you know."

Oh boy, did he. And he had to quit glancing toward the bedroom, or he'd drag her in there so she could show him her other skills.

The sun was already setting by the time they'd finished eating, and the only light in the cabin was the soft glow from the living room lamps. Mac sat down on the couch and lifted her feet to the coffee table, and before long, she had slumped to the right and was fast asleep. Across from her in the chair, Griff watched her sleep, as he'd done many times in the past. It never ceased to amaze him that she could be so beautiful even in deep slumber.

He yawned and leaned further back into the chair, wondering if he should try to get a little shuteye himself. It would be a long night, and more than likely, the attack would come much later. With no outside lights, a sneak attack gave the bad guys an advantage.

Just when he'd nixed that idea and decided he needed to stay alert, a sudden noise snagged his attention away from her, and he jumped from the chair. Racing to the corner of the room where he'd positioned her suitcase, he opened it and took out one of the two automatic weapons packed inside, along with a couple of magazine clips and hand grenades. Easing over to the curtain, he peeked out, expecting to see some sign that the party was about to begin.

But there was nothing. With the sun all but gone now, visibility was already beginning to be a problem. He scanned the trees that lined the driveway, but there was nothing out of the ordinary. Then a sudden movement caught his eye, and he jerked forward and aimed the gun, ready to shoot before he saw two squirrels run from the porch and scamper up a tree.

He forced himself to relax. He had to get a grip, but knowing they were sitting ducks made it hard. There was nothing to do but be patient and wait for the enemy to make their first move. He hoped he'd be able to make it their last.

"Griff?"

He turned slightly to see Mac rubbing her eyes and sitting upright on the couch. When she spotted the gun in his hands, she jumped up and ran toward him.

He held up his arm. "Guess my nerves are a little frazzled. I almost killed two baby squirrels." He shook his head. "God, I really could use another beer."

She stepped closer. "You can if you want. I know you well enough to know that two beers won't have any effect on your skills. I'd feel safer with you after an entire six-pack than I would with anyone else stone-cold sober in this situation."

He didn't know how to respond to that and lowered his head. He'd been mad at her for so long that it felt strange hearing her compliment him. He reminded himself that she was merely a teammate he was assigned to protect, and not Mac, the only woman he'd ever wanted to spend the rest of his life with. But she was standing so close now that he could smell the apricot shampoo she'd used that morning, a scent that conjured up memories of when their relationship was much different. He tried to take a step back, but he was already flush against the wall.

"Mac, I..."

She put her finger to his lips. "Don't talk. If today's going to be my last, I only want to remember the good things." She stood on her tiptoes and brushed her lips against his.

God help him. He tried to resist, but he wanted her so badly. The goddamn apricot scent overpowered his self-control, and he pulled her to him, crushing his lips against hers.

As her lips parted, he heard her moan slightly, which only broke down his defenses even further. She was so soft and warm against him, and when she pressed her body closer, he lost it and pulled her to him, filling his hands with her hair as his tongue probed her mouth.

Just when he was about to ignore the warning bells going off in his head and go for it, a sudden click startled them both. He felt her body stiffen when the electricity went out and the cabin was thrown into complete darkness.

## 12

"Stay down," he whispered as he handed her the AK-47. Crawling now, he inched his way across the floor to the suitcase and took out the other automatic weapon and the remaining magazines. "I'm going to see if I can spot anything from the side window."

He moved slowly into the bedroom and lifted himself up just enough to peer out of the window's edge. The bedroom faced the mountain road leading to the cabin and gave him the best view. Their plan was to use the stash of weapons to keep whoever was out there occupied long enough to give the SWEEPERS team time to get up the mountain. He hoped he and Mac would be able to hold them off that long.

He spotted a flash of light coming from just behind the tree out front, and he trained his weapon on the spot. Although he didn't know how many men were out there, it was a given the bad guys far outnumbered them. Their mission, if he had called it correctly, would be to take him out in a hurry, grab Mac, and then get off the mountain as quickly as possible.

If they wanted Mac alive, they'd have to be very careful about shooting randomly into the house. He wondered what they'd use to draw them out into the open, thanking the gods for the gas masks Dino had packed with the guns.

"You see anything?" Mac asked from the living room.

"One shooter behind the big oak tree out front. What about you?"

"I thought I saw movement a few minutes ago when a black car pulled up. Looks like a Caddy."

"How many can you see?"

"At least four." She met his gaze. "Tell me when to start shooting."

"Sit tight for now. Let them make the first move. More than likely they've already used heat sensors and know there are only two of us in the cabin. Right about now, they must be feeling a little cocky with the numbers advantage, thinking we're just curled up on the couch drinking hot chocolate."

He crawled back out to the living room and moved to the suitcase. "I'm thinking they'll use tear gas." Grabbing a gas mask, he tossed it her way. "Put it on. That stuff is potent." He reached for the other one and strapped it to his face.

"We look like something out of *Star Wars*," she said, apparently trying to lighten the mood before turning back to the window and raising her middle finger. "Bring it on, you slimy bastards."

If he could take anyone into battle with him, it would be her. She was a kick-ass-and-take-names kind of girl. They were silent as they waited for the enemy to make the first move. He glanced down at his watch, hoping Dino and his team were at least halfway up the mountain by now.

Just then, a canister crashed through the front

window and, as expected, tear gas poured out in a bil-
lowy cloud.

Griff took a grenade and handed Mac another before whispering, "They'll be waiting for us to come
running out of the front door. On my count, stand up
and hurl the grenade as hard as you can toward the
front Caddy. I'm gonna lob mine over near the tree."
He got to his feet but stayed low. "Okay, one, two,
three—go."

Griff pushed open the front door while both
ducked for cover. They threw the grenades seconds
apart. The first one exploded, flushing two men from
the tree line and lighting up an area of about fifty
yards of more. Griff blasted out a window with the AK-
47 and took them both out, along with another man
positioned further back, exposed by the unexpected
light. The explosion from the second grenade lifted
two more men into the air when it discharged next to
the Caddy. Again, the area lit up as their lifeless
bodies landed hard on the front porch steps.

"Five down and God only knows how many more
to go." Griff slumped down and high-fived Mac. "The
light show was compliments of GG, by the way. This
isn't the first time she's rigged a grenade."

"I'm liking her more every minute." Mac's voice
was sharp and crackling with excitement. "We just
stirred up a hornets' nest out there. They assumed
we'd be running toward them, not flinging grenades at
them."

"Yeah, they must be pissed off, knowing we were
waiting and that they've got a fight on their hands. Get
ready, Mac. The party's about to get nasty, and—"

Before he finished his sentence, a barrage of gunfire blew out all the windows. Griff pulled Mac down,
shielding her with his body. As quickly as it had be-

gun, the gunfire ended, and again there was total silence.

He lifted his body off hers, brushed off the shards of glass from his clothes, and then leaned against the wall. She sat up and followed suit. They stayed that way for several minutes, with only the sound of their breathing breaking the eerie silence.

"I guess it's wishful thinking to assume they've gone away," she said.

Griff shook his head. "No chance. These guys weren't prepared for our show of force, though. We definitely got their attention. They realize now that taking out a girl and her driver isn't going to be as easy as they thought."

"Think they're regrouping as we speak?" She inched her way over to the window to steal a peek. "I don't see anything."

"We need to stay inside and hold them off as long as we can to give the team more time to get here, but we should open the trapdoor and stay close to it so we can make a quick escape when the time is right. I have a feeling things are going to happen fast, and we need to be ready." He made his way to the corner and motioned for her to follow.

Once there, he lifted the rug, opened the trapdoor, and peered down into the dirt tunnel. Knowing this might very well be the thing that saved their lives, he wanted to make sure the bad guys hadn't found the entrance in the storage shed and were lying in wait for them. Everything looked the same. The flashlights they'd left after the trial run hadn't been moved, and there was nothing to indicate a breech.

"If I'm right about them using thermal detectors, they know we're both in the same room. That could work to our advantage, especially if their orders include taking you alive," he said before moving back to the wall.

"Do you think Petrović's out there?" She leaned closer.

"Probably not. I doubt Rashid is, either. This is the kind of grunt work they leave to trained killers. My hope is to take at least one of these guys alive. If he can lead us to Rashid, maybe Rashid will lead us to Petrović."

He heard her take a breath and slowly release it. He wished he could tell her the rescue team was close by, but he had no clue when they would get there. He hoped it was sooner rather than later.

"Griff?"

"Yeah."

"Promise me you'll kill me if you think we can't make it out of here alive." She shuddered. "I can't be near that man again."

"Quit talking nonsense, Mac. There's no way I'd ever let them march in here and take you alive," he replied, hoping she didn't detect the fear in his voice. In truth, he had no idea what would happen, but her asking him to put a bullet into her head was more than he could deal with right now.

"Promise me."

He threaded his fingers through his hair, and though he wasn't sure he could carry out her wishes, he nodded. "Okay. Quit being so morbid. I'm betting Dino and the crew will have these guys surrounded before it comes to that."

"I hope so, because—"

She screamed as a Molotov cocktail crashed through a blown-out window and landed across the room. Flames leaped up the old wooden walls. Before they could react, the entire room erupted into an inferno.

Griff grabbed her hand and pushed her toward the tunnel entrance. "Hurry. We don't have much time before the entire cabin goes up in flames."

She scurried down the ladder, and Griff followed, pulling the door shut before realizing it would make no difference. In a matter of minutes, there would be no cabin left standing. After jumping down the last two steps, he hesitated momentarily then grabbed the flashlight she held out to him.

"Let's go kick some ass," she said, leading the way with her own light. "They must be wondering why we haven't run out into their waiting arms by now."

They raced through the tunnel, and when they reached the other end, Griff grabbed her arm and whispered, "Let me go first. They may have scoped out this place and could be waiting to nab us." Cautiously, he climbed up the steps and lifted the trapdoor. There was no sign of anyone in the shed. A glance toward the door showed the four-wheeler positioned right where he'd first seen it and ready to go if necessary.

"It looks clear," he whispered before stepping out and then reaching down to help her.

"They have no clue we're here," she said, dusting the dirt from her clothes. "Right now, the element of surprise is in our favor." She walked over to the weapons container and opened it. "We may not make it out of here alive, but we're sure as hell gonna make someone's day miserable." She took out a Browning pistol and stuffed it into the back of her jeans before grabbing more magazines for her AK-47.

Griff walked beside her and picked up the RPG-7. "I remember the first time I fired a handheld rocket launcher. I was expecting a huge kickback and was surprised when there was very little. Make sure you're not behind me when I let this baby rip, though. The backblast can be bad." He made his way to the lone window on the other side of the building to get his first look at the enemy. With the landscape still illuminated from the grenades, he could see there were five identical Escalades parked in front of the house now, with men in camouflage hunkering down behind the vehicles, waiting for their prey to flee the burning house.

"Get ready, Mac. I counted about eight, but there's probably more. Because of the way they're positioned, I won't be able to take them all out. Whoever's left standing will be mad as hell. We better be ready to move quickly. When I fire the launcher, start up the engine on the four-wheeler and get ready to haul ass."

She nodded. "Got it."

He hoisted the weapon onto his right shoulder and aimed at the middle Escalade. "Here goes," he whispered before pulling the trigger.

In a matter of seconds, the car was thrown into the air along with three of the men. In the mayhem that followed, four more came running out from behind the house. Shouts in Arabic filled the air. No doubt they were in panic mode, wondering what in the hell had just happened. It didn't take them long to figure out that the attack had come from the shed. When they turned to face it, Griff threw two more grenades at them.

"Ready, Mac?" he shouted. "We can't wait any longer for the cavalry to show up."

After lobbing the final grenade, he pushed open the shed door and climbed on the four-wheeler behind her.

Mac pushed down on the thumb throttle, and the

front end rose into the air before dropping and stabilizing. All four tires gained traction, and the vehicle bolted from the shed, catching the remaining terrorists off guard. Griff sprayed gunfire as they pulled away, but the assailants were quickly beyond reach. Their offensive stand was over as soon as the Cadillacs were on the move. They'd have to shift into defensive mode, since there was no way the four-wheeler could outrun them.

Beyond the shed was what looked to be an overgrown pasture that had probably been home to farm animals at some point. The road running through it, if you could call it that, was narrow and rough, but it was their only chance to escape. Off-road was out of the question. No telling what pitfalls they'd encounter in the dense woods. Their only hope was that the crew would reach them in time.

"Where the hell is Dino?" he asked, disheartened that they'd been left to fight these guys alone. "We've got a good start, but they're already on our tail and closing fast." He heard a loud boom and saw first the lead Cadillac, and then the second in line, flip into the air and roll over. "What the—"

"There's a big red button on the dashboard that says PUSH ME, so I did," Mac said right before they hit a bump in the road, nearly propelling Griff off the back. "What happened?"

He adjusted his grip and grinned. "It must have fired something on the road behind us. Probably grenades. Remind me to thank GG the next time I see her." His grin turned into a frown when he spotted the remaining two Escalades dodging the obstacles by turning off the road into the thick brush and going around the overturned vehicles. One of them apparently got stuck in the thick brush and frantically revved up the engine, trying to get back on the road. "Let's hope this road doesn't lead to a dead end." No sooner had he said that than a dilapidated fence loomed ahead. Beyond that, they could see a rocky road leading up to the top of the mountain. "Shit!"

Mac plowed through the fence and made her way to the top, the rocks hurling them from side to side. As soon as she stopped, they both jumped off, shaken but not injured from the ride.

Mac reached the ledge first and peered over the side. "Oh my God!"

When Griff caught up to her, he immediately felt his pulse quicken. "Jesus!"

He could barely make out the bottom of the ravine —about a thousand feet below them. Unless they had wings, there was no way they would survive a fall from where they stood. He glanced around and saw the terrorists closing in on them. They had only minutes, and although he and Mac might be able to take out a few, there was no way they could get them all. This would not end up in their favor, and they'd definitely kill him before capturing her.

He remembered his promise to her. Could he really do as she'd asked? Did he have it in him to grab her hand and jump over the edge? At least that way they'd die together. He moved closer to her.

"There's a ledge about twelve or thirteen feet below us," she said, leaning far enough over the edge that he reached out and grabbed her arm to steady her. "If we can somehow get down there, we can press our backs into the mountain then hope they don't have the right angle to pick us off."

He leaned closer to see for himself and decided she was right. With a little luck, they might be able to hold off the bad guys long enough for the team to come sashaying in for the rescue. But if they tried to jump to the ledge and missed, they would surely die.

Then an idea popped into his head, and he turned to her. "Do you trust me?"

She peered into his eyes. "With my life."

"Good. Now take off your pants."

## 13

M ac cocked an eyebrow. "You want me to take
off my jeans?"

"Yes, hurry." Griff unzipped his own jeans and
pushed them down his legs.

She hastened to reposition the Browning pistol in
the inside pocket of her vest and quickly wriggled out
of her jeans. She felt the warm rush up her cheeks
when she noticed him giving her a once-over as she
stood in front of him, clad only in her underwear and
a thin blouse covered by a Kevlar vest.

He grabbed her jeans and tied the end of his pants
leg in a knot that he probably learned back in his
scouting days. As he turned away from her and tied
the other leg of his pants to the handlebar of the four-
wheeler, she stole a glance at his backside—and instantly regretted it as old memories of their time together bombarded her brain.

Quickly, she looked away and waited for his instructions. If she was right about what he was planning, she knew it was a long shot, but it just might
work.

After he finished, he made sure the emergency
brake on the vehicle was engaged, then he spotted a

large rock and wedged it against the left front tire. Next, he handed her the other end of the makeshift rope. "This isn't long enough to reach all the way to the ledge, but it'll put you close enough. Try to find a branch or something to grab once you let go. And for God's sake, don't look down."

*No chance of that happening.* Although she'd never been afraid of heights, this was the mother of them all.

"I can hear them coming. Hurry," he said.

She grabbed the end of her jeans and made eye contact with him while she positioned herself on the edge. Then she took a step backward, crying out when her feet left the mountain top. She fell about ten feet before the denim rope jerked and slammed her into the cliff wall with a thud that would definitely leave a bruise on her chin. She felt for anything to grab on to, but there was nothing. For a few seconds, she dangled helplessly, praying the makeshift rope would hold her weight. When she was able, she flattened her body against the side of the cliff and curled her hand around a protruding rock.

"Mac?"

"I'm okay," she said, her voice cracking.

She squeezed her eyes shut before doing the one thing he'd told her not to: she looked down. Immediately, she got lightheaded. The ledge was approximately two feet below, and she knew that with one slip of her foot, she'd fall to her death. Sucking in a deep breath and holding it, she let go of the rope, convinced there was no way she'd land on her feet.

But she did.

She looked up just as Griff took his first step off the cliff. When he let go of the rope, he landed crooked and fumbled to grab something to hang on to. She caught his arm at the moment his foot slipped off the ledge. With all the strength she could muster, she held on until he was able to grab a rock and pull himself back up. She didn't need to see his face to know he was thinking about what had almost happened.

No sooner had she breathed a sigh of relief than she heard loud voices above them.

"Dammit! They're already up there," Griff said.

She nodded toward her left hand at the turquois ring GG had given her and grinned. "I dare them to get on our rope and come down. One of them will be wearing a patch over an eye, if he lives to tell about it."

"Shh." Griff strained to hear the excited voices. "They're trying to decide what to do next."

Just then, several shots rang out, and both of them pressed their bodies into the wall as bullets whizzed past within inches of them.

"You were right about the angle," he said. "This will buy us a little time." He rolled his eyes. "Where in the hell is the team?"

"Something must've happened," she said, hoping that *something* wasn't as bad as she feared. "I think it's safe to say we're pretty much on our own here."

"Shh," he whispered again. "Hear that?" The sound of a helicopter moved closer. "Hope that's not reinforcements for them," Griff said, immediately bursting her bubble of hope.

As the chopper drew near, the voices above them grew louder and almost frantic. Griff and Mac understood why when they got their first look at the aircraft hovering over the side of the mountain. Emblazoned on the side of the Black Hawk was the USAF insignia.

The chopper sprayed the top of the mountain with firepower. Mac and Griff could only hang on and listen. It took about five minutes and a couple of explosions before the bird hovered directly over them. Mac held on to the rock with one hand and turned slightly to glance up in time to see both Ryan and Ty smiling down at her.

From out of nowhere, another helicopter appeared, and the Black Hawk banked sharply to the right and climbed, racing away with the other one hot on its tail.

"Oh God!" Mac said when she heard a loud explosion and saw a fireball light up the sky off to the left. It was too far away to tell which of the helicopters had exploded, but the surviving chopper was racing toward them. If this one held more terrorists, there was no way she and Griff could hide from them. They would be picked off like moving ducks at a carnival booth—except they couldn't even move. She pulled the pistol out of her pocket, prepared to fight to the end.

A rope descended from the hovering aircraft while she strained to figure out if these were friends or foes. Was she being rescued or taken prisoner? A smile crossed her lips when the U.S. insignia on the side came into view. Reaching out, she grabbed the lifeline.

Holding on with a tight grip, she nodded, and the helicopter slowly lifted her up to the mountain's edge. The bodies of the seven terrorists covered the landscape. She and Griff would not have stood a chance against such numbers. After she released the rope, she glanced up at a smiling Ryan, who saluted her from the cockpit before returning to pick up Griff.

"That's as close as I want to come to meeting my Maker," Griff said when he was dropped off, swiping the perspiration from his brow. "At least for now."

The helicopter landed about a hundred feet from them. Ryan exited the bird and ran toward them, with Ty right behind him.

"Where the hell have you guys been?" Griff barked.

Ryan made no bones about staring at Mac in her undies, but finally tore his eyes away and focused on Griff. "They blew up the mountain road and were waiting to ambush us," he explained. "We held them off until the helicopter arrived. After the pilot was able to land, we jumped aboard and got here as fast as we could."

"And not a minute too soon, I might add." Griff shook his head. "You guys really know how to make an entrance."

"If we'd have known we'd get to see Mac in her skivvies, we might have gotten here sooner," Ryan quipped.

Mac couldn't help herself and laughed. "Get a good look, big boy, because this is as close to my panties as you'll ever get."

"Oh, it's not the panties I want to be close to."

"Shut up!" she said playfully, before she pulled up the makeshift rope and untied her jeans. After slipping them over her hips, she patted Ryan on the back. "Thanks, Boom. You did good."

"What about me? I was the one who threw the rope out to you. And just because I didn't say so doesn't mean I'm not enjoying the show too," Ty joked, pointing to his cheek, prompting Mac to walk over and kiss the spot.

"You two need to get laid," Griff said, trying to sound gruff but not quite getting there. He slipped on his own jeans before grabbing Mac's hand and walking toward the waiting chopper. "Come on, fellas. We're ready to get off this fucking mountain."

"I LOST A LOT OF GOOD SOLDIERS," Rashid complained, "all because you wanted to keep the girl alive. Why is she so important to you, anyway?"

Petrović rolled his eyes, glad his Iranian counterpart couldn't see his face over the phone line. He hated dealing with such incompetence and longed to tell Rashid what he really thought—that it was none of his business why Petrović wanted Mac alive. It was beyond pathetic that Rashid's "soldiers" couldn't kill one driver and make a clean getaway with a woman.

"She's important to my research," Petrović said.

"She's an infidel and responsible for my brother's death. I'm sure of that. If I had my way, she'd be dead by now."

Petrović struggled to hold his tongue. Mac was extremely good at what she did, and Rashid was probably right in thinking she had somehow been involved in his brother's death. But Petrović wasn't about to say that. He didn't need Rashid doing anything stupid in the name of revenge and ruining everything. He had to have Mac alive, although he didn't expect her to come without a fight. And if he were being honest, he knew that death would probably be her ultimate destiny, but he wanted it to be at his hands, not some incompetent terrorist's.

"Have you made the wire transfer yet?" he asked, changing the subject.

"We're in the process of transferring the money from our sources now. It should be done by this afternoon."

"Good." Petrović rubbed his hands together in glee. The sooner that money hit his bank, the quicker he could begin executing his own plans—and *he* wouldn't fail.

"When are you arriving in the States?" Rashid asked.

"I'm already here," Petrović responded. "Arrived in Tampa early this morning. The canisters are coming on a freighter from Taiwan sometime today, and my guy at the port will have them to me by tomorrow afternoon."

"So we're still a go for Saturday?"

"Yes. When I have the canisters in my possession, I'll make the drive to Miami. With the Collins Brothers at the convention center Saturday afternoon, it will be perfect. My sources tell me the concert is sold out."

"How better to show the world our dominance and bring the United States to its knees then by watching twenty thousand screaming teenage girls die in a matter of seconds."

"That was a brilliant idea, Rashid. The CIA would never think you'd strike in Miami." Petrović pretended to laugh. "They must be falling all over each other trying to figure out which big city you'll hit."

It was clever, but Rashid hadn't been the one to think of it. With Miami's proximity to the Gulf, Petrović himself had chosen it and then effectively presented it to Rashid in a way that made the terrorist believe it had been his idea all along. And if the plan to leak the information over a supposedly secure line had worked, the CIA already knew that Miami would be the target of some kind of attack at the end of the week. Once Petrović got word that his bank account in the Cayman Islands was three hundred and eighty million dollars fatter, he'd make sure the exact location of the Miami decoy was leaked.

He closed the burner cell phone he'd purchased on the trip from the airport to the hotel and pulled out the battery. After dropping it into a pitcher of water, he reached into his duffel bag for another and laid it on the nightstand by his bed. Before stripping off his clothes, he hung the DO NOT DISTURB sign on the door. Although the red-eye from Colombia had been uneventful, he hadn't been able to sleep and now felt exhausted.

He climbed under the sheets, put on his sleep mask, and leaned back into the pillows. His last conscious thought before he drifted off to sleep was that if all went well, in a matter of days not only would he be a rich man, but he'd also have Mackenzie Conley in his grasp.

MAC STEPPED out of the shower and caught a glimpse of her naked body in the mirror. She knew she hadn't been eating well since she'd moved back to the East Coast, but she hadn't realized what a toll it had taken on her. If she wasn't careful, people would start commenting. But lately, she hadn't had an appetite and sometimes didn't eat all day, only to scarf down a sandwich and a package of peanut butter crackers with a glass of Merlot at night. She didn't need to be a nutritionist to know that ritual would have consequences sooner or later.

She dried off, then wrapped a towel around her chest before heading for the kitchen—if you could call it that. As soon as she and Griff were whisked off the mountain, they were brought to the SWEEPERS complex and stashed away in the living quarters reserved for the team when it was necessary to work around the clock. This one was made up of one big room with a bed in one corner, a couch in another, and a tiny kitchenette.

Even if she wanted to cook—which she didn't—
there was no way she could manage the small
cooktop that masqueraded as a stove. Fortunately, all
her meals were catered and delivered by an armed
soldier. Last night's offering had been barbecued
chicken, along with a baked potato and a huge salad.
It actually tasted really good, and she'd eaten more
than she had in a long time. A few more meals like
that, and she'd be back to her normal weight in no
time.

Maybe being cooped up in the small room had its
benefits after all.

The apartments were spread out over two floors in
a building to the right of the main one, and she wondered which room was Griff's. He'd balked at the idea
of being in protective custody, but in the end, Dino
won that argument.

She glanced at the clock on the nightstand. Seven
thirty. Dino had left word that there would be a
meeting in the conference room at eight. The last time
she was late, he'd made a verbal note of it. She didn't
want to be known as the never-on-time girl, although
of late, she'd earned that title.

She threw off the towel and hurried over to the
suitcase on the floor beside her bed. They hadn't even
allowed her to run by her apartment to throw a few of
her things together before they brought her here. Instead, they'd sent someone to do a little light packing
for her.

She lifted the suitcase off the floor and laid it on
the bed. When she opened it, she giggled, thinking
from the looks of it, Ryan had been the one delegated
to grab her clothes. Two pairs of panties, both thongs
she hadn't worn in ages, lay on top. Why she hadn't
just tossed them when she decided that hip huggers

were way more comfortable, she didn't know. She shook her head at the sight of the black lace bra.

*That boy definitely needs a couple of nights with a horny female.*

She picked up a pair of the panties and slipped them on, catching another glance at herself in the mirror. She really was getting too skinny. Digging in the suitcase, she pulled out a lightweight sweater and a pair of khaki slacks. At least whoever had ransacked her closet hadn't chosen a halter top and short shorts.

When she finished dressing, she blow-dried her hair, slapped on a little makeup, then headed for the door. It didn't surprise her to find an officer standing guard.

"My orders are to make sure you get to the director's office safely," he said, overtly taking an inventory of her body before he motioned for her to follow him.

For a second, Mac wondered if he might be the one who had chosen her undies, then decided it was definitely a Ryan Fitzpatrick thing.

Outside the building, she slid into the back seat of a waiting car with the young officer climbing in beside her. The ride across the property to headquarters only took a few minutes, and she began to feel nervous about seeing Griff for the first time since their harrowing episode hanging off the side of the Allegheny Mountain. Remembering how she'd kissed him when she thought they were going to die sent a warm flush crawling up her face. What had she been thinking? The man had made it perfectly clear that night in Cleveland that he wanted no part of a do-over with her.

And who could blame him? Even if she hadn't abandoned him two years ago after her captivity with Petrović, she could never be with any man again, especially not one she loved. The sociopath had made sure the shame he'd inflicted could never be undone.

As soon as she walked into the conference room, Griff gave her a half-smile. She nodded, hoping her face wasn't still rosy red.

Ryan grinned like the proverbial Cheshire Cat, stood, and waved at her. "Are you wearing the red or the black ones?"

"I knew you'd packed my clothes," she said, trying unsuccessfully to sound mad. "Did you get off when you touched all my lacy things?"

"Damn straight."

"Sit down, Fitzpatrick," Dino said before turning his attention to Mac. "Glad to see you finally made it." He poked his watch several times with his finger for emphasis. "Okay, let's get started. We have some new information that J-Lo was able to intercept this morning." He switched on the recorder in the middle of a conversation between two men.

"That's Petrović," Mac shouted, jumping from her chair.

"I thought as much," Dino said, stopping the recording. "But I knew you were the only one who could confirm it. Voice recognition identified the other guy as Rashid." He switched the recorder back on, and for the next few minutes, they listened in on the conversation.

The room was unusually quiet before Dino finally summarized what they'd all just heard. "It looks like the target is Children's Hospital near downtown Miami. Although they didn't specify a time, we think it will probably happen sometime between noon and four on Saturday."

"How did you come up with that?" Ty asked.

"It's visiting hours, and the hospital parking lot is

usually filled then. Plus on this particular Saturday, several members of the Miami Dolphins football team are stopping by to cheer up the kids. Their visit will give the terrorists the most bang for their buck."

"We need to get down there ASAP to make sure they don't have an opportunity to plant the gas," Ryan said.

"Already ahead of you. The chopper leaves in an hour. We'll stay in a downtown hotel until Saturday morning. The Florida National Guard is already on the scene. Hopefully, they'll be able to prevent the terrorists from getting in and out, although my guess is the bad guys don't care about getting out."

"So we just hang around the hotel and wait?" Mac asked.

"No. You guys will be glued to monitors in a secure area at the hospital, watching for anything out of the ordinary—especially you, Mac. J-Lo and his team are already on site, setting up additional security cameras and metal detectors. Every person coming into the building will be scanned. They're going to have to get really creative to get past us with biological weapons, and..." Dino stopped talking when he noticed Mac shaking her head.

"You have no idea how creative Petrović can be. I'm not sure we can stop him in time."

"The world is counting on you being wrong," Dino said, sitting down. "Any questions?" When no one responded, he turned off the recording. "Okay, let's meet back here in forty-five minutes. Pack only the necessities." A worried look crossed his face before he added, "We have to win this one, folks, or a lot of innocent children will pay with their lives."

## 14

The sun rose like an orange melon over the Gulf of Mexico as Mac stared out the hotel window, a steaming cup of coffee in her hand. She watched a lone fisherman cast his rod off a pier to her left and marveled at the fantastic view from her room. She squealed in delight when a large fish jumped out of the water.

They'd arrived in Miami two days ago and spent the better part of their time at Children's Hospital, sweeping the building for any sign of a biological weapon. Their search had uncovered nothing. Thanks to J-Lo and his team, twenty-five security cameras were in place in addition to the ones already operating. If there was a canister of nerve gas in the building, Petrović had pulled a Houdini and managed to sneak it in under the radar.

Since Mac was the biochemist of the group, her assignment was to hang out in the monitoring room while the team, along with Miami National Guard members, kept their eyes glued to the computer screens. At the first sign of anything even remotely suspicious, Mac was to order the entire hospital in lockdown while she attempted to drain the canisters of their lethal mixtures without allowing any of the gas to escape. Of course, there was still the possibility of a suicide bomber instead of a chemical attack. Not knowing which would come was unnerving.

Another reason Mac was delegated to the monitoring room was that she was the only one with any chance of recognizing Petrović. More than likely, he'd be disguised so well that even she wouldn't be able to pick him out of a crowd, unless she was close enough to look into his eyes—those same eyes that still haunted her.

She shivered, thinking of being that close to him again.

The night before, she and the rest of the team met at a Cajun restaurant and indulged in a local favorite: gumbo and crawfish. Knowing the lives of children might very well be in their hands had made for a somber group. But after a few pitchers of beer, the mood lightened somewhat. While not exactly a festive outing, it had been nice to share a few laughs and forget about Petrović and everything else she'd been through, if only for a few hours before they all headed to their rooms for a good night's rest.

Although Mac hadn't been able to build up enough courage to talk to Griff one-on-one at the restaurant, when she said something funny, he winked and tipped his glass to her. For a second, she'd let herself believe that things between them could go back to the way they used to be. But deep down, she knew that was impossible.

Even if there was no future for them, she had to tell him why she'd run—explain what Petrović had done to her when she was his prisoner and why she felt so dirty and scarred because of it. But she knew that would never happen, either. The shame was so deeply entrenched in her that she hadn't even been able to talk about it with the CIA-mandated therapist she'd seen after her rescue.

No, it was safer to keep her distance from Griff, since she always seemed to make a fool of herself when she was alone with him.

She tore her eyes from the view outside, walked over to the tray still sitting on her bed, and took the last swallow of orange juice. Their wake-up call that morning had been a hot breakfast with everything imaginable. She'd passed on the waffles but eaten a few bites of the eggs, which was all her queasy stomach would allow. In truth, she was more nervous than she let on. She knew how evasive Petrović could be, and she was terrified that he would find a way to isolate her. She vowed to stay close to the team at all times.

After showering and dressing, she joined the others downstairs, where they were led to a waiting van and transported to Miami Children's Hospital. Once there, security was so tight that even they were frisked before walking through the scanners.

As they crossed the lobby, the first thing she noticed was how deserted it was. The National Guard had arrived the day before and closed the hospital to visitors before evacuating children determined to be medically stable in the dead of night. The parents of those too critical to be transported were allowed to remain in their rooms. They, along with employees who had volunteered to stay, had been briefed about the possibility of a biological attack and were instructed on what to do if they heard the call for action over the hospital intercom. Thousands of gas masks had been flown in from Washington the night before and were ready if necessary in each room.

Mac and the rest of the team members rode the elevator to the eighth floor, where the entire front area had been transformed into a surveillance center. At least thirty monitors had been positioned in a large circle, each one manned by either a National Guard member or hospital security. And all were geared up in HAZMAT suits. Mac's job was to oversee the entire operation, and if anything suspicious came across the screen, she and her team would be dispatched to that area immediately.

After slipping into the white HAZMAT suit, she positioned herself in a chair located so she could see all the monitors at once. A hospital security officer brought her a cup of coffee, and she settled in for what she believed would be a long day.

Knowing Petrović the way she did, she realized he wouldn't be stupid enough to just walk through the front door with the canister. The more likely scenario was that he'd try to sneak past security with something that wouldn't catch the attention of the men guarding the doors and then somehow get the gas into the ventilation system, which would allow the deadly mixture to spread throughout the hospital quickly. But that would involve exposing himself, and she was positive he wasn't about to do that.

She racked her brain, trying to come up with other ways he could get into the hospital with the gas. The only other method he might use was contaminating the hospital's oxygen supply, which was delivered to a central source in the basement and pumped into each patient's room. Small canisters, similar to the ones she'd seen in Cleveland bearing his trademark serpent, were used when a patient was ambulatory and needed portable oxygen. But as soon as she thought of that possibility, she dispelled the notion, since only those patients receiving oxygen would be affected. Petrović was too big of a megalomaniac to "waste" his precious inventory on just a few. He was all about showing the world his power.

She took a sip of the hot coffee and leaned back in her chair. There was nothing more to do but wait for him to make his move.

And the wait was excruciating.

JOSEPH PETROVIĆ STOOD in front of the large computerized board at the end of a windowless room situated on the upper floor of Children's Hospital. Dressed in dark blue pants and a matching shirt with JOHN HARRISON embroidered over the right front pocket, he pretended to study the wall of screens that represented the hospital's entire information technology system. The mainframe computer sat in the middle of the room, emitting a soft hum as it controlled every computer in the hospital.

He looked up just as another man, dressed in the same type of uniform, walked into the room.

"Who are you?" the man asked, wrinkling his brow.

"John Harrison," Petrović responded without a hint of an accent.

"Where's Gunderson?"

"No idea. They didn't tell me that when they got my ass out of bed at seven this morning. Only said he hadn't shown up for work today." He shook his head. "I've been working straight nights for the past two weeks and was looking forward to a little R&R on my fishing boat this afternoon. Guess that'll have to wait until my next day off."

"Sorry, man. I wish they'd talked to me before they called you in. Most days it's pretty quiet down here, and with all the excitement today, it will be borderline boring. I could've made it without the extra help. Maybe after lunch you can sneak into the break room and catch a few Zs." He held out his hand. "David Cunningham."

Petrović shook it. "I appreciate that, David, and may take you up on it."

He walked to the other side of the room and sat down at the desk he knew belonged to Gunderson. Things so far were going much smoother than he'd hoped. Opening the drawer, he pulled out the laptop he'd placed there earlier and punched in a code. Immediately, the room designated as the security center popped onto the screen. It took only a few seconds before he spotted Mac leaning over the back of a chair, pointing out something to the woman sitting in front of the screen.

She was as beautiful as ever, even though the only part of her not decked out in a HAZMAT suit was her head. Just thinking about her caused his heart to race, and he took a few deep breaths in an attempt to normalize it. He would have a hard time being patient if he allowed himself to focus only on her. Quickly, he looked away from the screen and concentrated on a stack of papers on Gunderson's desk.

Pretending to be busy for the next ninety minutes, he was careful not to encourage further conversations with Cunningham. The less contact he made with the man, the better the chance of not being discovered. In a few hours his new friend would join Gunderson and Harrison in the land of the dead, anyway.

Movement on the laptop screen caught his attention, and he watched as one of the security team members jumped up and ran to where Mac was having a conversation with a woman in the middle of the room. He leaned in closer as the man, obviously excited, relayed something to Mac. Petrović didn't need to be a lip reader to know from her reaction that they must've spotted the lone canister he'd planted in the boiler room.

As Mac and two other men he remembered as her companions from Venezuela put on the special headgear and headed toward the elevator, he typed in another code, and the screen switched to the boiler room, where a group of men in full gear surrounded the main refrigerator system. He was proud of himself, remembering how easy it had been to plant the canister, as well as the cameras in both the boiler room and the security center.

He'd done his homework and knew that John Gunderson spent a lot of his free time in an off-track betting complex around the corner from his apartment. Petrović knew the man loved the ponies and was so far in debt he'd just recently begun working a second job at the local food mart to keep the goons from extracting payments from him in their own special way. Getting him to install the cameras at the hospital had been easy enough when Petrović flashed the green stuff. And since the man had worked at the hospital for the past twenty years, nobody thought it unusual when he roamed the various hospital departments.

Petrović's attention was diverted back to the monitor when Mac and the other two men came into view. Knowing it wouldn't take her more than a few minutes to realize there was nothing harmful in the canister, he opened the drawer and picked up the burner phone.

Already giddy thinking about finally achieving his goal, he dialed 911 before walking behind Cunningham and putting a bullet into the back of his head.

"BE CAREFUL WITH THAT," Mac said as Ryan lifted the canister from the large generator. "The less exposure, the better."

Ryan carefully laid the steel container on a nearby table, and Mac was in front of it immediately. Reaching for the bag with the equipment she'd need for preliminary testing, she pulled out a pair of gloves lined with impenetrable steel and put them on. Then she examined the canister. With her heart racing, she fully expected to see Petrović's distinctive calling card somewhere he knew she'd find it.

But there was no serpent, which she found odd. Before she could voice her concerns, Ty approached, visibly excited.

"Griff just got a call from Dino. A report came in that another canister is reported to be at the Miami Convention Center."

"The convention center?" Mac looked up, confused. "What's going on there at two in the afternoon?"

Both Ryan and Ty shrugged as one of the national guardsmen gasped.

They all turned to him. "What?" Mac asked.

"The Collins Brothers are in concert today. They're the rage among teenage girls right now. The doors opened at noon because they're expecting a huge crowd." His voice quivered. "Oh my God! My daughter's there with her two cousins."

Without thinking of the consequences, Mac turned to Ryan and Ty. "Go. I'm pretty sure this is a decoy, and Griff needs you both with him."

She choked back her words to keep from saying what had just flashed into her mind. Thousands of screaming teenage girls were probably crammed into the large convention center, waiting to hear the boy band sing their medley of songs. Thousands of innocent girls with no idea that they could be dead in a matter of seconds.

She turned to the security guard. "Go with them," she commanded him. When he shook his head, she added, "You won't be any good to us here if your mind is on the convention center. All that's left to do here is to get this canister into the lead container and inside the HAZMAT unit outside. I'll join you all at the convention center after that."

"I'm not leaving until you do," Ryan said.

"Me neither," Ty chimed in. "Griff gave us explicit instructions."

"That was before he knew about the convention center." She swallowed hard before she changed her mind. She was terrified to see them go, but she knew it was critical that they get to Griff as quickly as possible. "I'm the highest-ranking member of the team here, and I'm telling both of you to leave immediately for the convention center. There are more than enough military-trained officers surrounding me to make sure nothing happens."

"Mac, don't make us—"

"Go, Ryan Fitzpatrick. That's an order," she barked before softening. "You, too, Ty. I'll be right behind you. I promise."

Ryan stared her down before finally turning to one

of the guardsmen beside her. "If anything happens to her, it'll be your head. Got it?"

The man pointed to his automatic weapon and nodded just as two others rushed up carrying a large lead container.

"Tell Griff I'll be there in twenty minutes tops," Mac said as she waved them off. "Hurry. We're talking little girls here."

Reluctantly, both men turned and raced to the elevator. Mac focused her attention once again on the canister, rolling it over for one final check before sending it out to the HAZMAT unit. She was looking for something—anything—that remotely connected it to Petrović. When she lifted it up to place it in the lead box, she knew immediately it was either empty or held a lighter gas. Nerve gas was much heavier.

A horrifying thought flashed through her head that they'd been played—that the convention center had probably been the target all along. Saying a quick prayer that the team would get there in time to stop something catastrophic, she closed the lid of the container and turned to tell the guardsmen to take it directly to the van parked in the back of the hospital.

The gripping fear coursing through her body nearly paralyzed her when her eyes took in the scene surrounding her. Four of her five-man security team were lying facedown on the concrete floor. She reached for the phone she'd laid on the table when she was examining the canister, but before her fingers could close on it, she felt a needle prick the side of her neck.

Then her world went dark.

## 15

Griff pushed the gas pedal all the way to the floor in the borrowed police vehicle and turned on the siren and flashing lights. According to the dashboard GPS, the Miami Convention Center was a straight shot down Interstate 95, a little over eight miles away. As soon as the 911 call center had conveyed the message they'd received about the impending chemical attack at the arena, he and the remaining members of the team had piled into the cruiser and headed that way.

Although it was unlikely the terrorists had been able to plant two weapons of mass destruction in Miami in less than a week with so many security precautions in place, he knew it would be unwise to underestimate the bad guys. His gut told him Petrović was the puppet master behind all this and was again pulling the strings of the less intelligent but no less crazy jihadists. Still, the lives of all those children at the arena were too much of a risk to ignore the threat.

Swerving to miss a black sedan whose driver either hadn't heard his siren blaring or thought he could beat the police car through the intersection, Griff cursed under his breath. Before he'd left the command center back at the hotel, he'd put out the order for the local law enforcement acting as security detail for the concert to start evacuating the Collins Brothers and their fans. Hopefully, by the time he arrived, that would be well underway. He prayed there wouldn't be any serious injuries from the mass panic he knew would ensue during that process.

He glanced down at his watch, wishing the black cruiser had more horsepower. He chastised himself for not listening to the warning bells that had gone off in his head when intel had first intercepted talk of an attack at Miami Children's Hospital. It had been too easy, too convenient. But even if Mac and her team were on a wild goose chase over there, he'd had no choice but to dispatch them.

Almost to the arena now, he wondered how the HAZMAT extraction was going at the hospital. When he'd called Ryan to inform the team of the latest threat at the arena, he was told they'd already found a canister and Mac was in the process of deactivating it. He pushed away the idea that it might be the real thing and not merely a decoy. The thought of her so close to the deadly gas was too hard to think about.

Although he really wasn't worried about her skills, the niggling feeling that he and the guys were missing something kept playing in his mind. Why would a terrorist call to give them a heads-up about the threat at the arena? It made no sense, even if you imagined for a minute that one of the jihadists may have experienced a change of heart.

First of all, jihadists like these had no hearts. And secondly, killing innocent young people at the arena, mostly junior high girls who'd probably had to beg their parents to go to the concert in the first place, was all in a day's work to them.

So why the call?

As soon as he turned off the intersection and into the arena parking lot, he drove directly to the front gate, where the sight of thousands of young girls and a smaller number of boys fleeing the building triggered a sigh of relief. The city of Miami had responded with fifty or more buses waiting to take the concertgoers away from the arena. Several were already transporting many out of harm's way.

Two heavily armed national guardsmen ran up to Griff's car the second he pulled up.

"Come with us," one of them said, nearly dragging Griff from the vehicle in his haste to get him out. "They're waiting on you in the maintenance area."

They pushed through the crowd, making their way to the lower floor. By the time they reached the end of the hallway, Griff was huffing, swearing to himself to up his exercise regimen. It hadn't been that long since he had been cleared to return to duty after surviving the explosion at the bar, and he hadn't yet found the time to get back into a healthy routine. That was only part of the problem, though. Fast food every night wasn't exactly helpful, either, but after a sixteen-hour day at headquarters, a quick burger and fries or chicken tenders was all he could manage before collapsing into bed.

"Put these on, sir," the guardsman instructed, handing him and the other two men HAZMAT suits.

When he was dressed, the same guardsman led Griff to the lower floor and directed him into the maintenance area. Quickly scanning the large room, Griff spotted ten or twelve large HVAC units in the far corner, their noise—and the gas mask—making it impossible to hear what the guardsman was now saying to him.

Griff screamed to be heard above the racket. "Why the hell aren't these units turned off?"

"We were waiting on you, sir," a young cop said. He moved away from the air-conditioning units and stood directly in front of Griff. "We only arrived a few minutes ahead of you."

"Shut them down," Griff yelled. "If I'm right, they'll use the ventilation system to deliver the gas."

Immediately, four cops rushed to help two maintenance men who were already pulling levers to cut off the units.

"Over here," one of the officers shouted. "I think I've found something."

Griff took off in that direction, scanning the large exhaust hoses that snaked across the ceiling. Halfway there, his heart sank when he spotted a metal canister attached to the biggest of the HVAC units. But that didn't even describe the surge of terror that raced through his body when his eyes homed in on a very distinctive coiled-up snake emblem etched into the center of the large canister. He forced back the panic as he realized the emblem was the same one that had unnerved Mac so badly at the weapons fiasco in Cleveland that she'd nearly botched the mission.

Without a doubt, it was Petrović's logo.

"Don't touch that," he shouted, searching for the biochemist dispatched to the site with him as soon as the threat had been received.

"Where is it?" the chemist said, stepping from behind Griff.

"There." He pointed to the ominous canister, wishing Mac were here. He trusted her above everyone and would feel a lot better if she was the one disarming the weapon.

"I'll be damned. There were two canisters," a voice behind him said.

A sense of relief surged through his body when he realized it was Ryan. Now, Mac could take over and shut down the threat. Turning around to instruct her, he was shocked to see only Ryan and Ty. "Where's Mac?"

"She's at Children's disarming the other canister," Ty responded.

"You left her there by herself?" Griff was unable to hold back his rage. "I ordered you both to stay with her every minute."

"She was pretty sure the canister at Children's was empty, and she wanted us here with you to make sure all the kids got out safely." Ty's face fell. "Oh, God! You don't think..."

"Dammit, Ty! You were never to leave her side."

Ryan moved closer, unable to camouflage the growing fear on his face. "She pulled rank on us, Griff —said she was the officer in charge and it was a direct order." He grabbed his cell phone from his shirt pocket and called. The look of fear on his face escalated to pure terror. "It went directly to voice mail."

Griff's heart nearly stopped at the thought of Mac without any of her trusted team there to protect her. "Get back there now. And call me the minute you have eyes on her."

At that moment, the biochemist nudged him aside for a better look at the canister, and Griff was jolted back to the crisis at hand.

PETROVIĆ EASED the unconscious Mac to the floor then nodded at a man who walked down the ramp wearing gray coveralls with PROFESSIONAL LAUNDRY CLEANERS embroidered on the pocket and shoving a large rolling laundry cart. "Grab her feet, and help me get her in," he shouted to the guardsman standing at his side. Pointing to the camera directly above them, he said to both of them, "We've only got a narrow window before they realize the image on their screen is frozen."

He and the guardsman hoisted Mac into the cart and on top of a pile of white towels. Petrović covered her body with additional linens, then grabbed the two sets of gray coveralls complete with the same logo as the van driver's from the top. Nothing had been left to chance. Quickly, he pulled one pair up over his clothes. Before the guardsman zipped up his own coveralls, Petrović retrieved a small-caliber weapon from an ankle holster and, without missing a beat, shot the guardsman in the forehead. After he and the other man dragged the lifeless body out of range of the camera, he pulled the guardsman's coveralls off and shoved them in the laundry cart under the linen. Then they pushed it toward the landing dock to the waiting vehicle marked with the same logo as the uniforms.

As the two men loaded the basket carrying Mac into the belly of the white van, Petrović mentally patted himself on the back, marveling at how gullible American men were. It had only taken a few C-notes to get total cooperation. In their defense, not all had been enticed by the cash, but those few were no longer around to tell anyone of his intentions.

After closing the back door and sliding into the passenger side of the utility van, Petrović instructed the driver, wearing the same professional laundry uniform, to head toward Miami Port Division. Although he knew it would be highly improbable to think anyone could catch up to him after they figured it out, especially since he had two decoys in place, he kept glancing into the side mirror just in case he had underestimated his opponents or miscalculated the timeline.

Traffic was especially grueling, probably because of the commotion and panic happening at the convention center. It had been a stroke of genius diverting Mac's partners to the arena, and even though Rashid would be furious that his mission to bring death to the children at the concert was not going to be a cause for celebration that night, there was nothing he could do about it. The Arab had gladly paid the fee up front, and it was now safe and secure in a secret bank account. If all went well, Petrović would never see Rashid again.

As they rounded the corner at the harbor, Petrović directed the driver to the south side of the port, where the yacht he'd rented the week before sat ready and waiting at a private dock. He'd convinced the owner, a once-rich Cuban man named Huberto Diaz, that he was interested in buying it for an amount well above the asking price if it met his expectations. The man had fallen on hard times after his assets were frozen by the DEA following a raid on the yacht during one of his drug-smuggling runs, and he had nearly salivated over the offer. He would be waiting on board with the crew that Petrović himself had handpicked from a group of Cuban mercenaries who had come highly recommended.

"Over there."

After pulling the van closer to the dock, the driver cut the engine and jumped out to help unload the "package." Halfway to the yacht—named *El Letal*

*Cubano*, the lethal Cuban—four men emerged from the ship and rushed over to assist them. After transferring the laundry cart onto the ship, one of the new arrivals got behind the wheel of the van and drove it down a private ramp until it was totally underwater.

"Take her down to the infirmary," Petrović said as he waved to Diaz, who appeared at the helm and was now standing behind the ship's wheel.

Petrović walked up the ramp and waited until the mooring lines were all free from the bollards and the Cuban who'd driven the car into the sea had boarded the yacht before giving the go signal. One of the mercenaries he'd hired then executed the van driver and threw his body over the side before jumping onto the yacht and giving them a thumbs-up. When the yacht made its way out of the harbor and turned toward the open sea, Petrović felt the anxiety leaving his body. For the moment he was satisfied he'd taken care of the loose ends, even though there were still so many things that could go wrong.

But as hard as he tried, he couldn't stop the smile from forming at the corners of his lips. In about eight hours, *El Letal Cubano* would be in Cuban waters, and he could finally claim his mission was a success. Despite the recent restoration of diplomatic relationships between Cuba and the U.S., the restrictions still required a license for a boat of any kind to enter Cuban waters. Petrović knew that would take a lot of red tape, and hopefully, he would be long gone before a rescue boat could intercept them. His own license had only taken a few days after he'd greased the pockets of several government officials, both U.S. and Cuban.

His apprehension receded even more as the yacht cleared the harbor, and his thoughts again went to Mackenzie. How hard would it be to break her? In the end, the challenge was already creating fantasies in his head. He couldn't help but touch his arousal, unable to control his desire to be inside her.

And then she would finally be his.

RYAN SWERVED to avoid crashing into the SUV that stopped suddenly on Interstate 95, grazing the side of a pickup on his left. Traffic was a mess, and despite the siren and flashing lights, making it back to Miami Children's was nearly impossible. No doubt news of an impending chemical attack at the convention center had spread, and people were pouring out of the Gulf Coast casinos like gazelles fleeing a hungry lion. A multitude of vehicles jammed the freeway, leaving little or no place for them to get out of their way.

"Dammit!" Ryan said, jerking the steering wheel to the right and propelling the patrol car up onto the sidewalk. Laying on the horn the entire time, he inched his way past the pedestrians who were screaming and rushing to get out of his path.

"Over there." Ty stared at the dashboard before pointing to an almost completely hidden side road. "If this GPS is correct, it looks like that may knock off a few blocks."

Ryan made a sharp right turn and raced down the narrow alley. "What's taking them so long to get back to us? Didn't they tell you the video showed Mac still working on the canister in the basement?"

Ty nodded. "Yes, but for some reason they can't reach her or her security detail. The commander assured me they were on their way down there and promised to call the minute they spotted her." He made eye contact with Ryan and frowned. "I'm really starting to get a bad feeling about all this. Why wouldn't..." He stopped mid-sentence when his phone blared. Staring down at the screen, he said, "It's the hospital." He punched the accept call button and put it on speaker. "Tell me you found her."

"The basement's empty, and the canister's still on the table." The National Guard officer lowered his voice. "Neither Dr. Conley nor any of her security detail are there."

"Not there? How in the hell could she not be there? Didn't you have surveillance on her at all times?"

"We thought so," the man said. "But when I didn't find her or my men, I called upstairs to review the video. It was only then that they discovered the camera covering that part of the room had been disabled. It was frozen on a loop of her working on the canister with the men in her detail surrounding her. We've been paging her over the intercom for the past five minutes. So far, there's been no response from anywhere in the command center."

Ty shook his head. "They can't find her?"

"Tell him to keep looking and initiate a lockdown," Ryan said as he sped out of the alley and again drove the car down a busy sidewalk.

Ty met Ryan's eyes for a second before focusing back on the phone. "We should be there in about five or ten minutes. I repeat, lock down the hospital. Nobody gets in or out. Understood?"

"Yes sir, but—"

"But what?" Ty said. "Spit it out, man."

"Hold on. One of my men is yelling something from the far corner of the room."

They waited for what seemed like an eternity, crossing their fingers that the cop would come back and say he'd found Mac. When they heard the officer say, "Oh my God," in the background, they knew that wasn't going to happen.

"We found all five of her security detail in the corner, out of sight of the cameras. "They're all dead."

"And Dr. Conley?"

"Not here."

"Jesus!" A sickening moan escaped Ty's lips as he turned to Ryan. "He's got her."

## 16

Griff moved out of the way so that Dr. Jonathan Spicer could get closer to the canister, nodding a greeting to the biochemist when he passed.

"I need a fairly large table brought over," Spicer said as he set the toolbox on the ground and opened it. Pulling out a measuring tape, he checked the length and the diameter of the canister. "Also, have the team bring me a bomb disposal box big enough to house this two-and-a-half-foot sucker."

Three men behind him sprang into action and headed for the door, while two others returned with the table and placed it beside him.

"Are we sure this is the only canister?" Griff asked, not ready to assume the sociopath who planted this had stopped at one.

"You'd better hope so," Spicer said as he touched the outside of the canister with his lead gloves. "If the gas in this baby is anywhere close to the potency of the one this crazy asshole used in Brazil, it would take less than ten minutes to wipe out everyone in the center."

Griff turned to the commander of the National Guard. "Make sure your men check every nook and cranny in the arena. If the terrorists were able to plant a canister as big as this one in an area this open, they had to have had help. God only knows how many others they may have hidden."

"I just watched a movie where the bad guys put a bomb in the vending machine at a football stadium, and it was a disaster when it blew," one of the guardsmen said. "Just to be on the safe side, do you think we ought to bring in the bomb-sniffing dogs before we open any of the machines?"

"Good idea." Griff turned back to the canister. Glancing up, he followed the path of the copper tubing attached to the top as it snaked up and into the huge aluminum duct that delivered the cold air to the arena. He shivered, thinking how quickly the poisonous gas could have made its way to all those children.

Spicer was already wrapping a thick wire belt around the copper tubing closest to the insertion point into the HVAC unit. Then he used a special piece of equipment from the bag he'd brought to tighten it as much as he could, reminding Griff of a tourniquet placement on a bleeding limb. After maneuvering another one a few inches above the first, he tightened that one as well. When he was satisfied it was as tight as he could get it, the biochemist concentrated on the canister itself, obviously looking for the best way to dislodge it from the massive air conditioner.

"What's the holdup with the bomb box?" Spicer asked, his voice vibrating with impatience. "The faster we dismantle this thing and get it into the box, the better."

"Right here," a guardsman said as he and two others rushed over with a large steel box and placed it on the table. "That's one heavy mother."

"Open it and position it so the door is facing me," Spicer instructed them before turning to Griff. "It's probably about twenty pounds or so, maybe more with a heavier gas. Think you and I can get it into the box?"

Griff nodded and reached for his own pair of lead gloves. "Say the word."

After spraying the inner part of the canister where it was attached to the HVAC with an industrial-strength adhesive remover, Spicer attempted to pull it off. When it wouldn't budge, he sprayed it again, this time allowing a little more time before he tried to detach it.

When that still didn't work, he shouted over his shoulder, "Someone get me the dry ice from the HAZMAT van." Turning to Griff, he pointed to the canister. "Whatever the SOBs used on this was meant to make damn sure the vibrations of the air conditioner didn't jar the entire canister from the unit when it switched on and off automatically. Let's hope the dry ice can knock it loose. If not, as much as I hate the idea, we'll have to use heavy-duty equipment. There's no guarantee we won't crack the canister and release some of the gas if we do it that way."

"Why would that be so bad?" one of the guardsmen asked. "We're all suited up in protective gear and wearing gas masks."

Griff turned to the guard. "Because we have no idea what kind of gas this is or how long it can remain stable and linger in the air. The chemist who manufactured this and sold it to the terrorists would have had a Plan B as well as a Plan C in his arsenal. I wouldn't put anything past him."

A guardsman ran up with a small cooler and placed it on the table. Spicer reached in and grabbed a chunk of the dry ice. "Get a piece just like this, Griff, and do exactly what I do."

Griff placed the steaming ice on the connection point directly opposite from where Spencer had placed his. Within a few seconds, you could see the adhesive already beginning to disintegrate.

"Now put both hands on the canister and pull," Spicer said. He turned to the guardsman. "Get ready to shove a lead glove over the open end of the copper tubing as soon as it comes loose."

Miraculously, the canister broke free of the HVAC unit, and the two men cautiously did a one-eighty and placed it into the bomb box, being careful not to allow any of the gas to escape through the lead glove on the end of the delivery line. Only when it was safely locked up in the lead box and carted out to the HAZMAT van did the tension in Griff's body begin to subside.

"Wow! I had no idea dry ice could be so potent," he said when Spicer walked over and stood beside him.

"It's a powerful adhesive remover—able to break the bonds of virtually any chemical adhesive, but unfortunately, very toxic to humans and animals. It's actually pure, solidified carbon dioxide, and in a relatively short period, it can cause hypothermia, frostbite, and other conditions related to extremely cold temperatures. Not to mention that it's fatal if ingested or inhaled."

Griff glanced down at his gloves. "These are certainly lifesavers." Then he patted Spicer on the back. "Nice job today. Now go take care of that gas, and I'll finish cleaning up in here."

Spicer nodded. "We work well together. I only wish Mac had been here with us. She probably would have known to use the dry ice right off the bat and not wasted time with any other adhesive remover." With that, he turned and headed toward the exit.

*Mac!* With all the excitement going on there, Griff had forgotten for a few seconds that she'd been left alone at Miami Children's Hospital. His fears rushed back as a sense of unease washed over him, causing the hairs on his arms to stand at attention. Before he had time to react, his phone rang.

*Please let this be her, anxious to give me grief because I'm here with all the excitement and she's stuck in a base-ment with a dud.*

He pulled off the gloves and reached into his HAZMAT suit for the phone. It was Ty. The uneasi-ness increased, almost choking off his breath. He an-swered, but couldn't get any words to come out. When there was no response on the other end, it only made it worse.

"Griff?"

Swallowing hard, Griff finally found his voice. "Yeah. We have the situation under control here. Is Mac finished up over there?" Some stupid logic in his head told him that if he acted like he wasn't really worried, everything would somehow be okay, and they could all laugh about it over a pitcher of beer in the hotel bar later. But the awkward pause that followed shot that theory right out of his head, and he closed his eyes, bracing for bad news.

"The entire security detail is dead, and she's miss-ing. We think Petrović may have her."

Fearing the worst, he remembered the look on Mac's face the night he'd spent with her in the moun-tain cabin when Rashid's men had them surrounded. She'd looked directly into his eyes and made him promise he'd kill her before Petrović got his hands on her again. In that moment, he'd gotten the message loud and clear that whatever the bastard had done to her two years earlier must have been so horrific that she was willing to die before being anywhere near him. Although he had no idea what the man had used to terrorize her, Dino had hinted that it was something unimaginable. Griff had vowed to protect her no matter what.

Once again, he'd failed miserably.

"So, my friend, what do you think about my yacht so far? It's a beauty, no?" Huberto Diaz asked when Petrović approached the helm.

Petrović forced himself to pretend to be interested in the overweight yacht owner, who was now sucking on a fat cigar. "I have to admit, it's more than I'd hoped for."

In truth, he hadn't even taken a tour of the ship other than to oversee his men taking Mac down to the infirmary, where they'd strapped her to an examination table. "Let me know the minute we cross into Cuban waters," he said after glancing down at the many gauges across the ship's dashboard.

"Will do. You just sit back and enjoy the view," the portly Cuban responded, blowing a perfect smoke ring Petrović's way.

"Those things will kill you if you're not careful," Petrović replied, hoping his disgust with the Cuban didn't show in his voice. Once they reached their destination, the man would be dead anyway, so why not let him jack up his lungs with the noxious smoke?

Making his way to the front of the yacht, Petrović looked out over the water as the Port of Miami got smaller and smaller. Pulling a pair of high-powered binoculars from his pocket, he scanned the shoreline, looking for any signs of increased activity in the harbor. The fact that there was none was almost enough for him to let down his guard.

*Almost.*

Even though the cops were probably only now discovering the security footage they'd been watching had been doctored by one of the five dead guardsmen sprawled in the corner of the basement, there were still too many things that could go wrong. The decoy trucks would slow them down somewhat, but eventually, they'd come after him.

He jerked his attention toward the sky when a Coast Guard helicopter flew overhead, then closed his eyes in relief as the aircraft roared past in the opposite direction. Glancing down at his watch, he knew the next few hours would be critical. They were headed to a remote port off the southern coast of Cuba, where they would be protected by another band of rogue Cuban mercenaries. They'd be well insulated even if somehow the CIA was able to convince the Cuban authorities to bypass the red tape necessary and attempt to intercept them by land. Hours after arrival, he'd be on his way out of Cuba to his secret island, where nobody could find him or his precious "package."

His own crew on board could handle any assault coming from sea, especially since he'd made sure *El Letal Cubano* was equipped with sonar equipment that would make a U.S. submarine proud. No way a vessel could sneak up on them or get within five hundred yards undetected. And if one was stupid enough to try, it would be met with a guided missile that would send everyone in its path directly to hell.

There was no doubt in Petrović's mind that Mac's team would try desperately to rescue her once they realized she'd been kidnapped, but their attempts would be futile. He'd give anything to see the look on Griffin Bradley's face when he realized a missile was heading directly at him and his compadres if he attempted to intervene. He only wished there was a way he could share that visual with Mackenzie. Then maybe she'd finally realize that her boyfriend was not going to save her this time—that only Petrović had that power now.

"Joseph."

Petrović turned to the man who had somehow managed to walk up undetected and was now at his side. "Yes, Miguel, is there a problem?"

The leader of the mercenaries shook his head. "No, sir. We've stocked the cabinets with everything on your list. I just wanted you to know that, per your orders, we have the lady fully restrained in the infirmary and that she's starting to show signs of coming out the sedative."

Petrović patted him on the shoulder. "That's good news, my friend. Tell the men I'll be down there shortly and that they'll be able to head to the galley for a much-deserved celebration meal. My compliments to you for assembling such a competent team and for pulling this off without a hitch."

Miguel smiled. "Thank you, sir. Will there be anything else before you join us in sick bay?"

"No. You go ahead. I'll take over when I get there."

Petrović watched as the young Cuban walked away. Stocky with muscles that screamed of serious weightlifting, Miguel had not come cheap, but he'd proven himself to be well worth the cash layout. Petrović decided he might even try to convince the man to follow him to the deserted island he'd affectionately named Mackenzie's Hideaway. A replacement fortress for the one destroyed by the Navy SEALs several years before was being rebuilt there.

This one would be much smaller than the original one, mainly because he no longer needed a secret place to test his deadly chemicals. Centered on the island, it would offer a great view of the beach. The house would be ready within weeks, but in the meantime, he and Mackenzie would stay in a guard shack in the shadow of the trees, constructed and well stocked just last week.

With the millions from the jihadists added to the other money safely tucked away in his hidden account, Petrović was now free to enjoy the fruits of his labor. Fortified with the best security equipment money could buy and totally hidden from any satellite imagery, his new hideout was the ideal place to live out the rest of his life with the woman of his dreams.

And Miguel would be the perfect right-hand man to head his security detail—if Petrović could convince him. Money usually had a way of persuading even the most skeptical of people, and he hoped it would be no different with the head of the mercenaries.

Petrović placed the binoculars on the table near the guardrail and headed in the direction of the infirmary. As soon as he opened the door and walked in, he heard the commotion going on as his men tried to hold Mackenzie down. She was jerking violently, and for a second, he worried that she might be convulsing —that she was reacting badly to the strong sedative he'd plunged into her neck several hours earlier.

But the closer he got, the more he was able to dispel that notion when he realized that despite heavy leather restraints on both her legs and arms, she was still able to fight hard enough to rock the stainless-steel examining table. He chuckled to himself, thinking she hadn't lost the fire since his last encounter with her.

As he approached, one of the men grabbed her breast and squeezed, causing her to squirm even more, and when the soldier bent down to kiss her, she bit his lip hard enough to draw blood. The man slapped her face, leaving behind a beet-red outline of his hand across her cheek.

Without thinking twice, Petrović pulled out his gun and shot the offender in the back of the head. When the other soldiers turned toward him, stunned looks on their faces, he waved the gun in their direction. "Touch this woman in any way, and you will follow your comrade into hell."

One by one, they stepped back from the table and allowed him to move in. When his eyes connected with the now-quiet CIA biochemist, her body stiffened, and he could see fear flash across her face. When he was close enough, he bent down to speak to her, and she spat in his face. Without a word, he used his sleeve to wipe the spittle from his cheek, then reached in a cabinet behind him for a roll of duct tape. Slowly, he tore off a strip and placed it over her mouth, holding her eyes captive the entire time.

"Save your energy for later, love. I so enjoy a female with spunk and a healthy dose of fight in her." He bent down again and touched his lips to her forehead. "But make no mistake, Mackenzie Conley, I will make you see things my way, and when I do, you will enter a world like no other you've ever experienced. I'm already giddy just thinking about it."

17

Mac breathed in through her nose and slowly exhaled in an attempt to slow down her racing heart. She couldn't believe she'd ended up in the hands of this insane pervert. To her right, Petrović was busy doing something on the counter next to the table, his back to her. She shuddered, unable to see what he was preparing but sensing it was something that would make this nightmare even more terrifying.

Scanning the layout of the small room—at least what she could see lying flat on her back strapped to the table in the center of the room—she tried to formulate an escape plan. Whoever had helped Petrović kidnap her had stripped off the HAZMAT suit, leaving her in the jeans and t-shirt she'd worn underneath, and she shivered as the cold table penetrated the thin material. Glancing up, she eyeballed a large movable light directly above the table with a handle on the side, the kind you saw in operating rooms. Figuring this was some kind of examination room, given the light and the hard table she was on, she wondered if they were still somewhere at Children's Hospital. An unexpected swaying, along with a sudden queasy feeling and Petrović grabbing the edge of the cabinet for stability, made that highly unlikely.

Given the fact that she suffered from seasickness any time she was on a watercraft bigger than a ski boat, it was more than likely she was at sea. But headed where?

By the time Petrović turned to face her, she'd managed to calm her nerves somewhat, determined not to give him the satisfaction of knowing he had succeeded in putting the fear in her. From her previous encounter with him, she remembered that the more afraid she was of him, the more it turned him on.

*Sick bastard.*

"I see you've settled down, Mackenzie," he said, moving closer to the examination table.

Between his fingers caressing her restrained arm and her queasy stomach, it was all she could do not to throw up, which would be disastrous with her mouth taped shut. She forced herself to look up into the face of the most evil monster she'd ever encountered. And she'd come across a few horrific scumbags in her time at the agency. She couldn't speak, but even if the tape was removed, she wouldn't give him the satisfaction.

"Guess you're wondering where you are," he said in a low voice. "Suffice it to say, we're on our way to Cuba and then to a place where your friends will never find you."

She forced back a scream, then scolded herself for letting him successfully bait her—for giving him the ammo he'd use to control her, exactly like he'd done before.

She'd only seen Petrović without one of his many disguises a few times when he held her prisoner in Morocco. And only at night when he'd come to her bed. Looking at him now, she decided that some might find him attractive with his hazel eyes and shoulder-length dirty-blond hair that curled slightly on the ends.

Standing about five-eleven, he was wearing a gray uniform with PROFESSIONAL LAUNDRY CLEANERS embroidered on the pocket. She remembered vetting that company when they were preparing the hospital for a possible chemical attack. What had she missed? More than likely, that was how he'd gained access to the basement.

*And to me.*

No doubt he'd been the one who called in the tip about the deadly gas actually being at the convention center instead of the hospital. He'd chosen the perfect diversion to draw Ty and Ryan away from her, knowing she'd stay behind to make sure the canister they'd discovered wasn't armed. She said a silent prayer that Griff and the team had found and successfully deactivated the weapon at the convention center —if there even was a canister there. Knowing how devious Petrović was, it might have been just a ploy.

And it had worked.

Her thoughts were interrupted when Petrović touched her arm. The sickening smile on his face turned her stomach. "I've missed you, my sweet. I'd all but given up on ever seeing you again after you were taken from me. Then I saw your beautiful face in Venezuela and couldn't believe my eyes. It was like some higher power knew my deepest yearnings, knew I lived only to have you with me again." He teased his fingers along the edge of the duct tape, running his thumb over her covered mouth. "This must be uncomfortable and irritating to your soft, exquisite lips. Lips that will be mine forever in just a few hours." He leaned closer and whispered, "If you promise not to make a scene—not that anyone would hear you in the middle of the Caribbean Sea—I'll take this off."

She thought about this for a second before nodding, still trying desperately not to show fear. But when he pulled off the tape in one quick motion, she yelped, wishing she could punch the smirk off his face.

"There. Now we can have the conversation I've dreamed of every day for the entire two years we were apart." He brushed his lips lightly against hers.

It was all she could do not to bite down like she'd done to the other man earlier, or to spit out the taste of him on her lips, but common sense prevailed. If she was going to get away, she needed to play it cool. Her wits would be her weapon, and time her ally. She had to conjure ways to survive whatever he had in store until the team could figure out where she was and launch a rescue mission. But how did you fool the devil?

"Now, that wasn't so bad, was it?" he asked, straightening up and reaching behind him. When he turned back, he was holding an IV bag with attached tubing. "We should be in Cuban waters in about eight hours and on a plane to my secret fortress shortly thereafter. Restraints are necessary until then." He effortlessly inserted a needle into the crook of her elbow. She cringed, knowing his proficiency had come at the cost of countless unsuspecting victims.

"This bag is full of sugar and nutrients and will help keep you from getting dehydrated until we're on my private jet," he said, adjusting the flow. "Once we're airborne, we can replace it with the best champagne money can buy."

*Oh God!* If what he was saying was true, the team had a scant eight hours at best to find her. That wasn't enough time. Even if they knew where she was, they had to be at least two hours behind, possibly more. Before they could catch up, she'd be on her way to whatever godforsaken place he was taking her.

She closed her eyes, racking her brain for a way to fight back.

THE MOMENT GRIFF reached the emergency room entrance at Children's Hospital, he slammed on the brakes and jumped from the car. His feet barely touched the ground as he raced for the door. Flashing his badge at the two national guardsmen, he bolted through the entrance and toward the elevator, where he punched the down button with his fist. His heart pounded against his ribs as he waited an eternity for the elevator to arrive.

"Dammit! What's the holdup with this fucking thing?" he hollered to no one in particular.

Spying the stairwell, he was about to make a mad dash in that direction when the elevator door opened. He scrambled in and pounded on the lower-level button several times. "It's not true," he said to himself. "It's all a mistake. When the door opens, she'll be there, smiling, telling me that everything's okay." His voice cracked, and he stared at the ceiling through misty eyes. "So, why the hell am I crying?"

But reality hit him in the face the moment he stepped out onto the basement floor. National guardsmen and Miami's finest filled the room. Ryan and Ty stood next to the table that housed the suspected dud canister. Their faces said it all.

It was time for a gut check. Griff needed to suck it up and come up with a plan. Mac's life depended upon it. "That thing been checked out yet?" Griff asked, pointing to the decoy weapon.

"Yes, sir," a young guardsman responded. "Dr. Conley wanted the HAZMAT guys to transport it to the van just to be on the safe side, though." He paused and lowered his eyes. "That was before she..."

"Before she what?" Griff barked, knowing that whatever had happened to Mac was not the fault of the young man in front of him but unable to stop the frustration and feeling of helplessness that caused him to lash out.

"Before she disappeared and we realized the security camera had been rigged," the young man added sheepishly, taking a step backward, almost as if he knew the next barrage might not be verbal.

Griff glanced up at the camera in the corner to his left. "Is that the one?"

"Yes, sir."

"What about this one over the table?" He was desperate to find some logical explanation for how one person could dupe his entire team and some of the best-trained military troops in the State of Florida.

The young man shook his head. "Altered as well."

Griff threw his hands into the air. "Jesus! How could that happen with all the fucking security we have down here?" He looked at Ty, then Ryan. "Did you lock down the entire hospital?"

"As soon as we realized Mac was missing," Ryan responded.

"I want everyone questioned—including the janitors as well as the parents of the kids still here—to see if anyone noticed anything out of the ordinary. We're at a disadvantage, since we have no idea how much of a head start that psycho has, so it's critical for us to get answers now. Even a few minutes in his favor are too many."

"Already on it, boss," Ty said. "The only thing we've gathered so far is that they found the head of IT dead upstairs. We did locate another man who works in that department, though. He said there was a new guy on duty this morning. Introduced himself as John Harrison and said he'd been called in to replace Emil Gunderson, who normally works this shift. Said Gunderson had the flu or something. He's—"

"I want to talk to that new guy now," Griff interrupted.

Ryan stepped forward and stood directly in front of his boss. "That's just it, Griff. We can't locate him."

"We sent a couple of uniforms to Gunderson's house to check things out," Ty added. "We should be hearing from them any minute now. We also have a black-and-white on its way to Harrison's house."

Griff was already thinking ahead to the possible scenarios. It was just too coincidental for a new guy to be there on this particular day. He rubbed his forehead, frustrated they hadn't been more thorough with their instructions to hospital personnel. Time had been limited, and they thought they'd covered all the bases. At the very least, they should've made the employees more aware of the importance of reporting anything unusual today. "Good thinking, guys. Let me know the minute you hear something. In the meantime, see if our perp was caught on any of the footage before he disappeared."

"Already checked," Ty responded. "The guy managed to lower his head every time he got near our cameras, almost like he knew where every one of them was placed, even the hidden ones. All we can tell is that he's about six feet tall with a medium build and olive skin."

"Does that correlate with Gunderson's looks?"

Again Ty shook his head. "According to a picture in his personnel file, updated two years ago, Gunderson is a big German dude, fair-skinned with blondish hair. He also weighs over two hundred and fifty pounds."

"Shit!" Griff did a 360 around the room before turning back to his teammates. "Okay, we have to presume that Petrović's got Mac and that he's managed to escape unnoticed. How would he have done that?"

"Agent Bradley?" Griff turned to the guardsman now standing next to him. "Dr. Conley had a six-man detail protecting her. We've checked the entire basement but only found five bodies."

Ryan moved up next to Griff. "One of them went with us to the convention center. His daughter was at the concert, and Mac ordered him to go. Said he'd be useless to her if all he could think about was what was going on at the convention center."

It was just like Mac to worry more about the teenager than her own safety. "It's all starting to make sense to me. More than likely, Petrović had inside help from one or more of the law enforcement officers. Whoever it was made sure the cameras were jammed at precisely the right moment." He squinted and scanned the room, stopping at a ramp that led to a service door. "There. That's where he probably made his getaway, right under everyone's noses." He walked over to the area before continuing, "My guess is that as soon as the dirty cop or cops were no longer necessary, they were rewarded with a bullet to the back of the head." He pushed the button next to the door, and it opened into the delivery area in the back of the hospital. "Damn it," he said under his breath, knowing he was probably looking at Petrović's escape route.

"Mister, you can't be out here," a middle-aged man in uniform shouted from several feet away. "The hospital is in lockdown."

Griff reached into his shirt pocket and pulled out his ID. "How long have you been out here?"

The man grabbed the badge from Griff and studied it intensely for a moment before handing it back. "About four hours, Agent Bradley. Sorry I gave you a hard time."

"No problem." Excited that this might finally be the first big break he needed to figure out how Mac had disappeared, Griff asked, "Did you see any vehicles out here in the last few hours? An ambulance, maybe?"

The officer nodded. "No ambulance, but Professional Laundry Services was here making their daily pickup and delivery."

"They do it every day at this time?" Griff asked.

"Yes."

"Did you recognize any of the men from the laundry?"

The officer rubbed his forehead as if in deep thought. "I was busy surveilling the area and didn't pay much attention, since it wasn't anything unusual. But now that you mention it, I didn't recognize the guy. That, in itself, also isn't unusual, though, since they use a lot of different drivers. I remember thinking the company must spend a ton of cash just on new employee orientations alone. Figured it was a shitty— pardon the pun—job carrying off dirty hospital linens, and that's why they had such a frequent turnover rate."

Griff inched closer, if that was even possible, and

stared at the officer's name badge. "Think, Roscoe. It's important you tell me everything you can remember."

Roscoe wrinkled his brow. "Like I said, I was pre-occupied at the time and—"

"Any detail will help, even the small things that on their own wouldn't ordinarily catch your attention."

Roscoe rubbed his forehead again. "Sorry. I'm drawing a blank. There was nothing that caught my eye as being unusual. The truck pulled up, and the driver jumped out and waved to me, just like always, before he shoved an empty cart down the ramp. Ten minutes later, two guys wheeled the loaded cart back out and lifted it into the van."

"Two guys? I thought you said the driver took the empty cart into the hospital. Was there another man?" A sinking feeling paralyzed Griff as his brain switched to high alert. Either Petrović himself had been in the basement waiting for an opportunity to kidnap Mac, or he'd been in the *empty* laundry cart that was brought into the basement. Regardless, it had been too easy and never should have happened. His detailed security plan had been a class-A fuck-up.

"Well, shoot! I never thought about that," Roscoe muttered. "It didn't seem out of the ordinary until now."

"Did you at least see which direction the van went?"

The officer shook his head. "No, sir, but I happen to know the laundry is located in the south part of town."

"Ryan, get someone over there now to question the driver." Even as Griff barked out the command, he knew it would be a dead end. They wouldn't find the driver at Professional Laundry Services. He was certain now that Mac was in the hands of Joseph Petrović and that he had one helluva head start.

"Griff?"

He turned to face Ty.

"Just got the call. When the uniforms arrived at Harrison's house, they found the maintenance worker dead. Shot execution style. Still haven't located Gunderson, although his wife says he didn't come home last night and definitely does not have the flu. She filed a missing-person report about three hours ago, since she hasn't heard from him and can't reach him on his cell phone."

Griff inhaled sharply, hearing what in his heart he already knew. Despite their best laid plans, Petrović had managed to outsmart them. Griff had been outsmarted before, but never when the end result was catastrophic. This time Dr. Death had gotten away with a prize far more valuable than the money he'd probably received for the deadly chemical weapons.

This time he'd made off with the only woman Griff had ever loved. And Griff knew he had to get her back...or die trying.

## 18

"Get headquarters to download the video from all the traffic cameras in Miami. Tell them it's urgent that we find out where that laundry van headed," Griff said, already walking toward the police cruiser that was still idling in front of the ER door. "And get the hospital to fire up their helicopter. Tell them I'll meet the pilot in the helipad ASAP." He rubbed his forehead right above the left eye as if that would help him think. "I'll go crazy if I just stand by and wait for information to come to me."

"What do you want us to do, boss?" Ty asked.

"You and Ryan talk to the maintenance worker who was in contact with the *fake* Harrison this morning. See if he remembers anything else that might be helpful, although my guess is that it was Petrović in one of his many disguises. Then head up to the eighth-floor command post and wait for our guys in Virginia to transmit any info about the laundry truck. I want to know the minute you have something."

"What should we do if they spot the van?" Ryan asked, catching up with Griff as he and Ty rounded the corner and headed toward the helipad.

"Other than contacting me immediately, nothing.

Once we get the location, we'll follow discreetly to see what Petrović's next move is. We don't want to force him into doing something crazy. It's obvious the man is totally obsessed with Mac if he's willing to risk everything to kidnap her, and that makes him unstable. I wouldn't put anything past him at this point." He stopped to swallow, hating the next words he knew he had to voice. "Mac is our main priority here. We have to get to her before..." He choked on the words.

Ryan touched his shoulder. "We'll get her, Griff, just like we did the last time that prick abducted her." He slowed down as they got closer to the hospital helicopter, whose rotors were already winding up. "You find them, and we'll get her back. That's a promise."

Griff wished he felt even half of Ryan's confidence. Ordinarily, he was the one who rallied the others when their spirits were low, when it looked like a mission was failing. But this was no ordinary mission. Mac's life depended on them getting it right this time. And Petrović was no run-of-the-mill Al Qaeda operative willing to die. He had no convictions, no ethics. He'd probably kill his own mother without a smidgeon of remorse, and for no other reason than the sheer joy of watching another human suffer.

With his gut twisted into a knot, Griff climbed up into the helicopter.

"Martin Warner," the pilot said, handing Griff a headset before turning back to the dashboard. "Where to, Agent Bradley?"

Griff put on the headset, wishing he knew where to begin. "Not sure. Start off by heading toward Miami International. I'm fairly confident the man we're chasing won't try to escape using a commercial airliner—knowing it would be the first facility we'd shut down—but we can't ignore the possibility of him

using another aircraft. I know you've been briefed,
Warner, but let me go over it again so there's no question about what your role is in all this. We have a foreign national who has kidnapped one of our team
members, and we have to figure out in a hurry how he
plans to get that agent out of the country. I'm hoping
since you're no stranger to these skies, you may have
glimpsed a few private airstrips as you transported victims to the hospital."

Warner nodded. "There are several large ranch
houses close to the airport on the south side of town
with private hangars and airstrips. I'll head that way
now." He waited until Griff strapped himself in and
then gracefully lifted the bird off the ground. After
making a sharp U-turn in the air, he headed south.

Griff pulled out a pair of binoculars from under
his seat and began scanning the vehicles on the
ground, knowing the chance of actually spotting the
van was slim to none. Petrović had a pretty good head
start on them and, as much as Griff hated to admit it,
was a pro at evading the law.

After spending nearly twenty minutes in the air,
sometimes flying low enough to make out the models
of the cars without the binoculars, they'd passed over
five private airstrips and a small airport used by FedEx
and several other transportation companies with no
sign of the laundry truck. Griff tried hard not to be dis-
couraged, but it was all he could do to stay focused.
Even if they were on the right track, too much time
had passed since Petrović grabbed Mac. He could already be in the sky and well on his way to wherever he
was taking her.

"Call the tower and tell them to check if there's
been any aircraft taking off in the past thirty minutes

from small outlying airports. Have them search for flight plans as well."

As the pilot repeated the command to the tower, Griff lowered his head, knowing it would be a dead end. Even the most IQ-challenged perp wouldn't be stupid enough to file a flight plan when he was trying to outrun the cops.

He was jerked out of his thoughts when a familiar voice squawked over the intercom. "We found something."

"Bradley here. What do you have?" He tried not to let his hopes escalate.

"Griff, this is Ty. Since there was no new intel on Gunderson, I came out to the airport so I can relay any new information as fast as it comes in. Ryan stayed at the hospital waiting for orders for his next move. They found one of the laundry trucks parked in short-term parking."

"Anyone in it?"

"No. We're scanning all the footage in the gate area. I know we could never recognize Petrović, but if Mac's with him, we'll definitely pick her out of a crowd."

Griff was pretty sure the laundry truck was a decoy. Petrović was too smart to go to all the trouble of kidnapping Mac and then park the getaway truck in the highly visible parking area.

"What else can you tell me?"

"Traffic cams spotted another laundry van stopped in heavy traffic in downtown and another heading across town in the direction of the Miami Port Division. I've got several units on the way to check out both vehicles. They're waiting on instructions from you on what to do if they locate them."

"We should have known Petrović would have backup plans. Let me know—"

"Just heard from the unit downtown," Ty interrupted. "The van is empty, just like you suspected."

"Keep working both vehicles, although my gut tells me they're dead ends. Concentrate on the one heading toward the water."

*Shit! The prick is using a boat.*

Griff didn't have time to think this one through before he turned to the pilot. "Get to the harbor as quickly as you can." He waited while the helicopter changed directions before responding to Ty. "Find out what vessels have left Miami in the last half-hour."

"Already did. Five. One in particular got my attention."

"Stay on it. In the meantime, check all surveillance cameras around the area to see if we can spot the laundry van pulling into the harbor."

"Roger that. Hold on. New information coming in."

It was the longest two minutes in history, and Griff tapped nervously on the dashboard with his fingernails.

"Griff?"

"Yes, dammit. What is it?"

"A video camera picked up the laundry truck pulling into an area where the private yachts are docked. We have a witness who claims he saw a man drive the truck down the ramp into the water. The Coast Guard divers are on their way to check it out."

"Anything depart from there in the past thirty minutes?"

"One. *El Letal Cubano*. It left about twenty minutes ago."

"Bingo! The harbor is in our line of vision now. How do I find the pier?"

"It's long and empty, and two yachts are moored on either side of it," Ty reported.

"Got it," Warner said.

"I'll be on the pier. Have the Coast Guard meet me with their big guns. Let them know the crew on the yacht will be armed and extremely dangerous." Griff felt his spirits lift. "Good work, Ty."

For the first time since Mac disappeared, Griff had reason to hope—they were in pursuit, one step closer to saving her. But even as Warner looked for a place to land, Griff couldn't stop the uneasiness.

Did Petrović have the ability to track their approach? Was he so obsessed with Mac that he'd rather die *with* her than give her up? It had already been over four hours since she was abducted. Did the Coast Guard boats have the capability to reach her in time?

He curled his fingers around his automatic weapon under his jacket as he made an executive decision. "Head out to sea," he shouted to Warner. "It may be too late if we wait."

MAC OPENED HER EYES SLIGHTLY, and for a moment forgot that she was strapped to a metal table. She sensed she was alone, and after a glance around the room proved it, she tried unsuccessfully to sit up. The creep had made sure she wasn't able to move at all and had the IV dripping at a fast clip into her right arm, probably with a mild sedative in it to calm her down.

Another slow survey of the room confirmed her fear—there was no way to escape. Petrović had thought of everything. He'd locked her into a room with no windows and only one way out. She was pretty sure the door would sound an alarm even if she could get to it.

She lay helpless on the table. At least he'd turned off the overhead lamp that nearly blinded her earlier. The only illumination in the otherwise dark room now came from a wall fixture close to the door, similar to a night-light. Guess he figured she needed to rest for whatever he had planned.

She racked her brain for something—anything— that she could use to defend herself, but other than the cabinets, which she could see required a key to open, there was nothing. She tried hard not to think about the hopelessness of her situation, but it was a losing battle, and soon, a few tears escaped and made their way across her cheek, the salty taste yet another reminder that she was at his mercy. But surrender was not a part of her psyche. If she couldn't escape, she was determined to make sure Petrović didn't get another opportunity to terrorize her with his perverted sexual appetite. Death was always an option, one she wouldn't hesitate to choose.

As she pondered that fatal thought, an image of Griff's body next to hers in the cabin in the mountains flashed across her mind. It was as if their two years apart had never existed, that her ordeal with Petrović had only been a bad dream. But that feeling vanished when gunfire from the jihadists hired by Petrović had forced them to hit the floor. In that instant, he'd switched back to the Griff who saw her only as a team member—and his mission was her survival.

Another tear trickled down her face as she pictured the look in Griff's eyes when he promised to put a bullet in her skull before Petrović's men could capture her. *A little late, Griff.* Seemed it was all up to her now.

While she was contemplating ways to take her own life, the door opened. She heard Petrović's voice before she actually saw him. Staring hard into his eyes, she hoped he could read her determination— realize she would never surrender, never come willingly to his bed, something she knew he craved.

"Well, Mackenzie, it looks like you've had a restful sleep." He eased beside the table and stared down at her. "Maybe now we can have that talk, the one I've waited so long to have with you."

She wanted to spit in his face, to tell him the only thing she wanted was to see him in hell, but she realized anger was not the right approach. If she could convince him that her feelings had softened, he might allow her a little freedom. One unguarded moment would be all she'd need to go on the offensive, show him what years working undercover in the CIA had taught her.

"What do you want to talk about?" She tried to keep the growing contempt out of her voice.

He seemed to study her, as if unsure of her demeanor, then a sneer crossed his face and he shook his head. "Oh, my little vixen, somehow I doubt your sincerity." He snickered. "But you still have time to convince me. I'm satisfied to wait until I have you all alone before I make my demands. I'm positive that being in a place where no one on earth can help you will change your attitude toward me."

"I see now that there's no escape. I'll be spending the rest of my life with you," she said. "You've outwitted all of us and can now claim your prize. Is it still necessary that I be bound to this table, unable to respond to you?"

"Nice try, my darling, but until I have you on my island, I'm afraid you'll have to remain on this table."

She hoped he didn't notice the small glimmer of hope leave her. His island? "I understand, Joseph." Saying his first name out loud nearly gagged her. "It only tells me you're not reckless. Hopefully, I will prove to you I can be trusted and—"

"That would be beyond my wildest dreams," he interrupted. "The two of us growing old together."

She swallowed hard to keep the stomach acid gurgling up into her esophagus from choking off her air intake. Pointing to the IV bag, she said, "Joseph, I'm about to burst right now. I really need to use the bathroom."

He studied her and apparently decided there was no way she could escape. "Of course, Mackenzie, but I'll need to shackle your legs. I've seen you in action and doubt you have my best interests at heart." He winked. "You can push the IV pole yourself, though."

*Dammit!* Escape would be impossible if she couldn't even run.

She nodded. "Anyway, where would I go? I don't even know where I am."

"Halfway to Cuba, my dear," he said as he placed heavy chain shackles on her legs before unbuckling the leather restraints. "We should arrive in a few hours."

*Cuba?* Oh God, it was worse than she'd thought. How would Griff and the team find her in a country full of people who had no incentive to help? No law enforcement agreement with the U.S.?

She tried not to dwell on that as he unbuckled her arm restraints and helped her into an upright position. The room seemed to rotate for a few seconds before her equilibrium stabilized. Moving the IV pole around, Petrović held on to her as she stood by the side of the table and waited for the dizziness to pass. She couldn't be sure if the wooziness was because she'd been prone for so long or a result of whatever he'd added to the IV bag.

"The bathroom's over there." He pointed to the far corner. "I'll wait outside." He walked with her as she wheeled the IV in that direction.

When she tried to shut the door, he pushed it back on her. "Sorry, I've decided I'm not that trusting after all, love."

"Joseph, a girl needs privacy for this kind of thing. I'll only be a minute." She made a pouty face and forced her voice to sound playful.

He stepped away from the door. "I'm right here if you need me."

Once the door closed behind her, she made her way to the commode. She hadn't been lying. She had no idea how long it had been since her last trip to the bathroom, and she *was* about to burst. Afterward, as she was washing her hands at the sink, a harebrained idea popped into her head. Quietly, she moved back to the commode, then lifted the lid of the tank and stared down into the water as it filled.

*It just might work.*

Reaching into the tank, she grabbed the rubber ball and the brass handle that regulated the flow of water. With one quick snap, it was in her hand. Hobbling back to the sink as fast as she could with chains on her legs, she filled the ball with liquid antibacterial soap, then shoved the brass handle down the front of her jeans. Next, she slid the ball into the crook of her arm with the IV needle and opened the bathroom door. She hoped he didn't decide to do a body search.

But why would he? She'd only been in there a few minutes.

"Thank you for that, Joseph. I feel so much better now." She allowed him to grab her arm and help her back to the table. "I'm even getting a little hungry," she added, praying he would let down his guard a little more—long enough for her to go on the offensive.

When they got close to the table, she backed up so he could pick up her legs and help her up. As he bent over, she saw her opportunity and reacted quickly. Grabbing the rubber ball hidden in the crook of her elbow, she waited until he looked up, then squirted the soapy solution directly into his eyes. Squealing in pain, he slammed them shut and clawed at his face. It only took a second to yank the metal handle from her jeans and take aim at his carotid artery. But even though his eyes probably felt like they were on fire, somehow he must have sensed her next move and reacted by leaning backward, causing the hilt of the brass lever to plunge into the left side of his face instead, bringing on another cry of pain.

Before she could take aim and land another hit, he managed somehow to reach under the table. Immediately, the sound of the alarms filled the room, and within seconds, the door was flung open and three of his men rushed in.

"Grab her and return her to the table," Petrović said as he ran to the bathroom to rinse out his eyes.

As hard as she fought, she was no match for the three Cubans, and soon she was back on the table, fully restrained. They stood guard over her until Petrović came out of the bathroom and walked over. She knew there would be hell to pay, but right now it didn't matter. The sight of his red and swollen eyes, along with the two-inch gash in his cheek, still actively bleeding, made her laugh, which only angered him further.

He handed a key to the tallest of the Cubans, the obvious leader of the group. "Open that first cabinet and get me the first-aid kit," he said in a calm voice that belied the anger burning in his eyes.

After the man did as instructed, Petrović washed his cheek with peroxide, then applied several Steri-Strips to the wound before covering it with a bandage. "I'll have a physician sew this up when I'm back on land," he said, then dismissed the three soldiers. "Nice work getting here so quickly."

When they were gone and it was only he and Mac in the room, he approached the table and glared at her. "You're more like me than you think, Mackenzie —vicious and vindictive. We should make the perfect couple."

Mackenzie kept her mouth shut, not wanting to escalate the situation any further. Staying alive was her number one priority, and right now, she was on shaky ground.

He didn't wait for a reply. Instead, he turned to the cabinets and pulled out a smaller version of the IV bag. After drawing up a syringe of medicine from a vial, he injected it directly into the mini bag and added the IV tubing. Mac watched as he faced her and hung the new bag before pushing the needle into the existing IV.

"I thought I could make you see me in a different light without the use of force, but it's obvious that's not possible." He reached for the regulator and adjusted the drip. "Now, you can either see things my way or die knowing I was ready to give you everything. The choice is yours."

Despite her better judgment, she couldn't hold her tongue. "I'll die first," she blurted.

"Pity." He pointed to the IV bag. "That's heparin running into your veins. By the time we make it to Cuba, your clotting time will be at a lethal level. If you haven't changed your mind then, I'll watch you bleed to death."

He reached into the cabinet drawer, and when he turned back to Mac, he had a scalpel in his hand. She tried to fight the terror as he pushed up her jeans on both sides, but when he made a slash across one shin and then the other, she screamed.

A sickening smile covered his face. "Your choice, my dear."

## 19

"You realize I'm just a transport pilot, right?" Warner shot Griff a confused look. "Fortunately for us, the City of Miami invested in the AS365 N3 two years ago when a child died en route to Children's Hospital because it took too long to get there. This aircraft has fifteen percent more power and is considered one of the fastest in the world. It's nearly paid for itself already." He paused. "That being said, even if we do catch up to the yacht, how are we going to take on crew members as heavily armed as you told your guy a few minutes ago?"

Griff huffed, knowing Warner had just verbalized what he'd been thinking. If they somehow found the boat, there was nothing they could do except wait for help to arrive. But he also knew time was running out for Mac, and doing anything was better than doing nothing at all.

"Honestly, I don't know. I only have one gun, and I'm pretty sure you're unarmed, so we aren't equipped to do anything but search. But if we spot the ship, we can radio coordinates, get the right guys and armaments to take on the subjects." He tapped his watch. "My fear is that it will take the Coast Guard a couple of hours to get to us, and if my gut is right, that may be too late to save her."

"Her?"

Griff realized he hadn't disclosed that the kidnapped victim was a woman. "Dr. Mackenzie Conley, one of the best—if not *the* best—biochemical weapons experts in the world."

Warner whistled. "Wow! Are the terrorists looking to force her to work for them?"

Griff shook his head, wondering how much he should reveal to a civilian. "The details are classified."

Warner glared at him. "So, you're asking me to risk my life and I don't even get to know why?"

Griff turned away. "Trust me. You're better off not knowing all the details."

"That's for me to decide." Warner tilted the chopper before making a sharp turn to the right. "You either tell me or I'm heading home."

Warner was right. What he was being asked to do right now made him more than just a civilian. Griff decided to at least share some of the details leading up to the kidnapping.

"Okay. I'll talk as soon as you get this bird headed back in the right direction." When Warner hesitated, Griff turned to him. "As a fully credentialed law enforcement agent of the United States government, I'm ordering you to do as I command. If you refuse, you'll face a grand jury and a very pissed-off U.S. president."

After a few moments, Warner did as instructed. Griff measured his words carefully. "You probably haven't heard yet because the news is just breaking, but my team and I, along with the Miami police and the Florida National Guard, thwarted a massive terrorist attack today."

"Oh my God! Where?"

"At the convention center."

Warner sucked in a gulp of air. "Oh Christ! My daughter went there with her best friend to see the Collins Brothers." He slapped his forehead. "I didn't want her to go, told her she was too young for that scene, but she and my wife double-teamed me. I should have stood my ground. Oh God, if she was hurt or..." He turned to Griff, his expression pleading for reassurance that his worst fears hadn't materialized.

As much as he wanted to, Griff couldn't tell the man what he wanted to hear. "To my knowledge, there were no deaths. As for injuries, I haven't heard, but realistically, when mass panic erupts, people can get hurt in the rush to get out the doors." Before Warner could process that, Griff picked up the radio microphone. "What's your daughter's name?"

"Julia Warner, and her friend is Bella Martinez."

Griff pushed the button to speak. "Tower, this is Agent Griffin Bradley. I need someone to check to see if Julia Warner and Bella Martinez are on the injury list from the convention center." He paused. "And I'll need that information ASAP."

"Roger that."

Griff replaced the microphone. For the next few minutes, they remained silent, hoping for positive news. Griff continued to scan the water for any sight of the yacht. Other than two barges going the opposite way, he'd seen nothing that resembled a luxury craft.

"This terrorist attack," Warner said, his voice cracking. "Was it a suicide bomber?"

Keeping the truth under wraps would be impossible, considering the number of people involved in trying to stop it. "Not a bomb. Nerve gas."

"Holy Mother of God! Are you sure you got it before any leaked out?"

"Positive. I personally placed the canister of gas in a protective container and sent it to the waiting HAZMAT truck."

A hint of relief crossed Warner's face. "How did the bad guys get their hands on your biochemical expert?"

That was one question Griff didn't want to answer. Frustrated, he shook his head. The SWEEPERS unit was one of the most elite CIA teams operating undercover, and yet they'd been outplayed.

"Our intel picked up communications about a possible attack at Miami Children's Hospital," Griff said. "The entire team was there, along with the National Guard. Then, right after they discovered a canister attached to an air-conditioning unit, there was a 911 call saying that the attack would actually take place at the convention center."

"Isn't it unusual for the authorities to get an alert before a terrorist attack?"

Griff closed his eyes, wishing he had a good answer for that, wishing Ty and Ryan had stayed behind instead of leaving Mac with only the national guardsmen to defend her. But in his heart, he knew he would probably be mourning the death of his two team members right now if that had happened, and Petrović would still be on the run with Mac.

The man was that crafty.

"To answer your question, after Dr. Conley checked out the canister at the hospital, she was pretty sure it was a decoy. Then, when word came down that the attack was actually going to be at the convention center, she ordered the rest of the team to that site. Every available body would be needed to evacuate the concertgoers ahead of the chemical release. Five guardsmen stayed behind with her, and they were being monitored by security cameras at the command post, or so we thought. Our best guess is that one of the guards was in on the kidnapping and was killed, along with the others, when his services were no longer needed."

"The terrorists must have wanted her awfully bad to go to that much trouble," Warner said before turning toward Griff. "You implied earlier you had an idea where the yacht might be headed."

Griff welcomed the distraction and not having to explain Petrović's obsession with Mac. "You heard my team say the only yacht that sailed from the area where they found the getaway laundry truck was *El Letal Cubano*. I'm gonna take a wild guess and assume they're headed to Cuba. Even though our relationship with that country has changed somewhat in recent months, they're still under communist control and not very friendly. An uncooperative government could go out of their way to help our perp."

"I hear you." Warner made a sharp right turn and headed toward the Caribbean islands.

Just then, the radio squawked. "Griff?"

"Yeah, Ty, go ahead."

"One of the girls you asked about wasn't on the injured list, but the other, Bella Martinez, was trampled and is in the hospital with a couple of broken ribs and a collapsed lung. Julia is safe at home right now. However, there were close to fifty children injured in the stampede to get out of the building. Most have been treated at the hospital and released, but ten were admitted. Three are in critical condition."

"Damn the cold-hearted bastards who would hurt innocent children," Warner said. "Hope they rot in hell."

Griff nodded in agreement. If anything happened

to Mac, he would personally escort Petrović there himself.

Both men were quiet for the next hour or so, each deep in their own thoughts. The only sound was the roar of the rotors until Warner shouted, "Hey, over there. I see a ship."

Griff grabbed the binoculars and focused on the tiny dot several miles ahead. "How close are they to Cuba?"

Warner checked the dashboard. "Radar indicates about twenty-eight miles until they cross into Cuban waters. Looks like they're headed for Santiago de Cuba, a fairly large port on the southeastern tip of the island. I think we can reach them before they get there."

Griff tried to contain his excitement. Maybe it was the wrong ship. And even if it turned out to be the *El Letal Cubano*, there was no guarantee Mac was on board. He grabbed the radio mic. "Tower, this is Bradley," he said, trying not to shout. "We have a visual on what we think is the getaway ship." He relayed the coordinates. "Radar indicates we're approximately twenty-eight miles north of Cuban waters. Please dispatch those coordinates to the Florida Coast Guard. Make it a high priority."

Neither Warren nor Griff spoke as they closed in on the suspect ship. There was a long silence on the other end, and Griff waited anxiously. They were gaining on the yacht, but they were still too far away to make out the name on the stern. The radio interrupted Griff's concentration.

"Agent Bradley?"

"Speaking. Is the Coast Guard underway?"

"There's a problem."

"What the hell kind of problem? Come on, man. We're on the clock here."

"According to our agreement with Cuba, signed by our president, crossing into their airspace or territorial waters requires permission from their government."

Griff's anger level threatened to boil over. "Did you not hear me? We've found the ship that has a kidnapped United States citizen on board. Any delay may result in her losing her life."

"Sorry, sir. The Coast Guard can't act without causing an international incident. We can only make a call to Castro and try to—"

"Griff," Ty interrupted from out of nowhere. "I've put through a call to Dino. He's on the horn right now with the White House."

"For God's sakes, tell him we can't wait much longer." Griff closed his eyes and lowered his head in an attempt to bring down his blood pressure, which had to be off the charts.

"Agent Bradley?"

He opened his eyes and glanced at Warner, who handed him binoculars and pointed to the ship, now less than five miles away. A quick look made his heart jump. For the first time since this nightmare began, the feeling of helplessness was replaced with hope. The words *El Letal Cubano* were clearly visible across the stern.

"Fuck regulations," Warner said. "Get your gun out, Bradley. We're going down for a closer look."

PETROVIĆ SLAMMED the door to the cabin he'd set up as his quarters. *Dammit!* He hadn't expected Mackenzie to come without a fight, but he'd grossly underestimated her level of animosity toward him.

Animosity? It went well beyond that. The woman hated him so much that she'd rather die than be with him.

He rubbed the bandage on his cheek as the wound beneath it began to throb. She would've killed him if he hadn't moved quickly to defend himself. Clutching a bottle of scotch he'd brought up from the galley, he reached for a glass and poured a finger of the amber liquid. He followed that with another. Tilting his head back, he downed the contents, relishing the burning sensation that he hoped would ease the throbbing in his cheek.

Once again, he refilled the tumbler, slumped down in a chair, and let his mind wander, trying to decide what his next move should be. For weeks, he'd been so consumed with kidnapping Mackenzie and taking her back with him that he never imagined having to resort to a Plan B. He'd assumed when she realized there was no escape, that he *was* her destiny, she would eventually have no choice but to accept his love—maybe, in time, even come to love him back.

The look in her eyes and her attempt to plunge the shiv into his neck convinced him otherwise. Dr. Mackenzie Conley would kill him without blinking an eye if the opportunity ever presented itself. The sooner he accepted that, the better off he'd be.

He chugged half the scotch and set the glass on the table beside him. Although it hadn't totally eased the pain, at least it had calmed him down. If anything, it served to bolster his resolve.

This wasn't him. He'd never been one to give up without a fight, and he was not about to start now. There was nothing he couldn't achieve when he set his mind to it, and he'd prove that to Mackenzie. He had more tricks in his bag, and she'd soon see the futility of resisting him. By now, the loss of blood from the heparin drip and the leg wound would have made her weak and unable to physically strike out at him. She'd pose no problem when they transferred her to the awaiting aircraft in Cuba. And once she was secluded on the island off the coast of Grenada, she'd see things his way.

If not, he would deal with her then.

He stood, catching a glimpse of himself in the mirror as he started for the door. The old cliché about feeling like you'd been hit by a Mack truck popped into his brain, and he chuckled at the play on words. She definitely had surprised him with her strength when she'd whacked him with that steel handle.

By now, the liquor was working its magic, and he opened the door to return to the infirmary. Having made the decision not to give up on Mackenzie just yet, it was vital that he shut off the drip containing the heparin before she lost too much blood. He wanted her alive when they reached Cuba and boarded his plane.

As he headed in that direction, he nearly collided with Miguel, who suddenly appeared, obviously out of breath from running.

"Joseph, we've spotted a helicopter closing in on us," he said between gasps. "At first we thought it was simply a Cuban aircraft that had lost its way, but as it got closer, we could see a large red cross on its side." He crossed his arms to imitate the symbol. "It's an American medical transport vehicle."

Petrović narrowed his eyes. "Why is an American helicopter like that this far away from the Florida coast?"

"Possibly looking for your woman." Miguel waited for a response, and when he didn't get one, he continued, "So, what do you want us to do?"

For a moment, Petrović was silent. It had to be a mistake. How could the Americans have found his location so quickly? How did they even know he'd used the luxury yacht to escape? "Are you sure it's American?"

Miguel nodded. "MIAMI HOSPITAL RESCUE is written plainly on the side."

"Dammit!" Petrović slapped the wall hard enough to send a sharp pain from his fingertips all the way up to his jaw. He felt blood trickle from under the bandage onto his cheek. He'd probably jarred the Steri-Strips and reopened the wound. Swiping at the blood with his sleeve, he made a quick decision. "Get the RPG launcher and meet me on deck."

As the Cuban leader scrambled off to get the weapon, Petrović raced to the deck to see for himself. But before he made it topside, his gut told him it was not just a lost helicopter—that somehow, Mackenzie's team had to be involved.

*They have no idea who they're fucking with,* he mused as he made it to the deck level and ran to the back of the boat. After grabbing a pair of binoculars from the table, he got his first look at the helicopter now hovering a little over a mile back, almost like it was waiting for him to make the first move.

Miguel had been right. It was the helicopter from Miami Children's Hospital. Petrović figured he'd had a good six or seven hours' head start and that there'd be no way for anyone to track him until he was safely in the air on his way out of Cuba. And even if they had, he didn't think they'd catch up to him this quickly.

"We've just crossed into Cuban waters," Diaz said, startling him.

Petrović pivoted and faced the owner and captain of the yacht, who had sneaked up behind him.

"Who's in that helicopter?" Diaz asked.

"I have things under control here," Petrović said, "You can go back to your station and get ready to dock us soon."

Just then, Miguel ran up with the rocket launcher, followed by two of his men.

Diaz's mouth dropped open, and his eyes widened. "Mr. Petrović, I have no idea how you managed to sneak that weapon aboard my yacht, but I'm here to tell you that you can't use it. I'm already in trouble with the law, and there's no way I—" He stopped talking when Petrović shoved a gun in his face.

"Get back to your bridge," Petrović said. "This is my problem, and I'll deal with it."

The horrified captain turned and sprinted back to his station, tripping once and falling in the process. At another time that might have been a source of humor to Petrović, but he was too focused on the aircraft now flying straight at them. He grabbed the weapon from Miguel and balanced it on his shoulder, pointing it at the unsuspecting helicopter as it moved in closer. He took aim and fired. The rocket-propelled grenade struck the left side of the helicopter, sending it into a flaming downward spiral. Petrović only wished he could have seen the look on the faces of the crew at the moment of impact.

## 20

Mac opened her eyes, and for a second was disoriented before she remembered where she was and how she'd gotten there. Raising her head slightly, she caught a glimpse of the gashes Petrović had made across her lower legs. What had been a slight oozing before she'd fallen asleep had evolved into a healthy trickle that covered most of her ankles. It would only get worse as the steady flow of heparin lowered her body's ability to clot. She wouldn't last the night if the bleeding continued.

She wasn't afraid of dying. Hell, every day in the CIA brought that possibility, although she'd imagined her demise would come swiftly with little or no pain, a result of a terrorist's bullet. Never once had she pictured a slow, agonizing death while she was strapped to a gurney.

What was her alternative? Tell Petrović she'd changed her mind and that dying was no longer an option for her? That might buy her a little time, but he'd eventually see through the ruse. She'd soon be right back in the position she was in now—bleeding to death, rather than submitting to his demands.

When the door opened, she lifted her head up to

see the psycho himself walk into the room. Dressed in casual jeans and a button-down shirt now, he moved slowly toward her, his entire body menacing as he sauntered toward her. She met his stare with one of her own.

In another lifetime, she might have found him attractive—if you didn't know how deranged he was. But all she had to do was gaze into those greenish-brown eyes and see the evil radiating in her direction to squelch any decent thoughts she may have had about him.

His lips were drawn tight as he continued to approach the table. No matter what he did to her, she wouldn't give in. Fully expecting him to turn up the heparin and hasten her death, she braced herself. *Give me your best shot.* She shoved all thoughts of him out of her mind and replaced them with memories of Griff in their last embrace.

At the thought of him, a rush of warmth flowed throughout her body. How ironic—it took her dying to admit he was the one who made her the happiest, who made waking up each day worthwhile. She should never have pushed him away. If only she had told him and explained that she needed time to heal.

But after her ordeal in Morocco, she'd been so violated that she was certain no one could ever undo the damage, and she couldn't bring herself to face him. If she couldn't forgive herself, how could she expect him to do so? Like an idiot, she'd turned away, leaving the kindest, gentlest man she'd ever known standing hurt and confused outside her apartment. Shattered and afraid, she had run from her only chance at a future filled with love and laughter.

*And where did my foolishness get me? Two years of the most miserable time of my life.* Tears gathered in the corners of her eyes and spilled down the side of her face. *Looks like there'll be no more chance for us. Wish I could tell Griff I love him and that I'm not afraid to die.*

She closed her eyes as Petrović leaned closer to the table, the vision of Griff etched in her brain. When she reopened them he was standing over the table, his eyes holding her prisoner. She willed her mind to take her away from the present and what was about to happen. She wondered if there would be any pain. Knowing Petrović, she figured he would take extra measures to make sure there was.

"So, Mackenzie, have you changed your mind? Do you want to share your life with me?" Petrović asked.

His face was so close that she could feel his warm breath on her cheek, and she held back the urge to spit at him again. Instead, she stared deep into his eyes and whispered, "Never."

Expecting him to react with anger, she was surprised when he threw back his head and laughed. "Feisty...always feisty. Frankly, I wouldn't have it any other way." He reached up and turned off the heparin. "I've decided not to let you die, at least not yet. I'm confident in my ability to eventually persuade you to see things my way."

Looking up at him, she forced a smile. "With my dying breath, I'll curse your name." She turned her head just in time to avoid his lips.

"Although I like a challenge, I must say, this resistance of yours is getting old." He straightened up and stared down at her. "And if you're waiting for your friends to swoop down and save you...well, that ship has sailed." He sneered. "Or should I say, 'That bird has crashed.'"

It took a second for his meaning to sink in. "What do you mean? Was there a plane out there?"

He bent down closer to her face, obviously enjoying the fear that had replaced the smile as she speculated on what he meant. "It wasn't a plane. Let's just say your friends in the Miami hospital helicopter are sleeping with the fishes as we speak." He gave her a wink, then turned and walked out of the room, leaving her alone to deal with the reality of his parting words.

*He's lying—only trying to bait me.* There was no way the team could have found her so quickly. Even if that was a possibility, why would they use a helicopter from the hospital when they had access to some of the best military-grade aircraft in the world?

She tried to close off her mind, erase the image of the entire team drowning because of one man's obsession with her. Although her inner voice reasoned that Petrović had to be lying, in her heart, she knew he wasn't. Somehow he always managed to get his way, just like he'd managed to abduct her not once, but twice. And he was never going to give up trying to make her come willingly to his bed. No matter what he did to her, that was not even an option.

Glancing up at the IV, she tried to figure out a way to turn the heparin back on and run the deadly blood thinner wide open into her vein. A final act of in-your-face defiance. The frustration of knowing that was impossible with her arms restrained brought a blinding gush of tears.

She was helpless, and her team had paid the ultimate price because of her. Still, she prayed she was wrong.

*Please, God, don't let Griff be dead.*

"INCOMING," Griff yelled. A missile headed straight for them. "Brace your..."

The blast rocked the aircraft. Pieces of the chopper flew into the air. Warning bells wailed. Flames engulfed the outer hull. The craft spun out of control and plunged toward the sea.

Griff pressed against the dashboard for stability. He called to Warner, who was unresponsive.

*Shit!*

As the chopper plummeted from the sky, Griff caught a glimpse of the yacht. A man stood at the stern, a rocket launcher on his shoulder. He didn't fit the part of a serial killer, at least not the ones Griff was used to dealing with. Today, he'd been outplayed by a businessman. Although he'd never actually seen Petrović, Griff was willing to bet that was whom he had seen. That was his last thought before the chopper slammed into the water.

The impact was like hitting a concrete wall. After he regained his bearings and released his seatbelt, he checked on the pilot. Warner was frantically pulling on his seatbelt strap, unable to locate the release. Griff ran his hand under the seat and located the clasp. It had been pulled down and twisted, but it still worked.

All the while, the chopper continued its ride to the bottom of the abyss. Since the left side of the aircraft had sustained most of the damage from the RPG, Griff reasoned that would be the best side to exit. He positioned himself to kick it open. Drawing up his knees, he slammed his boots into the battered door.

Nothing.

Panic set in. They needed to hurry. Griff re-cocked his legs and kicked again. This time the hinges broke off and the door dropped down. In the sudden influx of seawater, they were able to exit through the hole and swim upward.

The surface was a long way up. With each stroke, Griff's arms grew heavier and heavier, and his chest burned like fire. It would take a miracle to save them, and Griff didn't see one coming.

He glanced to his right to make sure Warner was still with him. He wasn't. The pilot's head was slumped on his chest, and he was drifting downward. Griff reversed directions and grabbed him by the collar. The added weight acted like an anchor, and Griff didn't have the strength to save either of them.

Was this the way it would end, silently floating to a watery grave? It hardly seemed fitting, having survived missions involving some of the worst terrorist groups in the world. He tightened his hold on Warren. *Sorry, buddy, you don't deserve this.*

Guilt overcame him. This man would never enjoy his family again because of Griff. He had talked a civilian transportation pilot into a dangerous manhunt for a sophisticated international terrorist, one with a band of highly trained mercenaries armed with rocket launchers. *One hospital chopper and one automatic weapon against those odds? That's like a kid with a water gun fighting a well-equipped army.*

Had Warner stayed behind, he would be eating dinner with his wife and young daughter, celebrating they'd been spared what could have been a devastating terrorist attack. Instead, that same loving family would be planning his funeral in a few days.

Griff grabbed the unconscious man and pulled him closer. If they were going to die, at least they'd die together. Resigned to his fate, Griff slowly began to let the air seep from his mouth.

As he did so, countless images raced through his

head, everything and everybody. It was like his mind had drifted in a fast-moving dream. Foremost was an image of Mac. He hated that in the end, he had failed her. He would not be able to keep his promise—to stop Petrović for having her, or... He didn't want to think about taking her life.

As he released the last of the air from his lungs, he gave up the fight, content to let the sea have both him and Warner.

To his surprise, death had yet to claim him. Another image of Mac flashed into his brain, and with it, so many thoughts. He loved her—always had since the day she walked into headquarters and was introduced as Dinorelli's new protégée. He remembered being a little jealous because she had everything going for her. Handpicked by his boss right out of college, she was beautiful and smart as hell, and everyone at headquarters had fallen under her spell in a very short time. Although he tried his damnedest to not follow suit, it hadn't taken long for her to bewitch him as well.

Looking back, he should've been more understanding after she'd been rescued from Petrović's control the first time. Should've given her the time she needed to heal. Instead, he acted like a spoiled teenager who'd just been turned down for the prom.

What he wouldn't give to be able to tell her that now—to let her know that no matter what that madman had done to her, it truly didn't matter.

Like the gradual darkening of a movie screen, he was aware the end was upon him, but just before that final curtain lowered, he was grabbed from behind in a powerful chest hold and a mask was slapped over his face. Whatever was happening, he had no energy to fight back. His body went limp.

## 21

He was floating in the water, and he could see the light ahead. He moved toward it, wondering where it would lead him.

Then the light went out, and he was thrust into darkness. His body was lifted then lowered to a hard surface. With closed eyes, he inhaled deeply, wondering why heaven smelled like a freshly plowed field.

"Agent Bradley?"

Griff forced his eyes open. Staring down at him was a man dressed in full diving gear. He mustered every ounce of strength he could and attempted to push the man away. In his present state, Griff was helpless against Petrović or a highly paid assassin, a killer he was sure towered over him.

"Agent Bradley, I'm Captain Robert Livingston of the United States Navy. To my right is Commander Josh Fuentes."

Griff stole a look in the other direction. There, a man, also in full diving gear, was leaning over Martin Warner and administering CPR. It took a moment for Griff's brain to take this all in. Even then, he was still confused. The United States Navy? "How did you find us?"

"It wasn't easy. Let's just say you have friends in very high places."

Warner coughed, and the commander quickly rolled him on his side. A gush of water spurted from the pilot's mouth, followed by a gurgling sound and a noisy intake of air before his eyes finally opened. His reaction to the man looming over him in a slick black wetsuit was identical to Griff's initial one, and he struggled to get up.

"Whoa," Fuentes said, pushing Warner back down. "We're friendlies. No need to fight us."

"He's going to be okay," Captain Livingston said when he noticed the concerned look on Griff's face. "We've got a basic medical station set up downstairs, and I can assure you that Commander Fuentes is a highly trained trauma MD." He reached behind Griff's neck. "Do you think you can sit up and get some of the water out of your stomach?"

Griff nodded, and the captain helped him lift into a sitting position. Within seconds he threw up an enormous amount of seawater. A violent fit of coughing and uncontrollable shivering followed.

The captain handed him a towel. "Now that you've got that out of your system, you should feel a lot better. Let's take these wet clothes off and get you into something warmer."

Griff pulled off his shirt, waving off assistance from the captain. When the officer turned to lay it on the floor, Griff used those few seconds to size up the man who had saved his life. Captain Livingston was of average height, but it was obvious he believed in staying fit. Even in the wetsuit, he had the physique of an NFL defensive end, exactly the type you'd want on your side in a critical situation. Silently, Griff said a thank you to the powers that be for looking out for him and Warner.

But many unanswered questions crossed his mind. He'd need answers before he could let down his guard and get comfortable with his rescuers. For starters, how were they able to get to them so quickly? If memory served right, they hadn't seen a single military vessel anywhere near the helicopter crash site, nor had they passed any since they'd left the harbor. The only ship they'd seen was a cruise ship and a cargo barge flying a Canadian flag and stacked high with containers. "So how *did* you find us?" Griff asked.

Livingston slid a blue and gold Navy football jersey over Griff's head, giving credence to his earlier thought that the Navy officer might have been a football player in his earlier days. "The President of the United States personally called and gave me an explicit warning that I'd have to answer to him if anything happened to you. Seems he's extremely grateful to you and your team for thwarting a massive terrorist attack." The captain raised his eyebrows. "You don't say no to the head honcho himself."

Griff wrinkled his brow. "But how did you get here so quickly? I was told there could be no intervention without Castro's authorization, and even if he did grant temporary clearance, there's no way you could have gotten here so fast." He paused and shook his head. "So where in the hell did you come from?"

"There's no time for that now." Livingston reached for Griff's hand and helped him into a standing position. He grabbed a pair of sweatpants from the chair beside them and handed them over. "Put these on. We need to get down to the command center. There's a very worried team standing by to hear your voice and confirm that you're alive and well."

Griff did as instructed. Although the new outfit was much warmer, he still shivered.

Traversing the open deck of the ship only led to more questions.

The flag waving proudly in the wind was a Canadian one, causing him to speculate that this could be the cargo ship they'd passed earlier. But why would there be American soldiers on a shipping vessel flying a flag of another country? And if that wasn't confusing enough, why would there be a command center on board a ship hauling containers of who knew what?

He filed away his unanswered questions for now. There'd be time for them later. Right now, he had to talk to his guys to find out about Mac. Hopefully, a fully armed SWAT team had already been dispatched and would soon rain down the wrath of God on Petrović and his band of mercenaries. By Griff's calculations, *El Letal Cubano* was now in Cuban waters and might already be docked at Santiago de Cuba, making that rescue attempt more difficult. But even with a full-out attack by military elites, the reality was not comforting. Nothing short of a miracle would save Mac at this point, assuming she was still on the boat.

He followed Livingston past the shipping containers, down to the lower deck, and got his first look at what the captain called the command center. He'd been expecting a dashboard with coordinates and a VHF radio. Instead, computers lined the walls, each offering a variety of views of the ocean, above and below the water.

"Guess this only makes you all the more curious as to what we're doing in the middle of the Caribbean Sea, Agent Bradley."

"That would be an understatement." Griff cocked

his head. "And call me Bradley. You saved my life. I think we can drop the agent tag."

A smile crossed the officer's face as he handed Griff a satellite phone. "It's on speaker."

"Bradley here," Griff said into the phone.

"Griff! Oh my God, you're alive." Ryan's voice was loud and clear. "We thought you were a goner, especially when satellite images showed your helicopter crashing into the sea."

"Ryan, Mac's in big trouble, and there's very little time left. Did Dino send in the SEALs?"

There was a long pause, and Griff felt like a python had just circled his body and was constricting his chest, making breathing difficult.

"Ryan?" he squeaked out.

"Dino tried everything—even called in every favor he had in Washington. In the end, they couldn't justify creating a possible international incident, not when you don't know for sure that Mac is on the yacht."

"Bullshit! Listen to me. Petrović has her. I saw him on deck. He's the one who shot us down." Griff was shouting at this point. The snake was tightening its grip. Hysteria was setting in. He struggled to breathe, but he had to keep going, had to convince them. "She's running out of time. They've probably already docked in Cuba. While we sit around with our thumbs up our asses, she'll soon be on another ship or airborne, and we'll never see her again."

"Griff?"

His head shot up at the sound of the new voice. "Dino, please tell me help is on the way."

The dead silence on the other end was unnerving until Dino finally spoke. "I can't. I pleaded with everyone in Washington who has the power to issue the order. No one was willing to go out on a limb. It was all I could do to finagle your rescue. I'm out of options at this point."

Griff couldn't believe what he was hearing. "What in God's name are you thinking? We're talking about Mac here, not some unknown American in the hands of that crazy asshole. When you convinced her to rejoin the team to help capture Petrović, you knew she was still deeply scarred from her last encounter with him. You promised we would protect her. Do you remember that?"

"I wish I didn't," Dino said. "It's tearing me apart, but Mac knew the risks. As for you, Captain Livingston has orders to take you to Miami, where a C130 will fly you to headquarters for debriefing."

Anger escalated into a rage strong enough to rip apart the python compressing Griff's chest. "No way. Neither Captain Livingston nor the whole fucking Navy can make me go to Miami. I'm not leaving until I've done everything in my power to save Mac. That's more than you can say." He paused in an attempt to control his anger. It didn't work. "And another thing, Dinorelli, I've given the agency my best years, and I expected more in return. As far as I'm concerned, you can take this job and shove it." With that, he slammed the phone to the counter and turned to walk away.

Livingston picked up the phone and handed it to one of the sailors manning the wall of computers. "Deal with it." Then he caught up to Griff and grabbed his shoulder.

With a forceful jerk, Griff shook off his hand. "I'm not going anywhere, so don't try to persuade me. I refuse to abandon any of my team members, despite my orders. Unless you plan on physically restraining me, I'm going to lower a lifeboat and be on my way." He glared at the captain. "And before you consider stopping me, remember who warned you to make sure I came home in one piece. What do you think he'll say when I tell him you and your Navy hacks went out of your way to get me killed?" He snickered. "Who do you think he'll believe? Like you said, my team and I just thwarted a terrorist attack, for God's sake."

Livingston opened his mouth to speak, but Griff cut him off. "And be advised, I'm prepared to jump off this boat and swim all the way to Santiago de Cuba if I have to."

Livingston studied Griff's face before a hint of amusement creased the corners of his mouth. "I'm way ahead of you. I anticipated help coming, and I had the helmsman change directions. With or without your friends, we're on our way to Cuba as we speak."

Griff felt a flicker of hope for the first time since this ordeal began. "I can't thank you enough. I..." Then reality jumped in and doused the flame. "A man who is willing to kill an arena full of teenage girls is sick in the mind, but it would be foolish to underestimate him. We'll never make it to the port, and even if we do, I guarantee he has another escape route ready and waiting." He headed toward the side of the vessel, where a medium-sized lifeboat was secured.

Livingston laughed. "You CIA guys always did underestimate—What was it you called us? Oh yeah, Navy hacks. I can assure you no boat is getting into that harbor for hours."

Griff stopped abruptly and turned to face him. "What do you mean?"

Livingston's expression turned serious, but his eyes gave him away. "The passageway into the harbor is unusually narrow and lined with many international cargo ships waiting to unload and then reload before sailing back out to sea. Unfortunately, one of our ships miscalculated the turn into that waterway and plowed into a Chinese cargo ship carrying electrical appliances. What a mess that made."

Griff took a step closer to him. "Continue."

"There are washers, dryers—you name it—jamming the harbor, and by my estimation, it should take a good eight or nine hours at the very earliest to clear them. Not only did we get to poke the Chinese, but thanks to them, the stack-up of boats waiting to dock is now almost a mile long. There's not a chance in hell any of them will get in until the wee hours of the morning."

Griff closed his eyes for a moment, processing that information. If what Livingston had just told him was true, they had plenty of time to reach the yacht before it docked. But even with this new twist, there were other challenges. Since there was no way to surprise the crew on the yacht, he'd have to wait a few hours until darkness fell. With no option except to wait it out, he concentrated on how he could get on board the yacht unannounced.

"Seems I underestimated you, Captain. I'll need to borrow one of your diving suits and the lifeboat after all. If you can get me close enough to *El Letal Cubano*, I'll do the rest."

"Slow down, Griff. I have something you'll find a lot better than a lifeboat." Livingston waved toward the other side of the deck. "Since we have a little over an hour before we close in on the harbor, why don't we take a walk to where Commander Fuentes is looking after your helicopter pilot?" When Griff hesitated, Livingston added, "I promise we'll sit down afterwards with a nice cup of coffee, and I'll answer all your questions, or as many as I'm able to."

Griff followed him down to the lower deck. As they walked past the command center, he couldn't help staring at the high level of technology lining the walls. He wasn't sure he could wait much longer for answers to his many questions. Like why a Canadian cargo ship would require this kind of sophisticated equipment.

Those questions were set aside when they entered a back room, and he got his first look at Martin Warner since the divers had plucked them from a certain death. Sitting up in a hospital bed and drinking what looked like a steaming cup of coffee, the pilot smiled as soon as he saw Griff.

"Well, you're a pretty sight to behold," Warner said. "I thought we were goners."

Griff walked over and saluted him. This was the man who had bravely accompanied him, knowing how dangerous it would be. Without him, they'd probably still be back at the Miami harbor waiting for the Coast Guard to get clearance. "Thanks to the U.S. military, you and I can live to see another day."

"I'm not an American," Fuentes said, standing at attention and saluting Griff. "Commander Joshua Fuentes, Royal Canadian Navy."

Before Griff could respond, Livingston spoke up. "Another one of the things I'll try to explain in a few minutes. I just wanted you to see that your partner in crime was doing well."

Warner lowered his head. "I'm sorry we couldn't save your biochemical expert, Bradley. My gut tells me she's more to you than just a team member."

"My own stupidity kept me from realizing that myself. But I don't intend to let it end here. With Captain Livingston's help, I'm going to rescue her and bring her to safety. Or die trying."

Warner bolted into a sitting position. "I'm going with you."

Commander Fuentes reached out and forcibly pushed him back onto the bed. "You're not going anywhere, Martin. Are you forgetting it's been less than an hour since I pounded on your chest to revive you?"

Before Warner could protest, Griff shook his head. "While I appreciate the offer, I need to do this alone. I couldn't live with myself if something happened to you after everything I've already put you through." He patted the pilot's shoulder. "No, my friend, you're going to stay right here and get your strength back so you can take care of your family when you get home. They've been through a lot as well."

The mention of his family brought a smile to Warner's face. "Wait till I tell them about being shot down and then rescued by frigging Navy SEALs."

Livingston stepped forward to join Griff beside the bed. "Unfortunately, you can't do that, Mr. Warner. You and Agent Bradley have been unwittingly dropped right into the middle of a highly classified mission. As far as the world will know, you flew with him to find his team member, but an engine failure caused your helicopter to crash in the Caribbean Sea. Both of you were rescued by a Brazilian ship carrying a load of coffee to the Caymans." He paused briefly. "Sorry, but only the people in this room will ever know what a hero you are."

"I guess I'll just have to be satisfied knowing I helped in some small—"

"Hold on a minute," Griff interrupted. "Not everything about today is classified. By now the whole world is talking about the attempted terrorist attack at the convention center. When the media finds out you flew out to sea with me to save a kidnapped American hero with no regards for your own safety, you're going to find out how appreciative the country will be."

"I'll take it, although I wish you'd reconsider and let me go with you," Warner said, giving Griff a thumbs-up. "Do me a solid and go kill that bastard...slowly."

"I think we all want a part of that, Martin, but unfortunately, ROXI is a two-seater," Livingston said. "Since I'm the only one qualified to sit in the driver's seat, and Agent Bradley has a rescue awaiting him, you and Josh get to stay here and hold down the ship. Maybe if you're nice, he'll introduce you to his stash of good scotch."

"ROXI?"

Livingston nudged Griff toward the door. When they were in the hallway, he turned to him. "ROXI is the most advanced underwater vehicle the world has ever seen. Follow me to see for yourself." Halfway down the hall, Livingston asked, "Can I assume you're familiar with diving gear?"

"Certified as part of my basic training many years ago. Although it's been a while, I think I can still handle a tank."

"Good. Now if you'll come with me to the underbelly of this rig, we'll get you suited up and ready to go while I answer at least some of your questions."

## 22

"Cream or sugar, commander?"

"Just black." Griff settled into one of the two chairs in the small office. "As much as I could use a shot of whiskey right now, I need to keep my mind sharp to figure out a way onto that yacht."

"That will take skill with a heaping dose of luck, but I think you're up for the challenge," Livingston said. "The whiskey will come later, after you succeed in your mission. Let's finish this coffee then get you into that diving suit." He handed Griff the hot brew, then sat down behind the small desk with a cup of his own. "Guess you're wondering why an American soldier is on a freighter in the middle of the Caribbean with a Canadian officer?"

"I've run out of possible reasons in my head, none of which make any sense." Griff took a small sip.

Livingston cleared his throat before continuing, "I'm going to bypass the small talk and jump right to the heavy stuff and remind you just how clandestine our operation is. Even guys with your top-secret clearance aren't normally privy to this information." He pulled a file from the side drawer in the desk. From across the room, Griff could make out the word JUD on the front. "Joint Underwater Defense," the captain explained when he caught Griff looking. "The name speaks for itself."

"What kind of joint underwater defense could we possibly be doing with the Canadians? And defense against whom?"

"Be patient, Bradley. I'm not at liberty to explain everything, but I will give you enough that it makes sense." Livingston opened the file and studied it. "With the president's aggressive stance against the opioid epidemic in the United States, we've been looking at ways to fight back. None of our usual methods of combatting the flow of drugs into the States have worked."

"More like failed miserably," Griff added, remembering only recently that he'd seen a report citing opioid overdose as having surpassed automobile accidents as the number one cause of teenage deaths.

Livingston nodded. "Bad actors—like Russia, China, and Iran, to name a few—are still trying to find ways to arm the rebels. The powers that be decided the best way to do that was to patrol the Caribbean Sea and prevent contraband from ever reaching the islands in the first place and to keep said contraband from then being smuggled into the Gulf Coast states."

"You're looking for illegal guns?"

"Drugs, mostly, but occasionally, we see shipments of high-grade military-style weapons coming in, usually on Russian freighters. Even though we're no longer enemies, Russia would love nothing better than to arm Cubans against us."

Griff thought about this for a moment. "I get it that the information would be helpful, but short of stopping and boarding every cargo ship headed to the islands, there's no way you can possibly know what's in the containers."

"Oh, but that's where you're wrong, Bradley." Livingston smiled. "Have I mentioned ROXI?"

Griff straightened up in the chair. "You did. But unless you can explain how an AUV can see into the cargo hold of the massive barges transporting goods in and out of Cuba, I fail to see the relevance."

"ROXI isn't an AUV. Autonomous underwater vehicles, by their very name are unmanned--autonomous because they have no physical connection to their operator who's either onboard a ship or on land operating a remote. They're self-guiding and self-powered, and for decades they've provided the best information about deep-sea processes to oceanographers. They're also used for counterintelligence, surveillance, and reconnaissance."

He allowed Griff to digest that information. "ROXI is the brainchild of two German inventors named Reuter and Oppenheimer, who were working with the International Underwater Marine Exploration Division out of Zurich, initially searching for a better way to scan the bottom of the ocean with the naked eye. When they introduced the first one-man submersible to the world, it was instantly hailed as the greatest tool ever seen for improving the study of the sea."

He stopped to take another sip of coffee, then licked his lips. "It didn't take long for our guys in the Defense Department to realize how valuable this new invention could be in the game of—well, for lack of a better word, let's call it underwater espionage."

"Underwater espionage? Keep going, captain. You've definitely got my attention."

"I knew I would. Anyway, our government brought Reuter and Oppenheimer to the United States and whisked them off to a secret location, where they brainstormed with some of our best CIA and FBI agents, along with the most brilliant oceanographers on the U.S. payroll. It took three years before they agreed on a prototype and another two before ROXI, nicknamed for Reuter Oppenheimer eXplorer Initiative, went live."

"Any other countries have one of these?"

Livingston shook his head. "At a cost of over a hundred million to build it, the submersible you're about to see is the only one in existence—and the reason Reuter and Oppenheimer are now multimillionaires living out their retirement in style somewhere in the United States."

"I have to admit it sounds like something from the twenty-fifth century, but knowing a ship is carrying contraband and executing search and seizures on international waters are two different matters altogether. There would be one helluva global outcry."

"I agree. But we're not using search and seizure." Livingston checked his watch, took a gulp of his coffee, then set the cup on the desk. "It's almost time for us to join the long line of ships waiting to get into Santiago de Cuba. If you'll come with me, you'll get your first look at ROXI, and I can explain how she works. Then we'll work out the details of your rescue mission."

Griff followed him down an empty hallway with no apparent doors or exits, anxious to see the submersible that had the Navy officer so excited. When Livingston stopped directly in front of a framed picture of what looked to be a wheat field somewhere in the Midwest, Griff halted abruptly behind him, almost crashing into him.

"If you're curious about the smell on board, we're

carrying a load of wheat headed to the Cubans," Livingston said, pointing to the picture.

"So that's how you get away with being in these waters? I didn't think the U.S. had a trade agreement with Cuba."

"We don't, which is why this is a joint mission with our neighbors to the north. Among other things, wheat is the number one export out of Canada to Castro's government. Works great for us, don't you think?" Livingston touched the upper edge of the painting, and the wall swiveled open to reveal a small room about the size of Griff's living room.

More intrigued than ever now, Griff got his first glimpse of ROXI. About seven feet in length and four feet wide, the vehicle looked like something straight out of *Star Wars*. Blue in color with a huge viewing window in front, it rested on a raised floor in the middle of the room.

He did a slow walk around the submersible, noticing the incredible workmanship that had gone into the craft. But if he was impressed with the exterior, his amazement of modern-day technology only accelerated when he peered into the cockpit. Lining the entire dashboard were more computers and gauges than he'd seen in a Navy Hornet fighter jet.

Noticing Griff's reaction, Livingston opened the door and motioned for Griff to get in. Then he walked around to the other side and did the same.

"She's a beauty, no?" he asked. "And wait till you see what all she can do."

Griff slid onto the leather seat, which was the exact same blue color as the exterior, and glanced at the cockpit. "This thing has arms?"

"Among other useful features. Both are below the

passenger door and come in handy when we're next to a freighter and the water is rough."

"And how do you manage to get that close undetected?"

"The sonar-blocking system is one of a kind. I can attach to the side of a ship for stability without setting off any of their alarms. I'm in awe every time it happens."

"But that still doesn't explain how you're able to identify a ship carrying contraband from the legit ones. Surely it can't see through metal."

Livingston shrugged. "Wish it could, but no. I think I mentioned earlier that ROXI is a two-man submersible. I'm one of only five U.S. pilots trained to maneuver it close enough to any vessel so that whoever is with me can sneak on board under the cover of darkness and get a look at the cargo. If it's something suspicious, we report it to the Coast Guard, and before it gets into Cuban waters, they intercept it for one bogus reason or another." He paused for a second before continuing, "I'd give anything to see the looks on the bad guys' faces as they sit around a table trying to figure out how in the hell we can possibly know when they're carrying drugs."

Griff took another look at the dashboard, more in awe this time after hearing all the submersible could do. "One more question. How can someone get out of ROXI without the water pouring in?"

"Did I mention that we only go out at night for the fact-finding missions? Not only is security at a bare minimum, but we use the cover of darkness to bring ROXI above water without being detected. Then I lower the panel on the passenger side, which slides down, leaving enough clearance for my passenger to exit the vehicle and move away while I dive under the surface. Like I said, if the water is rough, I use the arms to attach to the ship." He knocked on the wooden dashboard. "It's been one hundred percent successful so far, and I don't anticipate any problems this time."

"Were you on patrol when you rescued me and Warner?"

The captain nodded. "Imagine my surprise when I got a call from your director asking for my help."

"Dinorelli?"

"That would be correct. Used to date the same girl when we were at the Academy. Hated it when he won her heart and married her."

So Dinorelli had at least reached out and tried to help, even though, in Griff's mind, he hadn't done enough to get the go-ahead to execute an all-out assault on the yacht with Petrović on it. At best he'd been negligent when the life of one of his own was in jeopardy.

Griff pushed that thought from his mind, trying to stay positive. He didn't need Dino and the team. He'd save Mac on his own. He hoped he was up to the task, because failure came with too many horrific consequences. "Tell me. How can I get on the yacht without getting my head blown off?"

Livingston's face turned serious. "I can't promise what will happen to you after you get on deck, but I can position you close enough to sneak onboard. What happens after that is up to you—and that luck I mentioned earlier, if it happens to come your way."

Griff took a moment to think that through before meeting Livingston's eyes. "Sounds good." He patted the dashboard. "When can I see ROXI do her thing?"

"Now is as good a time as any. It's not completely dark yet, but the sun will already be down and offer some measure of cover. Slide out. I'll get you that wet-suit, and we'll be on our way."

Griff was silent as he waited. What he wanted most was finally going to happen. By the end of the day, he'd either have Mac safely out of Petrović's hands...or he'd be fish bait.

As THE UNDERWATER craft approached the harbor, Griff's heart raced as fast as his thoughts. He peered through the window on the passenger side. Even though the only light in the murky water came from the ships lined up and waiting for the massive appliance jam to be cleared, he could tell they were under them.

"How will you know which yacht is the one with Mac aboard?"

Livingston turned toward him. "*El Letal Cubano* is a permanent blip on our radar, has been for about a year. The yacht is a pleasure craft owned by a Cuban national named Huberto Diaz. He makes a living transporting heroin to the States. Several months ago, we caught him offloading the contraband in Miami. Since then, we've locked the ship into our tracking system and monitored its every move. Diaz is currently out on bail and nearly broke. Word is he's looking to sell the yacht to pay his lawyers."

"That's probably how Petrović was able to convince him to let him use the yacht." Griff frowned. "Money's not a problem for him, and he'd use anybody to get what he wants."

Livingston slowed ROXI to a near-crawl and moved in closer to one of the ships. Then he turned off the headlights as he piloted the submersible upward until they broke the surface of the water and could see the lineup of ships behind them. "This is your yacht, Bradley." He maneuvered even closer before pushing a button on the dashboard.

Griff watched as two long arms unfolded from the pilot's side and silently attached to the yacht. "And they can't see or hear us?"

Livingston shook his head. "Since it will still be a few more hours until the harbor crews clear the waterway, hopefully, some of the crew members will be using the time to take their turn catching a few winks. We have no idea how many men are guarding the ship, so take the necessary precautions. Get ready to eject. Your best bet is to board the left side of the yacht where there are no ships, but even that will be difficult. Keep the transponder I gave you close by and use it if you get into trouble. I'll be ready to intercept the minute you jump overboard." He saluted Griff. "Godspeed."

Griff strapped the oxygen tank to his back and put the respirator into his mouth. After returning the salute, he pushed the eject button, noting that his entry into the open sea barely caused a ripple in the water. He dove under, while Livingston retracted ROXI's arms and disappeared.

Once on the left side, Griff inched as close to the yacht as possible and cautiously made his ascent. As soon as his head broke the top of the water, he pressed his body against the ship, in case someone was looking out over that side. Voices drifted down from the bow. He reversed directions and headed toward the stern again. He'd have to take his chances boarding from there.

A glance at the freighter directly behind *El Letal Cubano* revealed that no one was on deck. Like the captain had said, the crew had probably taken advantage of the downtime to catch a few Zs. At least, he hoped that was what they were doing. It would be disastrous if someone spotted him and sounded the alarm.

He found the anchor chain and shimmied up to where it met the bow. There he located a foothold and quickly kicked off his flippers before grabbing the gunwale and peeking over the side to make sure there were no guards on this end. Satisfied that it was deserted, he eased over onto the deck. There, he kept low and moved with stealth into the shadows of a large storage container located beneath an overhang that jutted out beneath the bridge.

Convinced there was only minimal light and no personnel, he allowed his breathing to normalize and settled in the far corner behind the container, a small distance from the wall. Then he shrugged off the diving equipment and stored it out of sight, hoping it wouldn't get noticed.

Reaching into the waterproof case fastened at his waist, he pulled out the Glock and the full clip Livingston had provided. With a round in the weapon and eight in the clip, he felt a little less defenseless. An additional four magazines were secured in place with Velcro. He hoped he didn't have to use them. As he rose to get a better look, he thumbed off the safety. Although the view wasn't the greatest, he was able to make out a stairwell in the center of the ship, probably leading to a galley and sleeping quarters. More than likely, that was where they were holding Mac.

The problem was, in order to get to the stairway, he'd have to come out into the open and be vulnerable for a few seconds. But that was a risk he'd have to take.

While Griff debated his move, the three distinct

voices he'd heard earlier escalated in volume from an upper deck behind the bridge. It sounded like they were speaking Spanish, and by the tone, they were arguing. Hopefully, they were concentrating more on whatever they were arguing about than on the other side of the boat, and he might be able to get to the stairway unnoticed. Maybe this was just the luck he needed, the luck Livingston had mentioned. He made a dash in that direction, but one of the goons caught sight of him.

"*QUE DEMONIOS ESTÀS HACIENDA*," the man yelled. Then all three joined in the pursuit, each one packing a gun.

Griff raised his weapon and fired off a round before racing back to the storage crate for protection. There was no way he could win in a firefight against the three armed Cubans. He looked back, expecting them to be charging toward him, but to his surprise, he saw all three of them on the ground.

"What the..." Before he had time to finish the sentence, a familiar face popped up from the side of the boat.

"Hello, Griff," Ty said, as he raised the barrel of his gun to his mouth and pretended to blow off smoke. "Looks like you got yourself into a little trouble." He shimmied over the side where Griff had boarded.

"Yeah. No way we'd let you have all the fun without us," Ryan said, climbing over after Ty.

"Am I glad to see you two," Griff said, coming out from behind the crate. "How in the hell did you get here?"

"Everyone onboard had to have heard the shots. We can do our celebrating later. Let's go find Mac."

## 23

Mac attempted to sit up when she heard three distinctive pops from somewhere outside the sick bay area. From an earlier conversation she'd overheard between Miguel, the head of the mercenaries, and Petrović, she knew there'd been some sort of accident in the harbor that was delaying the docking of all the ships. She also knew it was only a matter of time before they cleared that up and she'd be transported to a plane and whisked off to some godforsaken island with Petrović.

She vowed not to let that happen, and again glanced up at the heparin IV, trying to find a way to magically turn it back on. She'd resigned herself to do whatever was necessary to keep Petrović from winning —even if it meant suicide.

The three faint pops she'd heard sounded like gunshots to her trained ear, and she wondered if Petrović was taking care of loose ends now that he was so close to the finish line. No longer necessary to his mission, the crew would be a liability. Since he prided himself on his ability to stay invisible, leaving behind witnesses who had actually seen him out of disguise was not his modus operandi.

She realized time was running out for her. With no options left, not even suicide, she promised herself to never give up on finding a way to destroy Petrović if he managed to escape with her in tow. That revenge might not happen today, but rather when he least expected it. That would mean her acting skills would have to be Academy Award-worthy to gain his trust. Although the thought disgusted her, if she could cozy up to Omar Rashid in Romania, she could pretend that Petrović didn't physically make her sick. She jerked up, startled when the infirmary door was flung open and the man himself rushed in. She could tell by his facial expression that he was angry.

*Good,* she thought. Angry men made mistakes.

She waited as he walked over and restarted the heparin drip.

Confused, she continued to stare at him, biting her lower lip to keep from smiling when she noticed a trickle of blood coming from the bandage covering the spot where she'd nailed him with the homemade shiv. But her amusement quickly dissolved when he focused his attention back on her and she saw the unmistakable look in his eyes. A shudder that had nothing to do with the cold metal table made its way up her body.

"Unfortunately, my dear, we are under attack, and several of my men have been killed." He watched for her reaction.

She tried hard not to give him one. "Under attack by whom?"

"At this point, I can't say for sure. My guess is the Iranians out for revenge because I betrayed them in Miami." He paused. "Or it could be some sort of American attempt to rescue you."

"Why would you think my friends were trying to save me? You've already told me there's no chance of that happening—that you shot down my only hope of getting away."

He looked saddened by her response. "I never intended to kill you, Mackenzie, but all that's changed now." He adjusted the IV flow to a faster rate. "There's no way I'll let them take me alive, and unfortunately, if I can't have you, nobody can. Think of this as a Romeo and Juliet moment."

He turned away to open the cabinets. When he twisted back around, he held what she recognized as a brick of C-4 with wires of all colors protruding from the top. She watched in horror as he got on his knees and attached it to the underside of the table.

When he was upright again, he looked directly into her eyes. "Insurance, my love. Whoever is coming for you or me will find out the hard way that I don't play games."

"Leonardo, this is Miguel. What's going on up there? Was that a gunshot? Respond immediately," a voice squawked from the dead man's handheld radio.

Griff reached down and picked it up just as the same message was heard on the other men's walkie-talkies. "We have to move quickly," he said as he pocketed the radio. He then grabbed one of the soldier's automatic rifle and tucked his own weapon into his waistband. "I don't know how many are left, but I'd guess at least four or five. Petrović would have spared no expense to get to Mac." He glanced up at the helm, ready to take out whoever was piloting the yacht.

"Let me," Ty said, already heading in that direction. "This won't take long."

By the time Griff and Ryan started toward the staircase, Ty had rejoined them. "Talk about a chickenshit. Right before I slapped duct tape across his mouth, Captain Diaz swore he was only trying to sell his yacht and had nothing to do with the woman tied up below."

"So she is below." Griff took the lead and motioned for the other two to follow him down the steps, gun ready in case there was an army waiting at the bottom.

He hoped he wasn't leading them all into certain death, but they had no choice. Cautiously, he proceeded down a couple of steps, checking for any sign of hidden combatants.

He was surprised to find the long hallway completely empty and figured the soldiers who hadn't drawn watch duty were probably relaxing or still enjoying a siesta while they waited for the appliances to be removed from the harbor.

At the bottom of the stairs, Griff used his two fingers to communicate to his team. Ty moved to Griff's right and Ryan positioned himself on the other side. Silently, they made their way to the first door and opened it.

The room was empty.

The next one was the same, but when they charged through the third door, they caught two Cubans scrambling for their guns. A couple of quick shots wiped out that threat.

Griff pointed to the next room, and again signaled to get them to follow him. They were almost there when a shot from inside splintered the wood.

They pressed against the wall while Ty threw a

tear gas canister through the hole made by the gunshot. Within moments, a burly Cuban man opened the door and began firing with one hand, while swiping his eyes with the other.

Griff aimed and brought him down with one shot. If he'd counted right, that was six of them. He turned to Ryan and Ty and held up six fingers, then cocked his head to get them to advance to the next door.

There were only two doors left now, and the three of them approached cautiously. The first one opened into a kitchen area, and after a careful search that yielded no enemy soldiers, they headed down the hallway to the last door.

Griff's heart raced as they approached it, aware this had to be the place where Mac was being held prisoner—if she was on the yacht at all. He wouldn't let his mind add *or if she was still alive.*

Griff signaled Ryan, who stepped close and attached a low-grade explosive to the door to pop the latch. All three of them turned away and covered their ears as the door blew out into the hallway. Quickly, Griff led the way and raced in, getting his first look at the man nicknamed Dr. Death. About five eleven, Petrović stared back at him with a defiant, almost maniacal expression on his face. The dirty-blond hair and hard eyes that projected evil, even from a distance, were proof to Griff that the man in front of him was indeed Petrović.

And he was holding something in his hand.

Griff homed in on the IV running wide open into Mac's veins as she lay on the table, unmoving. Panic set in when he saw the steady stream of blood dripping off the bottom of the metal table. He started toward her but stopped abruptly when the man beside the table held up the object in his hand. A closer look told Griff it was a detonator.

"Stop right there," Petrović said. "You're Bradley, right?" When Griff didn't respond, he continued, "As you can see, Mackenzie is not looking so good right now. Unfortunately, the heparin's causing her to bleed out through her leg wounds."

Griff did his best to quickly assess the situation, noting that the room only had one door and no windows, presenting a challenge to an easy exit. But his many years of serving in the covert unit told him that there would not be an escape from here. Either he would walk out with Mac in his arms or they would all die today.

Seeing the smile on the arrogant prick's face, Griff struggled to maintain his cool. He prided himself on knowing when to take out a perpetrator, like he did in Morocco, when he shot the terrorist while he was holding a gun to a pregnant woman's head. He'd waited for the exact right moment when the guy let down his guard for only an instant.

But he couldn't pull the trigger now, not when Petrović could blow them all to hell. "I'm Bradley. And you must be Petrović," he said in as civil a voice as he could muster. Engaging Petrović in conversation would give them more time to assess exactly what they were up against. After Petrović nodded, Griff pointed to Mac, trying to buy time, trying to figure a way out of this. "You're willing to kill her?"

"Oh no, Bradley. It's you who will do that, unless you get both Mackenzie and me off the ship and into my private plane."

Griff smirked. "You're asking the impossible." He raised his gun and aimed directly between Petrović's eyes, then lowered it when the lunatic leaned over

Mac and placed his hand with the detonator above her face.

"Make it happen, or she dies. Look at her. She can't last much longer. She's lost a lot of blood and needs vitamin K." He squinted. "And if you think you can rescue her by taking me out, think again. She's lying on a brick of C-4, and no matter how fast you shoot, I'll still be able to press the button." He held up the detonator for emphasis.

*Dammit!* Griff had been trained to shoot for the "T," with the eyes being the horizontal part and the nose and mouth the vertical line. Although that shot would definitely kill Petrović, it didn't guarantee a "no reflex" reaction. He couldn't take the chance of that reflex allowing Petrović to push the button.

There was only one way to keep that from happening. Only one shot would prevent Petrović from pushing the detonator, a direct hit to the medulla oblongata, the part of the brainstem that controlled involuntary actions. Griff had seen training videos with sharpshooters aiming directly for the sweet spot under the nose and above the lips, but he'd never actually witnessed it or done it himself. He'd always scored high on his marksmanship reviews, but he wasn't confident enough in his ability to take that chance.

His gaze settled on Mac, and although he couldn't see her face, she was still not moving and was probably unconscious, sparing her from the fear that faced them all. He took a step closer to Petrović, who responded by holding up the detonator as a reminder of what he was capable of doing.

"You know I would never jeopardize a member of my team, so for now, you win. Turn off the IV, and I'll radio the authorities to begin working on your demands, although they can't do anything until the ships are able to get into the harbor."

Petrović frowned. "That should be soon, Bradley. For now, we'll simply have to wait." He pointed to Ty and Ryan. "Have your men lay down their weapons."

"Turn off the heparin first."

Petrović hesitated momentarily, then reached up and turned off the valve that regulated the IV flow. Griff nodded to his teammates, who placed their weapons on the ground as instructed.

"And give her vitamin K."

Petrović shook his head, his eyes narrowed. "I'm afraid you're not in a position to give me orders. Mackenzie is my trump card, so no vitamin K just yet."

Ryan moved up beside Griff. "From the way he's holding the detonator, be aware he may have added a kill switch," he said, his eyes never leaving the detonator in Petrović's hand.

"Very clever. I guess you'll just have to trust me."

Although Griff didn't know much about explosives, leaving all things bomb-related up to Ryan, who was the expert, he did know what a kill switch on a detonator meant. Instead of stopping the action, it actually activated it once the bomber's hand left the detonator. If Petrović did have a kill switch, it wouldn't matter one way or another if Griff was able to sever the brainstem. As soon as Petrović dropped the detonator, the bomb would go off.

Griff was getting desperate now, trying to decide what his next move should be. None of his choices guaranteed a good outcome. Not being a doctor, he had no idea how long Mac could live after losing all that blood, but now that the heparin was no longer running, he figured a few more minutes wouldn't make that much of a difference.

"What's it going to be, Bradley?"

"We wait," Griff replied. "Why is it so important to kidnap her? Surely a man like you, with all your power and wealth, could have any woman of his choosing." He knew that was laying on the bullshit, but he was trying to get Petrović to relax a little, maybe let down his guard.

"I think you already know the answer to that one. You judge me, yet you're no different than me. You stand ready to risk your own life, as well as those of your teammates, for the woman you love. Rather ironic, don't you think?"

Before Griff could respond, Ryan moved closer. When Griff glanced his way, the bomb expert shook his head, a signal that there was no kill switch, and then touched his finger to the spot under his nose.

"It's up to you whether this ends well, but if your friend takes another step, I'll blow us all up. I know Mackenzie will eventually learn to love me. That's why I haven't already killed her."

Petrović's eyes darted to the unconscious woman on the table, and kill switch or not, Griff knew he had to act quickly. He lifted his Glock and took aim. He hadn't realized he'd been holding his breath until the sound of the gunshot pushed the air from his lungs, and he gasped. As if in slow motion, he watched Petrović drop to the floor, a confused look coupled with shock spread across his face. The detonator landed right beside him.

Ryan was the first to react and ran to grab the device. "Shit! No kill switch, but it has a timer...and it's activated."

Ty pushed Petrović out of the way with his foot. Griff rushed to Mac and checked her pulse. It was weak and thready. Not good! He opened the cabinets, grabbed a new bag of fluids, and switched it with the one loaded with heparin. Then he bandaged the wounds on her legs, but the blood still seeped through.

With the new fluid now dripping wide open into her vein, he searched for the vitamin K. When he found the vial, he drew the lifesaving medicine up in a syringe and injected it directly into the tubing.

While he was doing that, both Ty and Ryan dropped to the floor and located the C-4 under the table.

"We got trouble," Ryan said. "Not only is this on a timer, the bastard's wired it like a land mine. If we lift Mac off the table, we all die."

"And we've only got eight minutes until it goes off," Ty added.

"Son of a bitch!"

At that moment, Mac opened her eyes. "Griff?"

"I'm here, Mac. We're all here. Save your strength and try to sleep. When you wake up, you'll be stateside and eating one of those greasy cheeseburgers you like." He wished he felt as confident as he was trying to make her feel. Waving off his two teammates, he pointed to the door. "You guys get off the boat and start moving the other freighters as far away from this yacht as possible. I'll stay behind to try to disarm the bomb."

"You?" Ryan asked. "We all know you're the best at just about everything, but even you have to admit that I'm the *bomb* when it comes to explosives. They don't call me Boom for nothing."

"I can't ask you to risk your life." Griff dropped to the floor. "Tell me what to do."

"No way I'm taking a chance on you blowing Mac

up." Ryan shoved Griff gently out of the way. "I'll need a light and something sharp."

Despite his reservations, Griff knew Ryan was right. There was none better when it came to explosives. He turned to Ty. "Go topside and begin clearing the boats around the yacht."

Ty shook his head. "I'm staying."

Griff was rarely at a loss for words. As his heart swelled with pride, he nodded. "Do your thing, Ryan. And God help us all."

"Already found them," Ty said, dropping to the floor and sliding under the table with Ryan.

"Watch and learn, pretty boy." Ryan grabbed the scalpel from Ty.

Ty directed the light to the top of the bomb, which was now showing seven and a half minutes on the timer.

With nothing else to do but wait, Griff was besieged by all the things that could go wrong. The best scenario still had Mac in critical condition and bleeding out. Even Ryan's cockiness couldn't hide the uncertainty in his voice. But he was willing to put his life on the line. So was Ty.

After a few minutes of total silence, Griff crouched down and whispered, "How much time?"

"A little over four minutes. This is like brain surgery."

Before Griff could react, Mac opened her eyes and moaned. Straightening up, he leaned over and kissed her on the forehead, trying desperately to think of something to say that would keep her calm. But he'd never been good at showing his emotions, had always used his training and skills to show what he meant. "I'm thinking about getting a dog. I need for you to help me pick one out," he blurted, mentally slapping himself for the absolutely lame attempt.

His self-critique was verified when he heard Ryan mutter, "What the fuck?" from under the table.

"Are we going to die?" Mac asked, her voice painfully weak.

So much for easing her fears. "Not to worry. I'm right here with you. Petrović is dead. He can never hurt you again." Griff bent down closer to her face. "I love you. Always have," he whispered, but she had already drifted back into unconsciousness.

"Hurry up, Ryan," Ty said. "Two minutes left."

"Shit!"

"What's wrong?"

"There are two red wires and I can't be sure which one to cut."

"Jesus, Ryan, if ever there was a time to be sure, this is it," Ty said.

"Done!" Ryan shouted triumphantly as he slid out from under the table.

Griff heard him, but it didn't register. "Done?"

Ryan was on his feet, shaking Griff by the shoulder. "Did you hear me? The worst part is over. Now for the ultimate test."

"I thought you disarmed it," Griff said.

"We still have to get her safely off the table. There may be a backup charge that we can't see," Ryan said.

Griff released her restraints. While he held her upper body, Ryan and Ty placed their hands under her lower half.

"On three," Ryan said.

None of them breathed until she was a few inches above the metal table and then lowered gently to the floor.

"Yes," Ty said. "Now, how in the hell are we going

to get her off this ship without alerting the Cuban authorities? I don't have to tell you how badly she needs medical attention."

"I know just the way to do that," Griff said. He reached into the pocket of his wetsuit and pulled out the transponder Captain Livingston had given him for emergencies. "Let's get her up on deck and ready for transport. Help will be arriving soon."

**24**

I n less than ten minutes, Griff felt the transponder vibrating, Livingston's signal that he was standing by for the rescue. Ryan and Ty carried Mac to the side of the boat, while Griff grabbed a mooring line and tied it under his shoulders. Then he positioned himself on the gunwale. "Hand her to me," he said. Once he had her secure in his arms, he turned and faced the water. Ryan and Ty gently lowered the two. The winds had calmed and the surface of the water posed no problem.

Griff freed himself from the rope and swam toward ROXI, a short distance away. As soon as he reached the submersible, the side door opened, and he slid Mac into the seat. "She's in bad shape and desperately needs blood. The bastard pumped her full of heparin, and despite getting vitamin K, she's still bleeding badly from two leg wounds."

Livingston reached over and placed an oxygen mask over Mac's mouth and nose before strapping her in. "Commander Fuentes will begin treating her as soon as I get back. A medical helicopter is on its way from Miami to transport her to the Navy hospital in

Virginia." He powered up ROXI. "Don't worry, Griff. You've done your thing. Now let us do ours."

"I want to go with her," Griff said, knowing that wasn't possible but hoping there might somehow be a way.

"You know this jewel can only carry two passengers. Besides, we need you with your team to wait for the authorities. They've already been instructed on what to tell them."

"Ty and Ryan are perfectly capable of handling that without me," Griff argued. "Can't you send one of your freighters to pick me up?"

Livingston shook his head. "We won't jeopardize the joint mission. If the Cubans see one of the Canadian freighters picking up an American after the incident on the yacht, there would be a lot of questions—ones we're not willing to answer." He waved Griff off. "We'll take care of her while you and the rest of your team handle the police. I promise you'll be able to join her soon."

As much as Griff wanted to protest further, he knew he was wasting time—a precious commodity that Mac didn't have. Resigned to the fact that he had to let her go, he moved away. The panel locked into position, and ROXI disappeared beneath the water. Griff swam to the back of the yacht. After he fastened the rope under his shoulders, Ryan and Ty hoisted him out of the water.

Back on deck, he turned to his men. "So what's our story?"

They both began to talk at once, before Ryan pointed to Ty. "You go first."

Ty nodded. "We had a quick talk with the owner of the yacht while you were gone. He's pretty shaken up.

Apparently he's awaiting a trial for drug trafficking, and—"

"Livingston mentioned that," Griff interrupted.

"We convinced him it was in his best interest to tell the Cuban officials that the three of us approached him about buying his yacht, and he took us on a test run."

"Ty did the perfect good cop/bad cop impersonation," Ryan added. "Just when the poor man was about to wet himself, the good cop threw him a bone." He turned to Ty. "Tell him how you did it."

Ty was obviously pleased with himself. "Before the bone, I mentioned that unless he told the authorities exactly what I instructed him to say, we'd let it slip that he was planning to unload a shipment of fentanyl to dealers in Cuba and was using us as part of the plan. The idiot had no idea we can't prove that, but he was so afraid that he would have agreed to anything."

Obviously impatient, Ryan picked up the story. "Then Ty told him we could make all his felony drug charges disappear. The guy couldn't agree fast enough."

"Anyway, back to the captain and the story he was to tell the authorities," Ty said. "He's going to say that while he was entertaining us as potential buyers, we were hijacked by the Cubans. They apparently received a tip that the yacht was carrying drugs. When they didn't find any, they went ballistic and decided to kill us and steal the yacht. The three of us managed to overpower them. Unfortunately, they were all killed in the shootout that followed."

"We went back and fired several rounds in the hallway with their guns to make it look authentic," Ty added.

Griff, deep in thought, wrinkled his brow. "What about Petrović?"

Ryan made the sign of the cross in jest. "As soon as you went overboard with Mac, we wrapped his body in a tarp, weighted him down, and threw him over the side. After the harbor mess is cleaned up, the Canadian freighter will send a diver to retrieve it. That way, after Rashid is no longer a threat, the president can stand in front of the White House and announce to the world that the U.S. military has tracked down and subsequently killed international enemies numbers one and two. Quite a notch for his belt."

"Who thought of this?" Without waiting for an answer, Griff continued, "It's actually quite a good explanation. If the terrorists think Petrović is still alive, they'll waste their time and effort trying to get their money back. I can only imagine how pissed they are that Petrović betrayed them and ruined their big plan to bring America to its knees."

Both Ty and Ryan got quiet before Ty finally spoke again. "They're definitely pissed. J-Lo and his merry band of intel gatherers picked up chatter about that. They also heard talk of them seeking revenge on Mac for making them lose their arms shipment. And somehow, Rashid managed to connect the dots. He figured out she was responsible for his brother's death a few years ago in Morocco."

"That's why Dino wasn't able to tell you that help was on the way," Ryan said. "He was afraid they might be listening in on the helicopter's frequency. Knowing your location, they could make their move on both Mac and Petrović, and Dino wanted the element of surprise."

"That makes me feel a lot better about Dino," Griff

said. "I thought he was abandoning both me and Mac."

"He'd never do that to Mac," Ryan said. "You—maybe." He fist-bumped Ty.

"Funny. So, what about the bomb?"

"We wrapped it up and put it in the tarp with the body. It would be hard to explain why it was onboard," Ty answered.

"You guys make me so damn proud," Griff said. "Although I still can't figure out how you got here so quickly, I'm definitely grateful."

"You have Dino to thank for that," Ty said. "He ordered a military helicopter to pick us up at Miami and transport us the minute you called in the coordinates."

"And again, he couldn't tell you because of the possibility that the terrorists might be listening," Ryan added. "When we got close enough to the harbor, we dropped into the water just in the nick of time to come to the rescue and save the old man in a bit of a jam."

"Old man, huh?"

Their attention was diverted by the sound of a motorboat approaching. The three of them looked over the side of the ship.

Five Cuban policemen approached. "Prepare to be boarded," someone called over a megaphone.

"Put on your best poker face," Griff instructed the others. "We've got one helluva story to sell."

❦

IT TOOK two days before the Cuban authorities finished their investigation and allowed the Americans to return home. During that time, there was zero communication with headquarters.

Griff nearly went crazy worrying about Mac. The

last update he'd had about her condition came from Dino the day she was airlifted from the Canadian freighter to the Naval Medical Center in Virginia. Even after receiving several units of blood, she was in guarded condition, in and out of consciousness. He'd sensed fear in Dino's voice, despite assurances that she was holding her own.

Finally allowed to leave Cuba, Griff, Ty, and Ryan boarded a plane from Havana to Miami, barely making their connecting flight to D.C. Upon arrival, they hopped the first cab they could find, shouting the entire way for the poor driver to go faster.

The cab hadn't rolled to a complete stop in front of the hospital before Griff jumped out. Ryan was right behind him. Ty stayed behind long enough to throw a fifty-dollar bill at the cab driver, apparently for the abuse he'd taken during the fifteen-mile drive from the airport. Within seconds, he caught up with the other two.

"We're looking for Mackenzie Conley," Griff said, stopping at the information desk and shifting nervously from one foot to another. He hated the smell of hospitals.

The receptionist glanced down at the computer and, after what seemed like an interminable delay, looked up at him. "Are you Agent Bradley?"

"Yes, where is she?"

The clerk lowered her eyes a second longer before again meeting his impatient gaze. "I've been instructed to direct you to the chapel, sir." She pointed to the elevators on her left. "Go to the second floor. The chapel is on your right."

Griff sprinted that way with Ty and Ryan close behind. His legs felt as if they might give way. Why were they sending him to the chapel? One look at Ty and

Ryan told him they were struggling with the same question.

As soon as the elevator door opened, they raced toward the chapel. Griff shoved through the heavy wooden door as if they were made of cardboard. The room was empty except for Director Dinorelli. He sat on the front pew and didn't bother to look back or acknowledge them.

Griff's heart sped up, and his entire body went cold. He forced his leaden legs to move. Standing beside Dino, he tapped his boss on the shoulder. "What's going on?"

Without looking up, the head of the SWEEPERS unit scooted over and patted the seat beside him. "Sit down, guys."

No one moved.

"I don't wanna sit. I want to see Mac," Griff blurted.

Dino finally made eye contact with Griff, who immediately shifted from anxiety to outright fear. He had known Dino for a long time, and that look on his face had always been a precursor to bad news.

"She had begun to rally. Vitals looked better, even though she still hadn't come out of the coma. The doctors were fairly optimistic, but said she wasn't out of the woods yet. They said recovery would probably take a few more days, since she'd lost nearly two-thirds of her blood when—"

"Dammit, Dino. Where is she?" Griff interrupted.

Dino's eyes grew sad, and he lowered his head. "I'm sorry, Griff. Apparently, she threw a blood clot this morning because of all the vitamin K they had to give her. She's gone."

The room began to spin as Griff's entire body went limp. Hands grabbed him from behind and prevented him from crashing to the floor.

Dino leaned over and gently pulled him down next to him. "You did everything you could to save her, but that psychopath made sure she wouldn't live. I'm so sorry."

Griff stared straight ahead at the altar. *Gone!* Mac was gone. His beautiful, courageous, funny Mac. His heart wrenched in pain, as if crushed by some invisible hand. And knowing he'd never gotten the chance to tell her that he loved her—that he'd *never* stopped loving her—only made the pain worse.

Now she'd never know.

He buried his head in his hands and sobbed, his unabashed sorrow exposed for all to see. After a while, he managed to compose himself and turned to Dino. "Where is she?"

"In the morgue. They're doing an autopsy, and then she'll be cremated, according to her directive on file at the agency. Because there's still a very real threat of a terrorist attack, I've set up a small memorial service to be held tomorrow at the chapel at Langley."

"Why Langley?" Ryan asked, dabbing at his own wet eyes.

"We can't take a chance of Rashid or any member of his terrorist group setting off a bomb at a civilian church. Remember, they're still reeling from a lost opportunity to strike the United States and will be looking for any way to make headlines."

Lost in his thoughts of Mac, Griff murmured to no one in particular, "I never got the chance to tell her..."

Dino put his arm around his shoulders. "She knew."

GRIFF SAT on the balcony of his apartment watching two children playing in the pool. He'd been out there since four in the morning, having tossed and turned most of the night. Sleeplessness had become the norm for him.

Since Mac's funeral, he hadn't bothered to shave, and he didn't care what he looked like. What was the point? Nothing mattered anymore. As for food, there were so many takeout containers in the trash, it was overflowing. But he wasn't up for a walk to the dumpsters. He was afraid he'd see someone and have to pretend to be normal.

He spent his days moping around, wishing Mac was still alive, but he knew nothing was going to bring her back. If he was ever to move on, to get his life back, he had to accept it. How the hell was he supposed to do that?

The future held no interest for him, not without her. And he blamed himself. He was supposed to keep her safe. What he wouldn't give for a redo of that horrible day at Miami Children's Hospital, when Petrović had out-schemed them and kidnapped her. Knowing how obsessed the man had been with her and how terrified she was of him, he should never have let her go to Miami in the first place. If only...

He shoved the table over with all the anger in him, sending the empty beer can clattering to the floor and causing two kids outside to stop playing and look up.

He didn't remember much about the memorial service at Langley. Seemed a part of him had died that day, too. He should have been the one in the urn.

His new, government-issued cell phone vibrated on the table, jarring him from his memories. Glancing at caller ID, he hesitated before picking it up. After a long one-on-one with his boss over way too many drinks following the service, he'd accepted that Dino had no other choice when he misled him about rescuing Mac. Since then, the director had been calling at least once a day, usually twice, to check up on him. He was tired of saying the same old thing every time.

*I'll be fine. I just need more time.*

*I'm working it out. I'll be back on the job soon.*

He wasn't sure he would ever be fine again or able to go back to work in the same office, knowing she wouldn't be there. He sucked in a gulp of air before he answered. "Hey, Dino. I'm okay. Really."

There was a moment of silence before the director replied, "You're not okay, and we both know it. This downward spiral you're in is going nowhere. You need to pull it together, man, and get on with your life. You'll never do that until you accept reality. Mac's dead."

Griff groaned. "How, exactly, do you propose I do that? I'm not sleeping and barely surviving. I would be a hazard to anyone unfortunate enough to depend on me during a mission. I would—"

"Don't you think I know that?" Dino interrupted. "I talked to Rutherford about you yesterday."

"You discussed me with the shrink? I don't need psychobabble, boss. I need Mac alive and laughing at the dumb things I do, like she always did."

"I want her back, too, but that's not going to happen." Dino's voice softened. "Rutherford suggested you get away for a few weeks. Clear your head. Get some closure."

"I suppose he thinks I need antidepressants as well," Griff said, more sarcastically than he intended. He knew Dino was only trying to be helpful.

"Who doesn't need to feel good? But no, he's aware you would never take them. Like I said, he does think a getaway would do you a world of good, though." He paused and waited for a reaction. When there was none, he continued, "Do you remember that little place where Lydia and I go wherever we need to escape the nine-to-five crazies?"

"The one by the ocean?"

"That's the one. I want you to go there and spend some time connecting with nature. Unleash your inhibitions. Cavort nude on the private beach, if that suits you. Smell the salt water. If, at the end of two weeks, you still aren't ready to come back to work, we'll figure out what to do next." His voice cracked. "I won't lose both you and Mac without a fight. I'm begging you to do this for my sake."

Griff's first instinct was to say no—to remind Dino that no amount of swimming naked in the sea would make him feel whole again—but he knew his boss was right. "Send me the information, and I'll call for a reservation."

"Already done," Dino said. "There's a rental car parked in your space at headquarters, so you don't even have to put the miles on your new truck. Key's under the rug."

Griff brushed the stubble on his chin. "Guess that means I'll have to shave."

"A cleanup would be good," Dino said.

"I'll do it only because it's you asking," Griff said, "but be forewarned, my phone stays here. If I'm going to spend time with nature, like you said, I don't want the damn thing ringing every hour with you guys checking to see if I'm okay."

"Fair enough. All I ask is that I'm the first call you make when you return."

"Fine." Griff disconnected then glanced around the apartment. He really should spend some time cleaning up before he left so he wouldn't come home to uninvited roaches—or worse.

"Screw it," he said.

Twenty minutes later, he had showered and shaved. Although somewhat leaner, he surprisingly looked human again. Maybe two weeks isolated on a deserted beach would be the perfect way to make his peace with Mac's death. If nothing else, maybe the sound of the waves splashing against the shore would lull him into a good night's rest.

On the way out the door, he took one more look around his apartment, then went back inside and called the cleaning service he used occasionally. Cockroaches, he could deal with, but rats? Not so much.

He drove to SWEEPERS headquarters in Granger. A tricked-out cherry-red Jeep Wrangler sat parked in his spot. Seeing it, he couldn't help but grin. Dino was really trying hard. Griff found the key exactly where it was supposed to be, climbed in, and cranked back the hardtop before heading south. Dino had even programed the GPS for his trip.

The eight-hour drive was uneventful, and he only stopped twice to heed nature's call and grab a burger. Once he turned off the interstate, he relied solely on the GPS as he drove the final forty miles on an isolated road that ran parallel to the ocean. Even in the dark, he could see how beautiful the view was with the full moon dancing on the shimmering water.

It was almost ten when he pulled up to the small cabin that sat about a hundred yards from a white, sandy beach bordering the water. After parking the car, he grabbed his suitcase and headed for the front door, anxious to see if the inside was as quaint and charming as the outside. Dino had said the key would be in the large flowerpot on the porch, but he couldn't find it.

*Great,* he thought. He didn't even have a phone to call anyone.

He walked around to the back the house, hoping to find a door open or a small window he could break. Glancing toward the water, he saw the view was amazing.

And then he saw her—a woman walking barefoot in the sand, coming his way. Although he couldn't see her face, there was something familiar about the way she walked.

A sudden jolt of electricity surged through his body as he stared. *How can it be?* Every nerve tingled. His breath caught in his throat. What he was seeing was not possible.

"Hello, Griff."

He closed his eyes and shook his head. *I must be losing my mind. Maybe I should have gotten a prescription from the company shrink.* When he opened them again, she was almost to the porch.

"Mac?" he said softly, afraid she might vanish at the sound of his voice.

She threw her hands in the air. "Who else would it be, Bradley?"

"But...but..." He dropped his suitcase and ran to her, crushing her against his body and holding on as if the light breeze might blow her away.

"Careful, hotshot. I'm still not one hundred percent."

He held her out so he could touch her cheek, still not convinced he wasn't hallucinating. But it wasn't an illusion. This was Mac, the woman he loved. Mac, somehow back from the dead, in his arms and smiling up at him. "How? Why? Oh, I don't give a damn. You're alive. That's all that matters. I've been waiting a long time to do this." He bent down and kissed her; unable to get enough of her. It left him dizzy and excited.

When he finally released her, she was smiling. "I've been waiting a long time for that very same thing. I guess it took my dying to knock some sense into us."

He stared into her eyes, still not convinced he wasn't imagining her. "Is it really you?"

"In the flesh."

"I still wish Dinorelli hadn't let me believe you were dead."

"He did it for my safety." She grabbed his hand. "Let's go inside. We'll have a stiff drink, and I'll tell you everything."

"I could definitely use one."

Inside, she poured the liquor and handed him a glass. Sitting on the couch, she waited for him to settle in beside her.

He downed the burning liquid in one gulp. "Now I'm ready."

She took a sip. "Intel picked up several conversations from the terrorist cell after I was airlifted to Miami. Seems Jamil Rashid was obsessed with getting revenge for his brother's death. J-Lo overheard them planning to take me out at the hospital."

"So Dinorelli faked your death and whisked you away to a safe house." Griff got up and refilled his glass, then brought the bottle over to refill hers.

"Yes. According to Dino, they're closing in on Rashid and his group. They even pinpointed his exact location once, but by the time they could confirm it and get the drones in position, he was gone."

"That still doesn't explain why I was kept in the dark. Does Dino have so little faith in me that he couldn't trust me?" He stopped and took another drink. "These last two weeks have been hell. Between grieving for you and blaming myself for not being able to save you—"

"I'm sorry." She laid her head on his shoulder. "Dino told me everything you were going through. I was hurting for you, too. But he knew the terrorists would be listening to any chatter, watching your every move. That's why he booked this cottage in his name, rented the Jeep himself. He even had a spook follow you for the first thirty minutes to make sure that even after all that, someone had not picked up your scent. You are the tops in your profession, but Dino wasn't about to trust your acting skills when it came to my life."

He ran his fingers through her hair. "Guess I can't blame him." He leaned over and kissed the top of her head, catching a whiff of the apricot shampoo she always used. "How long will you have to stay here?"

"Until Rashid is dead. That could be tomorrow, or it could be a week, maybe even a month from now." She cocked her head and gave him a mischievous look. "You gotta admit, this isn't a bad gig, as far as safe houses go."

He couldn't wait any longer and pulled her into his arms. "My biggest regret in all this was not telling you how I really felt. And then I thought I had lost that chance forever. The truth is I've loved you from the first day you walked into the office and gave me attitude. No matter what happens, you need to know that."

She lowered her eyes. "I thought you would never be able to see me as anything but damaged goods after what Petrović did to me." She raised her eyes to meet his, her eyes shiny with tears. "He used terror to control me, and God help me, I let him win."

Her eyes drifted to the door when there was a slight scratching noise. Griff scrambled off the couch, dove for his bag, and pulled out his weapon, certain the terrorists had somehow managed to follow him here. "Don't open the door," he screamed.

She turned and winked. "Put the gun away or you'll scare Roxy."

"Roxy?"

As soon as the door was opened, a golden retriever puppy bounded in, rushed over to him, and immediately began covering his face with sloppy kisses.

"Bet you thought I didn't remember your lame-ass comment back on the boat. Since you're the one who brought it up, I decided you needed another female around to teach you how to smooth-talk a lady."

"Point taken. Now will you get this mutt off me so I can do to you what she's doing to me?"